THE GARDEN-PARTY

KATHERINE MANSFIELD'S NEW ZEALAND STORIES

ILLUSTRATED EDITION

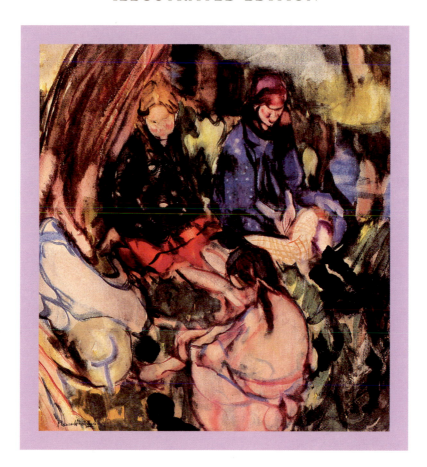

NEW AMSTERDAM

NEW YORK

The publishers would like to thank the Auckland
City Art Gallery, in particular the Director Dr T.
L. Rodney Wilson and the Curator of Historical
New Zealand Art Roger Blackley, for assistance
with research and provision of transparencies for
the reproduction of paintings from the Gallery
collection. Thanks are also due to the Auckland
Institute and Museum for permission to reproduce
flower paintings from the Botanical collection.

First published 1987

Stories selected and compiled by Michael Gifkins
© Century Hutchinson New Zealand Ltd

This edition published in the United States of
America, 1988, by New Amsterdam Books of New
York, Inc. by arrangement with Century
Hutchinson New Zealand, Ltd., Auckland, and
Alfred A. Knopf, Inc., New York.

NEW AMSTERDAM BOOKS
171 Madison Avenue
New York, NY 10016

ISBN 0-941533-38-7

Printed in Hong Kong

THE GARDEN-PARTY

Katherine Mansfield was born in Wellington, New Zealand, on 14 October, 1888. Between the ages of 15 and 17 and in the company of her sisters she attended Queen's College, London, returning to New Zealand at the end of 1906. With an allowance from her father she was back in London in 1908, determinedly embarked upon the career of a writer; her first published volume appeared in 1911. Illness, her work, and her relationship with John Middleton Murry occupied centre stage and by 1923 she was dead.

The stories of Katherine Mansfield are acknowledged to be amongst the finest in the *genre* and her critical reputation has continually evolved. It has long been accepted that many of her best pieces are based on memories of the country of her birth; certainly stories such as "Prelude", "The Doll's House" and "Her First Ball" are amongst the most greatly loved. Here, the larger part of the New Zealand stories is presented in illustrated form, making use of paintings principally by artists of her own country and active in and around the author's time. Special emphasis is given to the work of that other great expatriate New Zealand talent, Frances Hodgkins.

It might be argued that in the absence of specific reference, the stories chosen could be set almost anywhere at all. That is true, and it is a mark of their conviction and of the universality of Mansfield's themes that it should be so. Nonetheless there can be no doubt that they relate to precise locales clearly identifiable by reference to the known facts of the author's life, a life more fully documented than that of any New Zealand writer before or since.

The author's own life is of course present in the stories as more than that. There is the self-confidence of a major talent abroad, sustained by backward glances at a sun-filled antipodean childhood; there is recognition of the pain of loss and intimations of mortality; and then there is the gathering dark. For this reason the stories are arranged in the approximate order of their composition.

CONTENTS

The Auckland City Art Gallery first opened its doors in February 1888, the earliest permanent art gallery in New Zealand. Bequests from Sir George Grey and James Tannock Mackelvie formed the basis of the collection, which has been extended and enriched over the past hundred years.

It is fitting that the following selection of New Zealand and British pictures should celebrate the centenary of the Gallery, as well as the birth of Katherine Mansfield. Particularly appropriate is the inclusion of works by such talented expatriate artists as Raymond McIntyre, Rhona Haszard, Maud Sherwood and Frances Hodgkins.

A fellow exile of Mansfield's own generation, Frances Hodgkins is now acclaimed as one of New Zealand's greatest artists. The variety and scope of her pictures reproduced here reflect the strengths of the Gallery's representative Hodgkins collection, while forming an ideal complement to Katherine Mansfield's stories.

THE WOMAN AT THE STORE

ALL that day the heat was terrible. The wind blew close to the ground; it rooted among the tussock grass, slithered along the road, so that the white pumice dust swirled in our faces, settled and sifted over us and was like a dry-skin itching for growth on our bodies. The horses stumbled along, coughing and chuffing. The pack-horse was sick — with a big open sore rubbed under the belly. Now and again she stopped short, threw back her head, looked at us as though she were going to cry, and whinnied. Hundreds of larks shrilled; the sky was slate colour, and the sound of the larks reminded me of slate pencils scraping over its surface. There was nothing to be seen but wave after wave of tussock grass, patched with purple orchids and manuka bushes covered with thick spider webs.

Jo rode ahead. He wore a blue galatea shirt, corduroy trousers and riding boots. A white handkerchief, spotted with red — it looked as though his nose had been bleeding on it — was knotted round his throat. Wisps of white hair straggled from under his wideawake — his moustache and eyebrows were called white — he slouched in the saddle, grunting. Not once that day had he sung

> "I don't care, for don't you see,
>   My wife's mother was in front of me!"

It was the first day we had been without it for a month, and now there seemed something uncanny in his silence. Jim rode beside me, white as a clown; his black eyes glittered and he kept shooting out his tongue and moistening his lips. He was dressed in a Jaeger vest and a pair of blue duck trousers, fastened round the waist with a plaited leather belt. We had hardly spoken since dawn. At noon we had lunched off fly biscuits and apricots by the side of a swampy creek.

"My stomach feels like the crop of a hen," said Jo. "Now then, Jim, you're the bright boy of the party — where's this 'ere store you kep' on talking about. 'Oh yes,' you says, 'I know a fine store, with a paddock for the horses and a creek runnin' through, owned by a friend of mine who'll give yer a bottle of whisky before 'e shakes hands with yer.' I'd like ter see that place — merely as a matter of curiosity — not that I'd ever doubt yer word — as yer know very well — *but...*"

Jim laughed. "Don't forget there's a woman too, Jo, with blue eyes and yellow hair, who'll promise you something else before she shakes hands with you. Put that in your pipe and smoke it."

"The heat's making you balmy," said Jo. But he dug his knees into the horse. We shambled on. I half fell asleep and had a sort of uneasy dream that the horses were not moving forward at all — then that I was on a rocking-horse, and my old mother was scolding me for raising such a fearful dust from the drawing-room carpet. "You've entirely worn off the pattern of the carpet," I heard her saying, and she gave the reins a tug. I snivelled and woke to find Jim leaning over me, maliciously smiling.

"That was a case of all but," said he. "I just caught you. What's up? Been bye-bye?"

"No!" I raised my head. "Thank the Lord we're arriving somewhere."

We were on the brow of the hill, and below us there was a whare roofed with corrugated iron. It stood in a garden, rather far back from the road — a big paddock opposite, and a creek and a clump of young willow trees. A thin line of blue smoke stood up straight from the chimney of the whare; and as I looked a woman came out, followed by a child and a sheep dog — the woman carrying what appeared to me a black stick. She made gestures at us. The horses put on a final spurt, Jo took off his wideawake, shouted, threw out his chest, and began singing "I don't care, for don't you see..." The sun pushed through the pale clouds and shed a vivid light over the scene. It gleamed on the woman's yellow hair, over her flapping pinafore and the rifle she was carrying. The child hid behind her, and the yellow dog, a mangy beast, scuttled back into the whare, his tail between his legs. We drew reign and dismounted.

"Hallo," screamed the woman. "I thought you was three 'awks. My kid comes runnin' in ter me. 'Mumma,' says she. An' I comes out smart, I can tell yer. 'They'll be 'awks,' I says to her. Oh, the 'awks about 'ere, yer wouldn't believe."

The "kid" gave us the benefit of one eye from behind the woman's pinafore — then retired again.

"Where's your old man?" asked Jim.

The woman blinked rapidly, screwing up her face.

"Away shearin'. Bin away a month. I suppose ye're not goin' to stop, are yer? There's a storm comin' up."

"You bet we are," said Jo. "So you're on your lonely, missus?"

She stood, pleating the frills of her pinafore, and glancing from one to the other of us, like a hungry bird. I smiled at the thought of how Jim had pulled Jo's leg about her. Certainly her eyes were blue, and what hair she had was yellow, but ugly. She was a figure of fun. Looking at her, you felt there was nothing but sticks and wires under that pinafore — her front teeth were knocked out, she had red, pulpy hands and she wore on her feet a pair of dirty Bluchers.

"I'll go and turn out the horses," said Jim. "Got any embrocation? Poi's rubbed herself to hell!"

Walter Wright
Landscape

"'Arf a mo!" The woman stood silent a moment, her nostrils expanding as she breathed. Then she shouted violently, "I'd rather you didn't stop. . . . You *can't*, and there's the end of it. I don't let out that paddock any more. You'll have to go on; I ain't got nothing!"

"Well, I'm blest!" said Jo heavily. He pulled me aside. "Gone a bit off 'er dot," he whispered. "Too much alone, *you know*," very significantly. "Turn the sympathetic tap on 'er, she'll come round all right."

But there was no need — she had come round by herself.

"Stop if yer like!" she muttered, shrugging her shoulders. To me — "I'll give yer the embrocation if yer come along."

"Right-o, I'll take it down to them." We walked together up the garden path. It was planted on both sides with cabbages. They smelled like stale dish-water. Of flowers there were double poppies and sweet-williams. One little patch was divided off by pawa shells — presumably it belonged to the child — for she ran from her mother and began to grub in it with a broken clothes-peg. The yellow dog lay across the doorstep, biting fleas; the woman kicked him away.

"Gar-r, get away, you beast. . . the place ain't tidy. I 'aven't 'ad time ter fix things to-day — been ironing. Come right in."

It was a large room, the walls plastered with old pages of English periodicals. Queen Victoria's Jubilee appeared to be the most recent number. A table with an ironing board and wash-tub on it, some wooden forms, a black horsehair sofa and some broken cane chairs pushed against the walls. The mantelpiece above the stove was draped in pink paper, further ornamented with dried grasses and ferns and a coloured print of Richard Seddon. There were four doors — one, judging from the smell, led into the "Store", one on to the "backyard", through a third I saw the bedroom. Flies buzzed in circles round the ceiling, and treacle papers and bundles of dried clover were pinned to the window curtains.

I was alone in the room; she had gone into the store for the embrocation. I heard her stamping about and muttering to herself: "I got some, now where did I put that bottle? . . . It's behind the pickles. . . no, it ain't." I cleared a place on the table and sat there, swinging my legs. Down in the paddock I could hear Jo singing and the sound of hammer strokes as Jim drove in the tent pegs. It was sunset. There is no twilight in our New Zealand days, but a curious half-hour when everything appears grotesque — it frightens — as though the savage spirit of the country walked abroad and sneered at what it saw. Sitting alone in the hideous room I grew afraid. The woman next door was a long time finding that stuff. What was she doing in there? Once I thought I heard her bang her hands down on the counter, and once she half moaned, turning it into a cough and clearing her throat. I wanted to shout "Buck up!" but I kept silent.

"Good Lord, what a life!" I thought. "Imagine being here day in, day out, with that rat of a child and a mangy dog. Imagine bothering about ironing. *Mad*, of course she's mad! Wonder how long she's been here — wonder if I could get her to talk."

At that moment she poked her head round the door.

"Wot was it yer wanted?" she asked.

"Embrocation."

"Oh, I forgot. I got it, it was in front of the pickle jars."

She handed me the bottle.

"My, you do look tired, you do! Shall I knock yer up a few scones for supper! There's some tongue in the store, too, and I'll cook yer a cabbage if you fancy it."

"Right-o." I smiled at her. "Come down to the paddock and bring the kid for tea."

She shook her head, pursing up her mouth.

"Oh no. I don't fancy it. I'll send the kid down with the things and a billy of milk. Shall I knock up a few extry scones to take with yer ter-morrow?"

"Thanks."

She came and stood by the door.

"How old is the kid?"

"Six — come next Christmas. I 'ad a bit of trouble with 'er one way an' another. I 'adn't any milk till a month after she was born and she sickened like a cow."

"She's not like you — takes after her father?" Just as the woman had shouted her refusal at us before, she shouted at me then.

"No, she don't! She's the dead spit of me. Any fool could see that. Come on in now, Else, you stop messing in the dirt."

I met Jo climbing over the paddock fence.

"What's the old bitch got in the store?" he asked.

"Don't know — didn't look."

"Well, of all the fools. Jim's slanging you. What have you been doing all the time?"

"She couldn't find this stuff. Oh, my shakes, you are smart!"

Jo had washed, combed his wet hair in a line across his forehead, and buttoned a coat over his shirt. He grinned.

Jim snatched the embrocation from me. I went to the end of the paddock where the willows grew and bathed in the creek. The water was clear and soft as oil. Along the edges held by the grass and rushes white foam tumbled and bubbled. I lay in the water and looked up at the trees that were still a moment, then quivered lightly and again were still. The air smelt of rain. I forgot about the woman and the kid until I came back to the tent. Jim lay by the fire watching the billy boil.

I asked where Jo was, and if the kid had brought our supper.

"Pooh," said Jim, rolling over and looking up at the sky. "Didn't you see how Jo had been titivating? He said to me before he went up the whare, 'Dang it! she'll look better by night light — at any rate, my buck, she's female flesh!'"

"You had Jo about her looks — you had me too."

"No — look here. I can't make it out. It's four years since I came past this way and I stopped here two days. The husband was a pal of mine once, down the West Coast — a fine, big chap with a voice on him like a trombone. She's been barmaid down the Coast — as pretty as a wax doll. The coach used to come this way then once a fortnight, that was before they opened the railway up Napier way, and she had no end of a time! Told me once in a confidential moment that she knew one hundred and twenty-five different ways of kissing!"

"Oh, go on, Jim! She isn't the same woman!"

"'Course she is.....I can't make it out. What I think is the old man's cleared out and left her: that's all my eye about shearing. Sweet life! The only people who come through now are Maoris and sundowners!"

Through the dark we saw the gleam of the kid's pinafore. She trailed over to us with a basket in her hand, the milk billy in the other. I unpacked the basket, the child standing by.

"Come over here," said Jim, snapping his fingers at her.

She went, the lamp from the inside of the tent cast a bright light over her. A mean, undersized brat, with whitish hair and weak eyes. She stood, legs wide apart and her stomach protruding.

"What do you do all day?" asked Jim.

She scraped out one ear with her little finger, looked at the result and said, "Draw."

"Huh! What do you draw? Leave your ears alone!"

"Pictures."

"What on?"

"Bits of butter paper an' a pencil of my Mumma's."

"Boh! What a lot of words at one time!" Jim rolled his eyes at her. "Baa-lambs and moo-cows?"

"No, everything. I'll draw all of you when you're gone, and your horses and the tent, and that one" — she pointed to me — "with no clothes on in the creek. I looked at her where she couldn't see me from."

"Thanks very much. How ripping of you," said Jim. "Where's Dad?"

The kid pouted. "I won't tell you because I don't like yer face!" She started operations on the other ear.

"Here," I said. "Take the basket, get along home and tell the other man supper's ready."

"I don't want to."

"I'll give you a box on the ear if you don't," said Jim savagely.

"Hie! I'll tell Mumma. I'll tell Mumma." The kid fled.

We ate until we were full, and had arrived at the smoke stage before Jo came back,

14

Thomas Ryan
Champagne Pool, Wairakei Geyser Valley

very flushed and jaunty, a whisky bottle in his hand.

"'Ave a drink — you two!" he shouted, carrying off matters with a high hand. "'Ere, shove along the cups."

"One hundred and twenty-five different ways," I murmured to Jim.

"What's that? Oh! stow it!" said Jo. "Why 'ave you always got your knife into me. You gas like a kid at a Sunday School beano. She wants us to go there to-night and have a comfortable chat. I" — he waved his hand airily — "I got 'er round."

"Trust you for that," laughed Jim. "But did she tell you where the old man's got to?"

Jo looked up. "Shearing! You 'eard 'er, you fool!"

The woman had fixed up the room, even to a light bouquet of sweet-williams on the table. She and I sat one side of the table, Jo and Jim the other. An oil lamp was set between us, the whisky bottle and glasses, and a jug of water. The kid knelt against one of the forms, drawing on butter paper; I wondered, grimly, if she was attempting the creek episode. But Jo had been right about night time. The woman's hair was tumbled — two red spots burned in her cheeks — her eyes shone — and we knew that they were kissing feet under the table. She had changed the blue pinafore for a white calico dressing-jacket and a black skirt — the kid was decorated to the extent of a blue sateen hair ribbon. In the stifling room, with the flies buzzing against the ceiling and dropping on to the table, we got slowly drunk.

"Now listen to me," shouted the woman, banging her fist on the table. "It's six years since I was married, and four miscarriages. I says to 'im, I says, what do you think I'm doin' up 'ere? If you was back at the Coast I'd 'ave you lynched for child murder. Over and over I tells 'im — you've broken my spirit and spoiled my looks, and wot for — that's wot I'm driving at." She clutched her head with her hands and stared round at us. Speaking rapidly, "Oh, some days — an' months of them — I 'ear them two words knockin' inside me all the time — 'Wot for!' but sometimes I'll be cooking the spuds an' I lifts the lid off to give 'em a prong and I 'ears, quite suddin again, 'Wot for!' Oh! I don't mean only the spuds and the kid — I mean — I mean," she hiccoughed — "you know what I mean, Mr. Jo."

"I know," said Jo, scratching his head.

"Trouble with me is," she leaned across the table, "he left me too much alone. When the coach stopped coming, sometimes he'd go away days, sometimes he'd go away weeks, and leave me ter look after the store. Back 'e'd come — pleased as Punch. 'Oh, 'allo,' 'e'd say. "Ow are you gettin' on? Come and give us a kiss.' Sometimes I'd turn a bit nasty, and then 'e'd go off again, and if I took it all right, 'e'd wait till 'e could twist me round 'is finger, then 'e'd say, 'Well, so long, I'm off,' and do you think I could keep 'im? — not me!"

"Mumma," bleated the kid, "I made a picture of them on the 'ill, an' you an' me an' the dog down below."

"Shut your mouth!" said the woman.

A vivid flash of lightning played over the room — we heard the mutter of thunder.

"Good thing that's broke loose," said Jo. "I've 'ad it in me 'ead for three days."

"Where's your old man now?" asked Jim slowly.

The woman blubbered and dropped her head on to the table. "Jim, 'e's gone shearin' and left me alone again," she wailed.

"'Ere, look out for the glasses," said Jo. "Cheer-o, 'ave another drop. No good cryin' over spilt 'usbands! You, Jim, you blasted cuckoo!"

"Mr. Jo," said the woman, drying her eyes on her jacket frill, "you're a gent, an' if I was a secret woman I'd place any confidence in your 'ands. I don't mind if I do 'ave a glass on that."

Every moment the lightning grew more vivid and the thunder sounded nearer. Jim and I were silent — the kid never moved from her bench. She poked her tongue out and blew on her paper as she drew.

"It's the loneliness," said the woman, addressing Jo — he made sheep's eyes at her — "and bein' shut up 'ere like a broody 'en." He reached his hand across the table and held hers, and though the position looked most uncomfortable when they wanted to pass the water and whisky, their hands stuck together as though glued. I pushed back my chair and went over to the kid, who immediately sat flat down on her artistic achievements and made a face at me.

"You're not to look," said she.

"Oh, come on, don't be nasty!" Jim came over to us, and we were just drunk enough to wheedle the kid into showing us. And those drawings of hers were extraordinary and repulsively vulgar. The creations of a lunatic with a lunatic's cleverness. There was no doubt about it, the kid's mind was diseased. While she showed them to us, she worked herself up into a mad excitement, laughing and trembling, and shooting out her arms.

"Mumma," she yelled. "Now I'm going to draw them what you told me I never was to — now I am."

The woman rushed from the table and beat the child's head with the flat of her hand.

"I'll smack you with yer clothes turned up if yer dare say that again," she bawled.

Jo was too drunk to notice, but Jim caught her by the arm. The kid did not utter a cry. She drifted over to the window and began picking flies from the treacle paper.

We returned to the table — Jim and I sitting one side, the woman and Jo, touching shoulders, the other. We listened to the thunder, saying stupidly, "That was a near one," "There it goes again," and Jo, at a heavy hit, "Now we're off," "Steady on the brake," until rain began to fall, sharp as cannon shot on the iron roof.

"You'd better doss here for the night," said the woman.

"That's right," assented Jo, evidently in the know about this move.

"Bring up yer things from the tent. You two can doss in the store along with the kid — she's used to sleep in there and won't mind you."

"Oh, Mumma, I never did," interrupted the kid.

"Shut yer lies! An' Mr. Jo can 'ave this room."

It sounded a ridiculous arrangement, but it was useless to attempt to cross them, they were too far gone. While the woman sketched the plan of action, Jo sat, abnormally solemn and red, his eyes bulging, and pulling at his moustache.

"Give us a lantern," said Jim, "I'll go down to the paddock." We two went together. Rain whipped in our faces, the land was light as though a bush fire was raging. We behaved like two children let loose in the thick of an adventure, laughed and shouted to each other, and came back to the whare to find the kid already bedded in the counter of the store. The woman brought us a lamp. Jo took his bundle from Jim, the door was shut.

"Good night all," shouted Jo.

Jim and I sat on two sacks of potatoes. For the life of us we could not stop laughing. Strings of onions and half-hams dangled from the ceiling — wherever we looked there were advertisements for "Camp Coffee" and tinned meats. We pointed at them, tried to read them aloud — overcome with laughter and hiccoughs. The kid in the counter stared at us. She threw off her blanket and scrambled to the floor, where she stood in her grey flannel night-gown rubbing one leg against the other. We paid no attention to her.

"Wot are you laughing at?" she said uneasily.

"You!" shouted Jim. "The red tribe of you, my child."

She flew into a rage and beat herself with her hands. "I won't be laughed at, you curs — you." He swooped down upon the child and swung her on to the counter.

"Go to sleep, Miss Smarty — or make a drawing — here's a pencil — you can use Mumma's account book."

Through the rain we heard Jo creak over the boarding of the next room — the sound of a door being opened — then shut to.

"It's the loneliness," whispered Jim.

"One hundred and twenty-five different ways — alas! my poor brother!"

The kid tore out a page and flung it at me.

"There you are," she said. "Now I done it ter spite Mumma for shutting me up 'ere with you two. I done the one she told me I never ought to. I done the one she told me she'd shoot me if I did. Don't care! Don't care!"

The kid had drawn the picture of the woman shooting at a man with a rook rifle and then digging a hole to bury him in.

She jumped off the counter and squirmed about on the floor biting her nails.

Jim and I sat till dawn with the drawing beside us. The rain ceased, the little kid fell asleep, breathing loudly. We got up, stole out of the whare, down into the paddock. White clouds floated over a pink sky, a chill wind blew; the air smelled of wet grass. Just as we swung into the saddle Jo came out of the whare — he motioned to us to ride on.

"I'll pick you up later," he shouted.

A bend in the road, and the whole place disappeared.

OLE UNDERWOOD

To Anne Estelle Rice

DOWN the windy hill stalked Ole Underwood. He carried a black umbrella in one hand, in the other a red and white spotted handerchief knotted into a lump. He wore a black peaked cap like a pilot; gold rings gleamed in his ears and his little eyes snapped like two sparks. Like two sparks they glowed in the smoulder of his bearded face. On one side of the hill grew a forest of pines from the road right down to the sea. On the other side short tufted grass and little bushes of white manuka flower. The pine trees roared like waves in their topmost branches, their stems creaked like the timber of ships; in the windy air flew the white manuka flower. "Ah-k!" shouted Ole Underwood, shaking his umbrella at the wind bearing down upon him, beating him, half strangling him with his black cape. "Ah-k!" shouted the wind a hundred times as loud, and filled his mouth and nostrils with dust. Something inside Ole Underwood's breast beat like a hammer. One, two — one, two — never stopping, never changing. He couldn't do anything. It wasn't loud. No, it didn't make a noise — only a thud. One, two — one, two — like someone beating on an iron in a prison, someone in a secret place — bang — bang — bang — trying to get free. Do what he would, fumble at his coat, throw his arms about, spit, swear, he couldn't stop the noise. Stop! Stop! Stop! Ole Underwood began to shuffle and run.

Away below, the sea heaving against the stone walls, and the little town just out of its reach close packed together, the better to face the grey water. And up on the other side of the hill the prison with high red walls. Over all bulged the grey sky with black web-like clouds streaming.

Ole Underwood slackened his pace as he neared the town, and when he came to the first house he flourished his umbrella like a herald's staff and threw out his chest, his head glancing quickly from right to left. They were ugly little houses leading into the town, built of wood — two windows and a door, a stumpy veranda and a green mat of grass before. Under one veranda yellow hens huddled out of the wind. "Shoo!" shouted Ole Underwood, and laughed to see them fly, and laughed again at the woman who came to the door and shook a red, soapy fist at him. A little girl stood in another yard untwisting some rags from a clothes-line. When she saw Ole Underwood she let the clothes-prop fall and rushed screaming to the door, beating it screaming "Mumma — Mumma!" That started the hammer

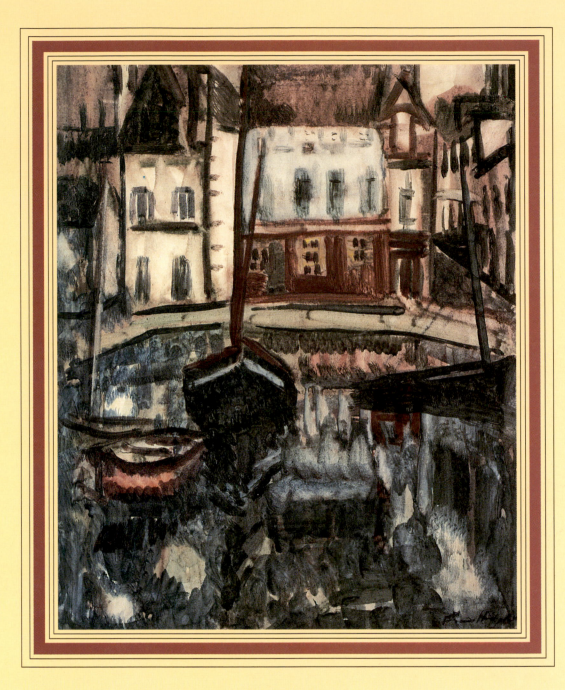

Frances Hodgkins
Concarneau: Dusk in the Port

in Ole Underwood's heart. Mum-ma — Mum-ma! He saw an old face with a trembling chin and grey hair nodding out of the window as they dragged him past. Mumma — Mumma! He looked up at the big red prison perched on the hill and he pulled a face as if he wanted to cry.

At the corner in front of the pub some carts were pulled up, some men sat in the porch of the pub drinking and talking. Ole Underwood wanted a drink. He slouched into the bar. It was half full of old and young men in big coats and top-boots with stock-whips in their hands. Behind the counter a big girl with red hair pulled the beer handles and cheeked the men. Ole Underwood sneaked to one side, like a cat. Nobody looked at him, only the men looked at each other, one or two of them nudged. The girl nodded and winked at the fellow she was serving. He took some money out of his knotted handkerchief and slipped it on to the counter. His hand shook. He didn't speak. The girl took no notice; she served everybody, went on with her talk, and then as if by accident shoved a mug towards him. A great big jar of red pinks stood on the bar counter. Ole Underwood stared at them as he drank and frowned at them. Red — red — red — red! beat the hammer. It was very warm in the bar and quiet as a pond, except for the talk and the girl. She kept on laughing. Ha! Ha! that was what the men liked to see, for she threw back her head and her great breasts lifted and shook to her laughter.

In one corner sat a stranger. He pointed at Ole Underwood. "Cracked!" said one of the men. "When he was a young fellow, thirty years ago, a man 'ere done in 'is woman, and 'e foun' out an' killed 'er. Got twenty years in quod up on the 'ill. Came out cracked."

"Oo done 'er in?" asked the man.

"Dunno. 'E dunno, nor nobody. 'E was a sailor till 'e marrid 'er. Cracked!" The man spat and smeared the spittle on the floor, shrugging his shoulders. "'E's 'armless enough."

Ole Underwood heard; he did not turn, but he shot out an old claw and crushed up the red pinks. "Uh-Uh! You ole beast! Uh! You ole swine!" screamed the girl, leaning across the counter and banging him with a tin jug. "Get art! Get art! Don' you never come 'ere no more!" Somebody kicked him: he scuttled like a rat.

He walked past the Chinamen's shops. The fruit and vegetables were all piled up against the windows. Bits of wooden cases, straw and old newspapers were strewn over the pavement. A woman flounced out of a shop and slushed a pail of slops over his feet. He peered in at the windows, at the Chinamen sitting in little groups on old barrels playing cards. They made him smile. He looked and looked, pressing his face against the glass and sniggering. They sat still with their long pigtails bound round their heads and their faces yellow as lemons. Some of them had knives in their belts, and one old man sat by himself on the floor plaiting his long crooked toes together. The Chinamen didn't mind Ole Underwood. When they saw him they nodded. He went to the door of a shop and cautiously opened it. In rushed the wind with him, scattering the cards. "Ya-Ya! Ya-Ya!" screamed the Chinamen, and Ole Underwood rushed off, the hammer beating quick and hard. Ya-Ya! He turned a corner out of sight. He thought he heard one of the Chinks after him, and he slipped into a timber-yard. There he lay panting....

Close by him, under another stack, there was a heap of yellow shavings. As he watched them they moved and a little grey cat unfolded herself and came out waving her tail. She trod delicately over to Ole Underwood and rubbed against his sleeve. The hammer in Ole Underwood's heart beat madly. It pounded up into his throat, and then it seemed to half stop and beat very, very faintly. "Kit! Kit! Kit!" That was what she used to call the little cat he brought her off the ship — "Kit! Kit! Kit!" — and stoop down with the saucer in her hands. "Ah! my God! my Lord!" Ole Underwood sat up and took the kitten in his arms and rocked to and fro, crushing it against his face. It was warm and soft, and it mewed faintly. He buried his eyes in its fur. My God! My Lord! He tucked the little cat in his coat and stole out of the woodyard and slouched down towards the wharves. As he came near the sea, Ole Underwood's nostrils expanded. The mad wind smelled of tar and ropes and slime and salt. He crossed the railway line, he crept behind the wharf-sheds and along the little cinder path that threaded through a patch of rank fennel to some stone drainpipes carrying the sewage into the sea. And he stared up at the wharves and at the ships with flags flying, and suddenly the old, old lust swept over Ole Underwood. "I will! I will! I will!" he muttered.

He tore the little cat out of his coat and swung it by its tail and flung it out to the sewer opening. The hammer beat loud and strong. He tossed his head, he was young again. He walked on to the wharves, past the wool-bales, past the loungers and the loafers to the extreme end of the wharves. The sea sucked against the wharf-poles as though it drank something from the land. One ship was loading wool. He heard a crane rattle and the shriek of a whistle. So he came to the little ship lying by herself with a bit of a plank for a gangway, and no sign of anybody — anybody at all. Ole Underwood looked once back at the town, at the prison perched like a red bird, at the black webby clouds trailing. Then he went up the gangway and on to the slippery deck. He grinned, and rolled in his walk, carrying high in his hand the red and white handkerchief. His ship! Mine! Mine! Mine! beat the hammer. There was a door latched open on the lee-side, labelled "State-room". He peered in. A man lay sleeping on a bunk — his bunk — a great big man in a seaman's coat with a long, fair beard and hair on the red pillow. And looking down upon him from the wall there shone her picture — his woman's picture — smiling and smiling at the big sleeping man.

How Pearl Button was Kidnapped

PEARL BUTTON swung on the little gate in front of the House of Boxes. It was the early afternoon of a sunshiny day with little winds playing hide-and-seek in it. They blew Pearl Button's pinafore frill into her mouth, and they blew the street dust all over the House of Boxes. Pearl watched it — like a cloud — like when mother peppered her fish and the top of the pepper-pot came off. She swung on the little gate, all alone, and she sang a small song. Two big women came walking down the street. One was dressed in red and the other was dressed in yellow and green. They had pink handkerchiefs over their heads, and both of them carried a big flax basket of ferns. They had no shoes and stockings on, and they came walking along, slowly, because they were so fat, and talking to each other and always smiling. Pearl stopped swinging, and when they saw her they stopped walking. They looked and looked at her and then they talked to each other, waving their arms and clapping their hands together. Pearl began to laugh.

The two women came up to her, keeping close to the hedge and looking in a frightened way towards the House of Boxes.

"Hallo, little girl!" said one.

Pearl said, "Hallo!"

"You all alone by yourself?"

Pearl nodded.

"Where's your mother?"

"In the kitching, ironing-because-it's-Tuesday."

The women smiled at her and Pearl smiled back. "Oh," she said, "haven't you got very white teeth indeed! Do it again."

The dark women laughed, and again they talked to each other with funny words and wavings of the hands. "What's your name?" they asked her.

"Pearl Button."

"You coming with us, Pearl Button? We got beautiful things to show you," whispered one of the women. So Pearl got down from the gate and she slipped out into the road. And she walked between the two dark women down the windy road, taking little running steps to keep up, and wondering what they had in their House of Boxes.

They walked a long way. "You tired?" asked one of the women, bending down to Pearl. Pearl shook her head. They walked much further. "You not tired?" asked the other woman. And Pearl shook her head again, but tears shook from her eyes at the same time and her lips trembled. One of the women gave over her flax basket of ferns and caught Pearl Button up in her arms, and walked with Pearl Button's head against her shoulder and her dusty little legs dangling. She was softer than a bed and she had a nice smell — a smell that made you bury your head and breathe and breathe it. . . .

They set Pearl Button down in a log room full of other people the same colour as they were — and all these people came close to her and looked at her, nodding and laughing and throwing up their eyes. The woman who had carried Pearl took off her hair ribbon and shook her curls loose. There was a cry from the other women, and they crowded close and some of them ran a finger through Pearl's yellow curls, very gently, and one of them, a young one, lifted all Pearl's hair and kissed the back of her little white neck. Pearl felt shy but happy at the same time. There were some men on the floor, smoking, with rugs and feather mats round their shoulders. One of them made a funny face at her and he pulled a great big peach out of his pocket and set it on the floor, and flicked it with his finger as though it were a marble. It rolled right over to her. Pearl picked it up. "Please can I eat it?" she asked. At that they all laughed and clapped their hands, and the man with the funny face made another at her and pulled a pear out of his pocket and sent it bobbling over the floor. Pearl laughed. The women sat on the floor and Pearl sat down too. The floor was very dusty. She carefully pulled up her pinafore and dress and sat on her petticoat as she had been taught to sit in dusty places, and she ate the fruit, the juice running all down her front.

"Oh!" she said in a very frightened voice to one of the women, "I've spilt all the juice!"

"That doesn't matter at all," said the woman patting her cheek. A man came into the room with a long whip in his hand. He shouted something. They all got up, shouting, laughing, wrapping themselves up in rugs and blankets and feather mats. Pearl was carried again, this time into a great cart, and she sat on the lap of one of her women with the driver beside her. It was a green cart with a red pony and a black pony. It went very fast out of the town. The driver stood up and waved the whip round his head. Pearl peered over the shoulder of her woman. Other carts were behind like a procession. She waved at them. Then the country came. First fields of short grass with sheep on them and little bushes of white flowers and pink briar rose baskets — then big trees on both sides of the road — and nothing to be seen except big trees. Pearl tried to look through them but it was quite dark. Birds were singing. She nestled closer in the big lap. The woman was warm as a cat, and she moved up and down when she breathed, just like purring. Pearl played with a green ornament round her neck, and the woman took the little hand and kissed each of her fingers and then turned it over and kissed the dimples. Pearl had never been happy like this before. On the top of a big hill they stopped. The driving man turned to Pearl and said, "Look, look!" and pointed with his whip.

And down at the bottom of the hill was something perfectly different — a great big piece of blue water was creeping over the land. She screamed and clutched at the big woman.

Girolamo Pieri Nerli
Study: Head of a Girl

"What is it, what is it?"

"Why," said the woman, "it's the sea."

"Will it hurt us — is it coming?"

"Ai-e, no, it doesn't come to us. It's very beautiful. You look again."

Pearl looked. "You're sure it can't come," she said.

"Ai-e, no. It stays in its place," said the big woman. Waves with white tops came leaping over the blue. Pearl watched them break on a long piece of land covered with garden-path shells. They drove round a corner.

There were some little houses down close to the sea, with wood fences round them and gardens inside. They comforted her. Pink and red and blue washing hung over the fences, and as they came near more people came out, and five yellow dogs with long thin tails. All the people were fat and laughing, with little naked babies holding on to them or rolling about in the gardens like puppies. Pearl was lifted down and taken into a tiny house with only one room and a veranda. There was a girl there with two pieces of black hair down to her feet. She was setting the dinner on the floor. "It *is* a funny place," said Pearl, watching the pretty girl while the women unbuttoned her little drawers for her. She was very hungry. She ate meat and vegetables and fruit and the woman gave her milk out of a green cup. And it was quite silent except for the sea outside and the laughs of the two women watching her. "Haven't you got any Houses of Boxes?" she said. "Don't you all live in a row? Don't the men go to offices? Aren't there any nasty things?"

They took off her shoes and stockings, her pinafore and dress. She walked about in her petticoat and then she walked outside with the grass pushing between her toes. The two women came out with different sorts of baskets. They took her hands. Over a little paddock, through a fence, and then on warm sand with brown grass in it they went down to the sea. Pearl held back when the sand grew wet, but the women coaxed, "Nothing to hurt, very beautiful. You come." They dug in the sand and found some shells which they threw into the baskets. The sand was wet as mud pies. Pearl forgot her fright and began digging too. She got hot and wet, and suddenly over her feet broke a little line of foam. "Oo, oo!" she shrieked, dabbling with her feet. "Lovely, lovely!" She paddled in the shallow water. It was warm. She made a cup of her hands and caught some of it. But it stopped being blue in her hands. She was so excited that she rushed over to her woman and flung her little thin arms round the woman's neck, hugging her, kissing. . . .

Suddenly the girl gave a frightful scream. The woman raised herself and Pearl slipped down on the sand and looked towards the land. Little men in blue coats — little blue men came running, running towards her with shouts and whistlings — a crowd of little blue men to carry her back to the House of Boxes.

NEW DRESSES

MRS. CARSFIELD and her mother sat at the dining-room table putting the finishing touches to some green cashmere dresses. They were to be worn by the two Misses Carsfield at church on the following day, with apple-green sashes, and straw hats with ribbon tails. Mrs. Carsfield had set her heart on it, and this being a late night for Henry, who was attending a meeting of the Political League, she and the old mother had the dining-room to themselves and could make "a peaceful litter" as she expressed it. The red cloth was taken off the table — where stood the wedding-present sewing-machine, a brown work-basket, the "material," and some torn fashion journals. Mrs. Carsfield worked the machine, slowly for she feared the green thread would give out, and had a sort of tired hope that it might last longer if she was careful to use a little at a time; the old woman sat in a rocking-chair, her skirt turned back, and her felt-slippered feet on a hassock, tying the machine threads and stitching some narrow lace on the necks and cuffs. The gas jet flickered. Now and again the old woman glanced up at the jet and said, "There's water in the pipe, Anne, that's what's the matter," then was silent, to say again a moment later, "There must be water in that pipe, Anne," and again, with quite a burst of energy, "*Now* there is — I'm *certain* of it."

Anne frowned at the sewing-machine. "The way mother *harps* on things — it gets frightfully on my nerves," she thought. "And always when there's no earthly opportunity to better a thing. . . . I suppose it's old age — but most aggravating." Aloud she said: "Mother, I'm having a really substantial hem in this dress of Rose's — the child has got so leggy lately. And don't put any lace on Helen's cuffs; it will make a distinction, and besides she's so careless about rubbing her hands on anything grubby."

"Oh, there's plenty," said the old woman. "I'll put it a little higher up." And she wondered why Anne had such a down on Helen — Henry was just the same. They seemed to want to hurt Helen's feelings — the distinction was merely an excuse.

"Well," said Mrs. Carsfield, "You didn't see Helen's clothes when I took them off to-night. Black from head to foot after a week. And when I compared them before her eyes with Rose's she merely shrugged, you know that habit she's got, and began stuttering. I really shall have to see Dr. Malcolm about her stuttering, if only to give her a good fright.

I believe it's merely an affection she's picked up at school — that she can help it."

"Anne, you know she's always stuttered. You did just the same when you were her age, she's highly strung." The old woman took off her spectacles, breathed on them, and rubbed them with a corner of her sewing apron.

"Well, the last thing in the world to do her any good is to let her imagine *that*," answered Anne, shaking out one of the green frocks and pricking at the pleats with her needle. "She is treated exactly like Rose, and the Boy hasn't a nerve. Did you see him when I put him on the rocking-horse to-day, for the first time? He simply gurgled with joy. He's more the image of his father every day."

"Yes, he certainly is a thorough Carsfield," assented the old woman, nodding her head.

"Now that's another thing about Helen," said Anne. "The peculiar way she treats Boy, staring at him and frightening him as she does. You remember when he was a baby how she used to take away his bottle to see what he would do? Rose is perfect with the child — but Helen . . ."

The old woman put down her work on the table. A little silence fell, and through the silence the loud ticking of the dining-room clock. She wanted to speak her mind to Anne once and for all about the way she and Henry were treating Helen, ruining the child, but the ticking noise distracted her. She could not think of the words and sat there stupidly, her brain going *tick, tick* to the dining-room clock.

"How loudly that clock ticks," was all she said.

"Oh, there's mother — off the subject again — giving me no help or encouragement," thought Anne. She glanced at the clock.

"Mother, if you've finished that frock, would you go into the kitchen and heat up some coffee and perhaps cut a plate of ham. Henry will be in directly. I'm practically through with this second frock by myself." She held it up for inspection. "Aren't they charming? They ought to last the children a good two years, and then I expect they'll do for school — lengthened, and perhaps dyed."

"I'm glad we decided on the more expensive material," said the old woman.

Left alone in the dining-room Anne's frown deepened and her mouth drooped — a sharp line showed from nose to chin. She breathed deeply and pushed back her hair. There seemed to be no air in the room, she felt stuffed up, and it seemed so useless to be tiring herself out with fine sewing for Helen. One never got through with children and never had any gratitude from them — except Rose — who was exceptional. Another sign of old age in mother was her absurd point of view about Helen and her "touchiness" on the subject. There was one thing, Mrs. Carsfield said to herself. She was determined to keep Helen apart from Boy. He had all his father's sensitiveness to unsympathetic influences. A blessing that the girls were at school all day!

At last the dresses were finished and folded over the back of the chair. She carried the sewing-machine over to the bookshelves, spread the tablecloth, and went over to the window. The blind was up, she could see the garden quite plainly: there must be a moon about. And then she caught sight of something shining on the garden seat. A book, yes, it must be a book, left there to get soaked through by the dew. She went out into the hall, put on her goloshes, gathered up her skirt, and ran into the garden. Yes, it was a book. She picked it up carefully. Damp already — and the cover bulging. She shrugged her shoulders in the way that her little daughter had caught from her. In the shadowy garden that smelled of grass and rose leaves Anne's heart hardened. Then the gate clicked and she saw Henry striding up the front path.

"Henry!" she called.

"Hullo," he cried, "what on earth are you doing down there....Moon-gazing, Anne?" She ran forward and kissed him.

"Oh, look at this book," she said. "Helen's been leaving it about again. My dear, how you smell of cigars!"

Said Henry: "You've got to smoke a decent cigar when you're with these other chaps. Looks so bad if you don't. But come inside Anne; you haven't got anything on. Let the book go hang! You're cold, my dear, you're shivering." He put his arm round her shoulder. "See the moon over there, by the chimney? Fine night. By Jove! I had the fellows roaring to-night — I made a colossal joke. One of them said: 'Life is a game of cards,' and I, without thinking, just straight out..." Henry paused by the door and held up a finger. "I said...well, I've forgotten the exact words, but they shouted, my dear, simply shouted. No, I'll remember what I said in bed to-night; you know I always do."

"I'll take this book into the kitchen to dry on the stove-rack," said Anne, and she thought, as she banged the pages, "Henry has been drinking beer again, that means indigestion to-morrow. No use mentioning Helen to-night."

When Henry had finished the supper he lay back in the chair, picking his teeth, and patted his knee for Anne to come and sit there.

"Hullo," he said, jumping her up and down, "what's the green fandangles on the chair back? What have you and mother been up to, eh?"

Said Anne airily, casting a most careless glance at the green dresses, "Only some frocks for the children. Remnants for Sunday."

The old woman put the plate and cup and saucer together, then lighted a candle.

"I think I'll go to bed," she said cheerfully.

"Oh, dear me, how unwise of mother," thought Anne. "She makes Henry suspect by going away like that, as she always does if there's any unpleasantness brewing."

"No, don't go to bed yet, mother," cried Henry jovially. "Let's have a look at the things." She passed him over the dresses, faintly smiling. Henry rubbed them through his fingers.

"So these are the remnants, are they, Anne? Don't feel much like the Sunday trousers my mother used to make me out of an ironing blanket. How much did you pay for this a yard, Anne?"

Anne took the dresses from him and played with a button of his waistcoat.

"Forget the exact price, darling. Mother and I rather skimped them, even though they were so cheap. What can great big men bother about clothes...? Was Lumley there to-night?"

"Yes, he says their kid was a bit bandy-legged at just the same age as Boy. He told me of a new kind of chair for children that the draper has just got in — makes them sit with their legs straight. By the way, have you got this month's draper's bill?"

She had been waiting for that — had known it was coming. She slipped off his knee and yawned.

"Oh, dear me," she said, "I think I'll follow mother. Bed's the place for me." She stared at Henry vacantly. "Bill — bill did you say, dear? Oh, I'll look it out in the morning."

"No, Anne, hold on." Henry got up and went over to the cupboard where the bill file was kept. "To-morrow's no good — because it's Sunday. I want to get that account off my chest before I turn in. Sit down there — in the rocking chair — you needn't stand!"

She dropped into the chair and began humming, all the while her thoughts coldly busy and her eyes fixed on her husband's broad back as he bent over the cupboard door. He dawdled over finding the file.

"He's keeping me in suspense on purpose," she thought. "We can afford it — otherwise why should I do it? I know our income and our expenditure. I'm not a fool. They're a hell upon earth every month, these bills." And she thought of her bed upstairs, yearned for it, imagining she had never felt so tired in her life.

"Here we are!" said Henry. He slammed the file on the table.

"Draw up your chair...."

"Clayton: Seven yards green cashmere at five shillings a yard — thirty-five shillings." He read the item twice — then folded the sheet over and bent towards Anne. He was flushed and his breath smelt of beer. She knew exactly how he took things in that mood, and she raised her eyebrows and nodded.

"Do you mean to tell me," stormed Henry, "that lot over there cost thirty-five shillings — that stuff you've been mucking up for the children. Good God! Anybody would think you'd married a millionaire. You could buy your mother a trousseau with that money. You're making yourself a laughing-stock for the whole town. How do you think I can buy Boy a chair or anything else — if you chuck away my earnings like that? Time and again you impress upon me the impossibility of keeping Helen decent; and then you go decking her out the next moment in thirty-five shillings' worth of green cashmere...."

On and on stormed the voice.

"He'll have calmed down in the morning, when the beer's worked off," thought Anne, and later, as she toiled up to bed, "When he sees how they'll last, he'll understand...."

A brilliant Sunday morning. Henry and Anne, quite reconciled, sitting in the dining-room waiting for church time to the tune of Carsfield junior, who steadily thumped the shelf of his high chair with a gravy spoon given him from the breakfast table by his father.

Frances Hodgkins
The Edwardians

"That beggar's got muscle," said Henry proudly. "I've timed him by my watch. He's kept that up for five minutes without stopping."

"Extraordinary," said Anne, buttoning her gloves. "I think he's had that spoon almost long enough now, dear, don't you? I'm so afraid of him putting it into his mouth."

"Oh, I've got an eye on him." Henry stood over his small son. "Go it, old man. Tell mother boys like to kick up a row."

Anne kept silence. At any rate, it would keep his eye off the children when they came down in those cashmeres. She was still wondering if she had drummed into their minds often enough the supreme importance of being careful and of taking them off immediately after church before dinner, and why Helen was fidgety when she was pulled about at all, when the door opened and the old woman ushered them in, complete to the straw hats with ribbon tails.

She could not help thrilling, they looked so very superior — Rose carrying her prayer-book in a white case embroidered with a pink woollen cross. But she feigned indifference immediately and the lateness of the hour. Not a word more on the subject from Henry, even with the thirty-five shillings' work walking hand in hand before him all the way to church. Anne decided that was really generous and noble of him. She looked up at him walking with the shoulders thrown back. How fine he looked in that long black coat with the white silk tie just showing! And the children looked worthy of him. She squeezed his hand in church, conveying by that silent pressure "It was for your sake I made the dresses; of course, you can't understand that, but *really*, Henry." And she fully believed it.

On their way home the Carsfield family met Doctor Malcolm out walking with a black dog carrying his stick in its mouth. Doctor Malcolm stopped and asked after Boy so intelligently that Henry invited him to dinner.

"Come and pick a bone with us and see Boy for yourself," he said. And Doctor Malcolm accepted. He walked beside Henry and shouted over his shoulder, "Helen, keep an eye on *my* boy baby, will you, and see he doesn't swallow that walking-stick. Because, if he does, a tree will grow right out of his mouth or it will go to his tail and make it so stiff that a wag will knock you into kingdom come!"

"Oh, Doctor Malcolm!" laughed Helen, stooping over the dog. "Come along, doggie, give it up, there's a good boy!"

"Helen, your dress!" warned Anne.

"Yes, indeed," said Doctor Malcolm. "They are looking top-notchers to-day — the two young ladies."

"Well, it really *is* Rose's colour," said Anne. "Her complexion is so much more vivid than Helen's."

Rose blushed. Doctor Malcolm's eyes twinkled, and he kept a tight rein on himself saying she looked like a tomato in a lettuce salad.

"That child wants taken down a peg," he decided. "Give me Helen every time. She'll come to her own yet and lead them just the dance they need."

Boy was having his midday sleep when they arrived home, and Doctor Malcolm begged that Helen might show him round the garden. Henry, repenting already of his generosity,

Frances Hodgkins
Bridesmaids

gladly assented, and Anne went into the kitchen to interview the servant girl.

"Mumma, let me come too and taste the gravy," begged Rose.

"Huh!" muttered Doctor Malcolm. "Good riddance."

He established himself on the garden bench — put up his feet and took off his hat to give the sun "a chance of growing a second crop," he told Helen.

She asked soberly: "Doctor Malcolm, do you really like my dress."

"Of course I do, my lady. Don't you?"

"Oh yes, I'd like to be born and die in it. But it was such a fuss — tryings on, you know, and pullings, and 'don'ts'. I believe mother would kill me if it got hurt. I even knelt on my petticoat all through church because of dust on the hassock."

"Bad as that!" asked Doctor Malcolm, rolling his eyes at Helen.

"Oh, *far* worse," said the child, then burst into laughter and shouted "Hellish!" dancing over the lawn.

"Take care, they'll hear you, Helen."

"Oh, booh! It's just dirty old cashmere — serve them right. They can't see me if they're not here to see and so it doesn't matter. It's only with them I feel funny."

"Haven't you got to remove your finery before dinner?"

"No, because you're here."

"Oh my prophetic soul!" groaned Doctor Malcolm.

Coffee was served in the garden. The servant girl brought out some cane chairs and a rug for Boy. The children were told to go away and play.

"Leave off worrying Doctor Malcolm, Helen," said Henry. "You mustn't be a plague to people who are not members of your own family." Helen pouted and dragged over to the swing for comfort. She swung high, and thought Doctor Malcolm was a most beautiful man — and wondered if his dog had finished the plate of bones in the back yard. Decided to go and see. Slower she swung, then took a flying leap; her tight skirt caught a nail — there was a sharp, tearing sound — quickly she glanced at the others — they had not noticed — and then at the frock — at a hole big enough to stick her hand through. She felt neither frightened nor sorry. "I'll go and change it," she thought.

"Helen, where are you going to?" called Anne.

"Into the house for a book."

The old woman noticed that the child held her skirt in a peculiar way. Her petticoat string must have come untied. But she made no remark. Once in the bedroom Helen unbuttoned the frock, slipped out of it, and wondered what to do next. Hide it somewhere — she glanced all round the room — there was nowhere safe from them. Except the top of the cupboard — but even standing on a chair she could not throw so high — it fell back on top of her every time — the horrid, hateful thing. Then her eyes lighted on her school satchel hanging on the end of the bedpost. Wrap it in her school pinafore — put it in the bottom of the bag with the pencil case on top. They'd never look there. She returned to the garden in the every-day dress — but forgot about the book.

"A-ah," said Anne, smiling ironically. "What a new leaf for Doctor Malcolm's benefit! Look, mother, Helen has changed without being told to."

"Come here, dear, and be done up properly." She whispered to Helen: "Where did you leave your dress?"

"Left it on the side of the bed. *Where* I took it off," sang Helen.

Doctor Malcolm was talking to Henry of the advantages derived from public school education for the sons of commercial men, but he had his eye on the scene and, watching Helen, he smelt a rat — smelt a Hamelin tribe of them.

Confusion and consternation reigned. One of the green cashmeres had disappeared — spirited off the face of the earth — during the time that Helen took it off and the children's tea.

"Show me the exact spot," scolded Mrs. Carsfield for the twentieth time. "Helen, tell the truth."

"Mumma, I *swear* I left it on the floor."

"Well, it's no good swearing if it's not there. It can't have been stolen!"

"I did see a very funny-looking man in a white cap walking up and down the road and staring in the windows as I came up to change." Sharply Anne eyed her daughter.

"Now," she said, "I *know* you are telling lies."

She turned to the old woman, in her voice something of pride and joyous satisfaction. "You hear, mother — this cock-and-bull story?"

When they were near the end of the bed Helen blushed and turned away from them. And now and again she wanted to shout "I tore it, I tore it," and she fancied she had said it and seen their faces, just as sometimes in bed she dreamed she had got up and dressed. But as the evening wore on she grew quite careless — glad only of one thing — people had to go to sleep at night. Viciously she stared at the sun shining through the window space and making a pattern of the curtain on the bare nursery table with a whole egg-cup full of water to herself. . . .

Henry visited their bedroom the last thing. She heard him come creaking into their room and hid under the bedclothes. But Rose betrayed her.

"Helen's not asleep," piped Rose.

Henry sat by the bedside pulling his moustache.

"If it were not Sunday, Helen, I would whip you. As it is, and I must be at the office early to-morrow, I shall give you a sound smacking after tea in the evening

35

. . . . Do you hear me?"

She grunted.

"You love your father and mother,
don't you?"

No answer.

Rose gave Helen a dig with her foot.

"Well," said Henry, sighing deeply, "I suppose you love Jesus?"

"Rose has scratched my leg with her toe-nail," answered Helen.

Henry strode out of the room and flung himself on to his own bed with his outdoor boots on the starched bolster, Anne noticed, but he was too overcome for her to venture a protest. The old woman was in the bedroom, too, idly combing the hairs from Anne's brush. Henry told them the story, and was gratified to observe Anne's tears.

"It *is* Rose's turn for her toe-nails after the bath next Saturday," commented the old woman.

In the middle of the night Henry dug his elbow into Mrs. Carsfield.

"I've got an idea," he said. "Malcolm's at the bottom of this."

"No . . . how . . . why . . . where . . . bottom of what?"

"Those damned green dresses."

"Wouldn't be surprised," she managed to articulate, thinking "imagine his rage if I woke *him* up to tell him an idiotic thing like that!"

"Is Mrs. Carsfield at home?" asked Doctor Malcolm.

"No, sir, she's out visiting," answered the servant girl.

"Is Mr. Carsfield anywhere about?"

"Oh no, sir, he's never home midday."

"Show me into the drawing-room."

The servant girl opened the drawing-room door, cocked her eye at the doctor's bag. She wished he would leave it in the hall — even if she could only *feel* the outside without opening it. . . . But the doctor kept it in his hand.

The old woman sat in the drawing-room, a roll of knitting on her lap. Her head had fallen back — her mouth was open — she was asleep and quietly snoring. She started up at the sound of the doctor's footsteps and straightened her cap.

"Oh, Doctor — you *did* take me by surprise. I was dreaming that Henry had bought Anne five little canaries. Please sit down!"

"No, thanks. I just popped in on the chance of catching you alone. . . . You see this bag?"

The old woman nodded.

"Now, are you any good at opening bags?"

"Well, my husband was a great traveller and once I spent a whole night in a railway train."

"Well, have a go at opening this one."

The old woman knelt on the floor — her fingers trembled.

"There's nothing startling inside?" she asked.

Christopher Perkins
Wellington

"Well, it won't bite exactly," said Doctor Malcolm.

The catch sprang open — the bag yawned like a toothless mouth, and she saw, folded in its depths — green cashmere — with narrow lace on the neck and sleeves.

"Fancy that!" said the old woman mildly. "May I take it out, Doctor?" She professed neither astonishment nor pleasure — and Malcolm felt disappointed.

"Helen's dress," he said, and bending towards her, raised his voice. "That young spark's Sunday rig-out."

"I'm not deaf, Doctor," answer the old woman. "Yes, I thought it looked like it. I told Anne only this morning it was bound to turn up somewhere." She shook the crumpled frock and looked it over. "Things always do if you give them time; I've noticed that so often — it's such a blessing."

"You know Lindsay — the postman? Gastric ulcers — called there this morning. . . . Saw this brought in by Lena, who'd got it from Helen on her way to school. Said the kid fished it out of her satchel rolled in a pinafore and said her mother had told her to give it away because it did not fit her. When I saw the tear I understood yesterday's 'new leaf', as Mrs. Carsfield put it. Was up to the dodge in a jiffy. Got the dress — bought some stuff at Clayton's and made my sister Bertha sew it while I had dinner. I knew what would be happening this end of the line — and I knew you'd see Helen through for the sake of getting one in at Henry."

"How thoughtful of you, Doctor!" said the old woman. "I'll tell Anne I found it under my dolman."

"Yes, that's your ticket," said Doctor Malcolm.

"But, of course, Helen would have forgotten the whipping by to-morrow morning and I'd promised her a new doll. . . ." The old woman spoke regretfully.

Doctor Malcolm snapped his bag together. "It's no good talking to the old bird," he thought, "she doesn't take in half I say. Don't seem to have got any forrader than doing Helen out of a doll."

PRELUDE

I

THERE was not an inch of room for Lottie and Kezia in the buggy. When Pat swung them on top of the luggage they wobbled; the grandmother's lap was full and Linda Burnell could not possibly have held a lump of a child on hers for any distance. Isabel, very superior, was perched beside the new handy-man on the driver's seat. Holdalls, bags and boxes were piled upon the floor. "These are absolute necessities that I will not let out of my sight for one instant," said Linda Burnell, her voice trembling with fatigue and excitement.

Lottie and Kezia stood on the patch of lawn just inside the gate all ready for the fray in their coats with brass anchor buttons and little round caps with battleship ribbons. Hand in hand, they stared with round solemn eyes, first at the absolute necessities and then at their mother.

"We shall simply have to leave them. That is all. We shall simply have to cast them off," said Linda Burnell. A strange little laugh flew from her lips; she leaned back against the buttoned leather cushions and shut her eyes, her lips trembling with laughter. Happily at that moment Mrs. Samuel Josephs, who had been watching the scene from behind her drawing-room blind, waddled down the garden path.

"Why nod leave the chudren with be for the afterdoon, Brs. Burnell? They could go on the dray with the storeban when he comes in the eveding. Those thigs on the path have to go, dod't they?"

"Yes, everything outside the house is supposed to go," said Linda Burnell, and she waved a white hand at the tables and chairs standing on their heads on the front lawn. How absurd they looked! Either they ought to be the other way up, or Lottie and Kezia ought to stand on their heads, too. And she longed to say: "Stand on your heads, children, and wait for the storeman." It seemed to her that would be so exquisitely funny that she could not attend to Mrs. Samuel Josephs.

The fat creaking body leaned across the gate, and the big jelly of a face smiled. "Dod't you worry, Brs. Burnell. Loddie and Kezia can have tea with by chudren in the dursery, and I'll see theb on the dray afterwards."

The grandmother considered. "Yes, it really is quite the best plan. We are very obliged to you, Mrs. Samuel Josephs. Children, say 'thank you' to Mrs. Samuel Josephs."

Two subdued chirrups: "Thank you, Mrs. Samuel Josephs."

"And be good little girls, and — come closer — " they advanced, "don't forget to tell Mrs. Samuel Josephs when you want to..."

"No, granma."

"Dod't worry, Brs. Burnell."

At the last moment Kezia let go Lottie's hand and darted towards the buggy.

"I want to kiss my granma good-bye again."

But she was too late. The buggy rolled off up the road, Isabel bursting with pride, her nose turned up at all the world, Linda Burnell prostrated, and the grandmother rummaging among the very curious oddments she had had put in her black silk reticule at the last moment, for something to give her daughter. The buggy twinkled away in the sunlight and fine golden dust up the hill and over. Kezia bit her lip, but Lottie, carefully finding her handkerchief first, set up a wail.

"Mother! Granma!"

Mrs. Samuel Josephs, like a huge warm black silk tea-cosy, enveloped her.

"It's all right, by dear. Be a brave child. You come and blay in the dursery!"

She put her arm round weeping Lottie and led her away. Kezia followed, making a face at Mrs. Samuel Josephs' placket, which was undone as usual, with two long pink corset laces hanging out of it....

Lottie's weeping died down as she mounted the stairs, but the sight of her at the nursery door with swollen eyes and a blob of a nose gave great satisfaction to the S. J.'s, who sat on two benches before a long table covered with American cloth and set out with immense plates of bread and dripping and two brown jugs that faintly steamed.

"Hullo! You've been crying!"

"Ooh! Your eyes have gone right in."

"Doesn't her nose look funny."

"You're all red-and-patchy."

Lottie was quite a success. She felt it and swelled, smiling timidly.

"Go and sid by Zaidee, ducky," said Mrs. Samuel Josephs, "and Kezia, you sid ad the end by Boses."

Moses grinned and gave her a nip as she sat down; but she pretended not to notice. She did hate boys.

"Which will you have?" asked Stanley, leaning across the table very politely, and smiling at her. "Which will you have to begin with — strawberries and cream or bread and dripping?"

"Strawberries and cream, please," said she.

"Ah-h-h-h." How they all laughed and beat the table with their teaspoons. Wasn't that a take-in! Wasn't it now! Didn't he fox her! Good old Stan!

"Ma! She thought it was real."

Even Mrs. Samuel Josephs, pouring out the milk and water, could not help smiling. "You bustn't tease theb on their last day," she wheezed.

But Kezia bit a big piece out of her bread and dripping, and then stood the piece up on her plate. With the bite out it made a dear little sort of a gate. Pooh! She didn't care! A tear rolled down her cheek, but she wasn't crying. She couldn't have cried in front of those awful Samuel Josephs. She sat with her head bent, and as the tear dripped slowly down, she caught it with a neat little whisk of her tongue and ate it before any of them had seen.

II

After tea Kezia wandered back to their own house. Slowly she walked up the back steps, and through the scullery into the kitchen. Nothing was left in it but a lump of gritty yellow soap in one corner of the kitchen window-sill and a piece of flannel stained with a blue bag in another. The fire-place was choked up with rubbish. She poked among it but found nothing except a hair-tidy with a heart painted on it that had belonged to the servant girl. Even that she left lying, and she trailed through the narrow passage into the drawing-room. The Venetian blind was pulled down but not drawn close. Long pencil rays of sunlight shone through and the wavy shadow of a bush outside danced on the gold lines. Now it was still, now it began to flutter again, and now it came almost as far as her feet. Zoom! Zoom! a blue-bottle knocked against the ceiling; the carpet-tacks had little bits of red fluff sticking to them.

The dining-room window had a square of coloured glass at each corner. One was blue and one was yellow. Kezia bent down to have one more look at a blue lawn with blue arum lilies growing at the gate, and then at a yellow lawn with yellow lilies and a yellow fence. As she looked a little Chinese Lottie came out on to the lawn and began to dust the tables and chairs with a corner of her pinafore. Was that really Lottie? Kezia was not quite sure until she had looked through the ordinary window.

Upstairs in her father's and mother's room she found a pill box black and shiny outside and red in, holding a blob of cotton wool.

"I could keep a bird's egg in that," she decided.

In the servant girl's room there was a stay-button stuck in a crack of the floor, and in another crack some beads and a long needle. She knew there was nothing in her grandmother's room; she had watched her pack. She went over to the window and leaned against it, pressing her hands against the pane.

Kezia liked to stand so before the window. She liked the feeling of the cold shining glass against her hot palms, and she liked to watch the funny white tops that came on her fingers when she pressed them hard against the pane. As she stood there, the day flickered out and dark came. With the dark crept the wind snuffling and howling. The windows of the empty house shook, a creaking came from the walls and floors, a piece of loose iron on the roof banged forlornly. Kezia was suddenly quite, quite still, with wide open eyes and knees pressed together. She was frightened. She wanted to call Lottie and to go on calling all the while she ran downstairs and out of the house. But IT was just behind her, waiting at the door, at the head of the stairs, at the bottom of the stairs, hiding in the passage, ready to dart out at the back door. But Lottie was at the back door, too.

Roland Wakelin
Landscape

"Kezia!" she called cheerfully. "The storeman's here. Everything is on the dray and three horses, Kezia. Mrs. Samuel Josephs has given us a big shawl to wear round us, and she says to button up your coat. She won't come out because of asthma."

Lottie was very important.

"Now then, you kids," called the storeman. He hooked his big thumbs under their arms and up they swung. Lottie arranged the shawl "most beautifully" and the storeman tucked up their feet in a piece of old blanket.

"Lift up. Easy does it."

They might have been a couple of young ponies. The storeman felt over the cords holding his load, unhooked the brakechain from the wheel, and whistling, he swung up beside them.

"Keep close to me," said Lottie, "because otherwise you pull the shawl away from my side, Kezia."

But Kezia edged up to the storeman. He towered beside her big as a giant and he smelled of nuts and new wooden boxes.

III

It was the first time that Lottie and Kezia had ever been out so late. Everything looked different — the painted wooden houses far smaller than they did by day, the gardens far bigger and wilder. Bright stars speckled the sky and the moon hung over the harbour dabbling the waves with gold. They could see the lighthouse shining on Quarantine Island, and the green lights on the old coal hulks.

"There comes the Picton boat," said the storeman, pointing to a little steamer all hung with bright beads.

But when they reached the top of the hill and began to go down the other side the harbour disappeared, and although they were still in the town they were quite lost. Other carts rattled past. Everybody knew the storeman.

"Night, Fred."

"Night O," he shouted.

Kezia liked very much to hear him. Whenever a cart appeared in the distance she looked up and waited for his voice. He was an old friend; and she and her grandmother had often been to his place to buy grapes. The storeman lived alone in a cottage that had a glasshouse against one wall built by himself. All the glasshouse was spanned and arched over with one beautiful vine. He took her brown basket from her, lined it with three large leaves, and then he felt in his belt for a little horn knife, reached up and snapped off a big blue cluster and laid it on the leaves so tenderly that Kezia held her breath to watch. He was a very big man. He wore brown velvet trousers, and he had a long brown beard. But he never wore a collar, not even on Sunday. The back of his neck was burnt bright red.

"Where are we now?" Every few minutes one of the children asked him the question.

"Why, this is Hawk Street, or Charlotte Crescent."

"Of course it is," Lottie pricked up her ears at the last name; she always felt that Charlotte Crescent belonged specially to her. Very few people had streets with the same name as theirs.

"Look, Kezia, there is Charlotte Crescent. Doesn't it look different?" Now everything familiar was left behind. Now the big dray rattled into unknown country, along new roads with high clay banks on either side, up steep, steep hills, down into bushy valleys, through wide shallow rivers. Further and further. Lottie's head wagged; she drooped, she slipped half into Kezia's lap and lay there. But Kezia could not open her eyes wide enough. The wind blew and she shivered; but her cheeks and ears burned.

"Do stars ever blow about?" she asked.

"Not to notice," said the storeman.

"We've got a nuncle and a naunt living near our new house," said Kezia. "They have got two children, Pip, the eldest is called, and the youngest's name is Rags. He's got a ram. He has to feed it with a nenamuel teapot and a glove top over the spout. He's going to show us. What is the difference between a ram and a sheep?"

"Well, a ram has horns and runs for you."

Kezia considered. "I don't want to see it frightfully," she said. "I hate rushing animals like dogs and parrots. I often dream that animals rush at me — even camels — and while they are rushing, their heads swell e-enormous."

The storeman said nothing. Kezia peered up at him, screwing up her eyes. Then she put her finger out and stroked his sleeve; it felt hairy. "Are we near?" she asked.

"Not far off, now," answered the storeman. "Getting tired?"

"Well, I'm not an atom bit sleepy," said Kezia. "But my eyes keep curling up in such a funny sort of way." She gave a long sigh, and to stop her eyes from curling she shut them. . . . When she opened them again they were clanking through a drive that cut through the garden like a whip-lash, looping suddenly an island of green, and behind the island, but out of sight until you came upon it, was the house. It was long and low built, with a pillared veranda and balcony all the way round. The soft white bulk of it lay stretched upon the green garden like a sleeping beast. And now one and now another of the windows leaped into light. Someone was walking through the empty rooms carrying a lamp. From the window downstairs the light of a fire flickered. A strange beautiful excitement seemed to stream from the house in quivery ripples.

"Where are we?" said Lottie, sitting up. Her reefer cap was all on one side and on her cheek there was the print of an anchor button she had pressed against while sleeping. Tenderly the storeman lifted her, set her cap straight, and pulled down her crumpled clothes. She stood blinking on the lowest veranda step watching Kezia, who seemed to come flying through the air to her feet.

"Ooh!" cried Kezia, flinging up her arms. The grandmother came out of the dark hall carrying a little lamp. She was smiling.

"You found your way in the dark?" said she.

"Perfectly well."

But Lottie staggered on the lowest veranda step like a bird fallen out of the nest. If she stood still for a moment she fell asleep; if she leaned against anything her eyes closed. She could not walk another step.

"Kezia," said the grandmother, "can I trust you to carry the lamp?"

"Yes, my granma."

The old woman bent down and gave the bright breathing thing into her hands and then she caught up drunken Lottie. "This way."

Through a square hall filled with bales and hundreds of parrots (but the parrots were only on the wall-paper) down a narrow passage where the parrots persisted in flying past Kezia with her lamp.

"Be very quiet," warned the grandmother, putting down Lottie and opening the dining-room door. "Poor little mother has got such a headache."

Linda Burnell, in a long cane chair, with her feet on a hassock and a plaid over her knees, lay before a crackling fire. Burnell and Beryl sat at the table in the middle of the room eating a dish of fried chops and drinking tea out of a brown china teapot. Over the back of her mother's chair leaned Isabel. She had a comb in her fingers and in a gentle absorbed fashion she was combing the curls from her mother's forehead. Outside the pool of lamp and firelight the room stretched dark and bare to the hollow windows.

"Are those the children?" But Linda did not really care; she did not even open her eyes to see.

"Put down the lamp, Kezia," said Aunt Beryl, "or we shall have the house on fire before we are out of the packing cases. More tea, Stanley?"

"Well, you might just give me five-eighths of a cup," said Burnell, leaning across the table. "Have another chop, Beryl. Tip-top meat, isn't it? Not too lean and not too fat." He turned to his wife. "You're sure you won't change your mind, Linda darling?"

"The very thought of it is enough." She raised one eyebrow in the way she had. The grandmother brought the children bread and milk and they sat up to table, flushed and sleepy behind the wavy steam.

"I had meat for my supper," said Isabel, still combing gently.

"I had a whole chop for my supper, the bone and all and Worcester sauce. Didn't I, father?"

"Oh, don't boast, Isabel," said Aunt Beryl.

Isabel looked astounded. "I wasn't boasting, was I, Mummy? I never thought of boasting. I thought they would like to know. I only meant to tell them."

"Very well. That's enough," said Burnell. He pushed back his plate, took a tooth-pick out of his pocket and began picking his strong white teeth.

"You might see that Fred has a bite of something in the kitchen before he goes, will you, mother?"

"Yes, Stanley." The old woman turned to go.

"Oh, hold on half a jiffy. I suppose nobody knows where my slippers were put? I suppose I shall not be able to get at them for a month or two — what?"

"Yes," came from Linda. "In the top of the canvas holdall marked 'urgent necessities'."

"Well, you might get them for me, will you, mother?"

"Yes, Stanley."

Burnell got up, stretched himself, and going over to the fire he turned his back to it and lifted up his coat tails.

"By Jove, this is a pretty pickle. Eh, Beryl?"

Beryl, sipping tea, her elbows on the table, smiled over the cup at him. She wore an unfamiliar pink pinafore; the sleeves of her blouse were rolled up to her shoulders showing her lovely freckled arms, and she had let her hair fall down her back in a long pigtail.

"How long do you think it will take to get straight — couple of weeks — eh?" he chaffed.

"Good heavens, no," said Beryl airily. "The worst is over already. The servant girl and I have simply slaved all day, and ever since mother came she has worked like a horse, too. We have never sat down for a moment. We have had a day."

Stanley scented a rebuke.

"Well, I suppose you did not expect me to rush away from the office and nail carpets — did you?"

"Certainly not," laughed Beryl. She put down her cup and ran out of the dining-room.

"What the hell does she expect us to do?" asked Stanley. "Sit down and fan herself with a palm-leaf fan while I have a gang of professionals to do the job? By Jove, if she can't do a hand's turn occasionally without shouting about it in return for..."

And he gloomed as the chops began to fight the tea in his sensitive stomach. But Linda put up a hand and dragged him down to the side of her long chair.

"This is a wretched time for you, old boy," she said. Her cheeks were very white, but she smiled and curled her fingers into the big red hand she held. Burnell became quiet. Suddenly he began to whistle "Pure as a lily, joyous and free" — a good sign.

"Think you're going to like it?" he asked.

"I don't want to tell you, but I think I ought to, mother," said Isabel. "Kezia is drinking tea out of Aunt Beryl's cup.

IV

They were taken off to bed by the grandmother. She went first with a candle; the stairs rang to their climbing feet. Isabel and Lottie lay in a room to themselves, Kezia curled in her grandmother's soft bed.

"Aren't there going to be any sheets, my granma?"

"No, not to-night."

"It's tickly," said Kezia, "but it's like Indians." She dragged her grandmother down to her and kissed her under the chin. "Come to bed soon and be my Indian brave."

"What a silly you are," said the old woman, tucking her in as she loved to be tucked.

"Aren't you going to leave me a candle?"

"No. Sh-h. Go to sleep."

"Well, can I have the door left open?"

She rolled herself up into a round but she did not go to sleep. From all over the house came the sound of steps. The house itself creaked and popped. Loud whispering voices came from downstairs. Once she heard Aunt Beryl's rush of high laughter, and once she heard a loud trumpeting from Burnell blowing his nose. Outside the window hundreds of black cats with yellow eyes sat in the sky watching her — but she was not frightened.

Harold Gilman
Mother and Child

Lottie was saying to Isabel:

"I'm going to say my prayers in bed to-night."

"No, you can't Lottie." Isabel was very firm. "God only excuses you saying your prayers in bed if you've got a temperature." So Lottie yielded:

"Gentle Jesus meek anmile,
Look pon a little chile.
Pity me, simple Lizzie,
Suffer me to come to thee."

And then they lay down back to back, their little behinds just touching, and fell asleep.

Standing in a pool of moonlight Beryl Fairfield undressed herself. She was tired, but she pretended to be more tired than she really was — letting her clothes fall, pushing back with a languid gesture her warm, heavy hair.

"Oh, how tired I am — very tired."

She shut her eyes a moment, but her lips smiled. Her breath rose and fell in her breast like two fanning wings. The window was wide open; it was warm, and somewhere out there in the garden a young man, dark and slender, with mocking eyes, tiptoed among the bushes, and gathered the flowers into a big bouquet, and slipped under her window and held it up to her. She saw herself bending forward. He thrust his head among the bright waxy flowers, sly and laughing. "No, no," said Beryl. She turned from the window and dropped her nightgown over her head.

"How frightfully unreasonable Stanley is sometimes," she thought, buttoning. And then, as she lay down, there came the old thought, the cruel thought — ah, if only she had money of her own.

A young man, immensely rich, has just arrived from England. He meets her quite by chance.... The new governor is unmarried.... There is a ball at Government house.... Who is that exquisite creature in *eau-de-nil* satin? Beryl Fairfield....

"The thing that pleases me," said Stanley, leaning against the side of the bed and giving himself a good scratch on his shoulders and back before turning in, "is that I've got the place dirt cheap, Linda. I was talking about it to little Wally Bell to-day and he said he simply could not understand why they had accepted my figure. You see land about here is bound to become more and more valuable...in about ten years' time... of course we shall have to go very slow and cut down expenses as fine as possible. Not asleep — are you?"

"No, dear, I've heard every word," said Linda.

He sprang into bed, leaned over her and blew out the candle.

"Good night, Mr. Business Man," said she, and she took hold of his head by the ears and gave him a quick kiss. Her faint far-away voice seemed to come from a deep well.

"Good night, darling." He slipped his arm under her neck and drew her to him.

"Yes, clasp me," said the faint voice from the deep well.

Pat the handy-man sprawled in his little room behind the kitchen. His sponge-bag, coat and trousers hung from the door-peg like a hanged man. From the edge of the blanket his twisted toes protruded, and on the floor beside him there was an empty cane bird-cage. He looked like a comic picture.

"Honk, honk," came from the servant girl. She had adenoids.

Last to go to bed was the grandmother.

"What. Not asleep yet?"

"No, I'm waiting for you," said Kezia. The old woman sighed and lay down beside her. Kezia thrust her head under her grandmother's arm and gave a little squeak. But the old woman only pressed her faintly, and sighed again, took out her teeth, and put them in a glass of water beside her on the floor.

In the garden some tiny owls, perched on the branches of a lace-bark tree, called: "More pork; more pork." And far away in the bush there sounded a harsh rapid chatter: "Ha-ha-ha . . . Ha-ha-ha."

V

Dawn came sharp and chill with red clouds on a faint green sky and drops of water on every leaf and blade. A breeze blew over the garden, dropping dew and dropping petals, shivered over the drenched paddocks, and was lost in the sombre bush. In the sky some tiny stars floated for a moment and then they were gone — they were dissolved like bubbles. And plain to be heard in the early quiet was the sound of the creek in the paddock running over the brown stones, running in and out of the sandy hollows, hiding under clumps of dark berry bushes, spilling into a swamp of yellow water flowers and cresses.

And then at the first beam of sun the birds began. Big cheeky birds, starlings and mynahs, whistled on the lawns, the little birds, the goldfinches and linnets and fan-tails, flicked from bough to bough. A lovely kingfisher perched on the paddock fence preening his rich beauty, and a *tui* sang his three notes and laughed and sang them again.

"How loud the birds are," said Linda in her dream. She was walking with her father through a green paddock sprinkled with daisies. Suddenly he bent down and parted the grasses and showed her a tiny ball of fluff just at her feet. "Oh, papa, the darling." She made a cup of her hands and caught the tiny bird and stroked its head with her finger. It was quite tame. But a funny thing happened. As she stroked it began to swell, it ruffled and pouched, it grew bigger and bigger and its round eyes seemed to smile knowingly at her. Now her arms were hardly wide enough to hold it and she dropped it into her apron. It had become a baby with a big naked head and a gaping bird-mouth, opening and shutting. Her father broke into a loud clattering laugh and she woke to see Burnell standing by the windows rattling the Venetian blind up to the very top.

"Hullo," he said. "Didn't wake you, did I? Nothing much wrong with the weather this morning."

He was enormously pleased. Weather like this set a final seal on his bargain. He felt, somehow, that he had bought the lovely day, too — got it chucked in dirt cheap with the house and ground. He dashed off to his bath and Linda turned over and raised herself on one elbow to see the room by daylight. All the furniture had found a place — all the old paraphernalia, as she expressed it. Even the photographs were on the mantelpiece and the medicine bottles on the shelf above the washstand. Her clothes lay across a chair — her outdoor things, a purple cape and a round hat with a plume in it. Looking at them she wished that she was going away from this house, too. And she saw herself driving away from them all in a little buggy, driving away from everybody and not even waving.

Back came Stanley girt with a towel, glowing and slapping his thighs. He pitched the wet towel on top of her hat and cape, and standing firm in the exact centre of a square of sunlight he began to do his exercises. Deep breathing, bending and squatting like a frog and shooting out his legs. He was so delighted with his firm, obedient body that he hit himself on the chest and gave a loud "Ah." But this amazing vigour seemed to set him worlds away from Linda. She lay on the white tumbled bed and watched him as if from the clouds.

"Oh, damn! Oh, blast!" said Stanley, who had butted into a crisp white shirt only to find that some idiot had fastened the neck-band and he was caught. He stalked over to Linda waving his arms.

"You look like a big fat turkey," said she.

"Fat. I like that," said Stanley. "I haven't square inch of fat on me. Feel that."

"It's rock — it's iron," mocked she.

"You'd be surprised," said Stanley, as though this were intensely interesting, "at the number of chaps at the club who have got a corporation. Young chaps, you know — men of my age." He began parting his bushy ginger hair, his blue eyes fixed and round in the glass, his knees bent, because the dressing-table was always — confound it — a bit too low for him. "Little Wally Bell, for instance," and he straightened, describing upon himself an enormous curve with the hairbrush. "I must say I've a perfect horror…"

"My dear, don't worry. You'll never be fat. You are far too energetic."

"Yes, yes, I suppose that's true," said he, comforted for the hundredth time, and taking a pearl penknife out of his pocket he began to pare his nails.

"Breakfast, Stanley." Beryl was at the door. "Oh, Linda, mother says you are not to get up yet." She popped her head in at the door. She had a big piece of syringa stuck through her hair.

"Everything we left on the veranda last night is simply sopping this morning. You should see poor dear mother wringing out the tables and the chairs. However, there is no harm done — " this with the faintest glance at Stanley.

"Have you told Pat to have the buggy round in time? It's a good six and a half miles to the office."

"I can imagine what this early start for the office will be like," thought Linda. "It will be very high pressure indeed."

"Pat, Pat." She heard the servant girl calling. But Pat was evidently hard to find; the silly voice went baa-baaing through the garden.

Linda did not rest again until the final slam of the front door told her that Stanley was really gone.

Later she heard her children playing in the garden. Lottie's stolid, compact little voice cried: "Ke-zia. Isa-bel." She was always getting lost or losing people only to find them again to her great surprise, round the next tree or the next corner. "Oh, there you are after all." They had been turned out after breakfast and told not to come back to the house until they were called. Isabel wheeled a neat pramload of prim dolls and Lottie was allowed for a great treat to walk beside her holding the doll's parasol over the face of the wax one.

"Where are you going to, Kezia?" asked Isabel, who longed to find some light and menial duty that Kezia might perform and so be roped in under her government.

"Oh, just away," said Kezia. . . .

Then she did not hear them any more. What a glare there was in the room. She hated blinds pulled up to the top at any time, but in the morning it was intolerable. She turned over to the wall and idly, with one finger, she traced a poppy on the wall-paper with a leaf and a stem and a fat bursting bud. In the quiet, and under her tracing finger, the poppy seemed to come alive. She could feel the sticky, silky petals, the stem, hairy like a gooseberry skin, the rough leaf and the tight glazed bud. Things had a habit of coming alive like that. Not only large substantial things like furniture but curtains and the patterns of stuffs and the fringes of quilts and cushions. How often she had seen the tassel fringe of her quilt change into a funny procession of dancers with priests attending. . . . For there were some tassels that did not dance at all but walked stately, bent forward as if praying or chanting. How often the medicine bottles had turned into a row of little men with brown top-hats on; and the washstand jug had a way of sitting in the basin like a fat bird in a round nest.

"I dreamed about birds last night," thought Linda. What was it? She had forgotten. But the strangest part of this coming alive of things was what they did. They listened, they seemed to swell out with some mysterious important content, and when they were full she felt that they smiled. But it was not for her, only, their sly secret smile; they were members of a secret society and they smiled among themselves. Sometimes, when she had fallen asleep in the daytime, she woke and could not lift a finger, could not even turn her eyes to left or right because THEY were there; sometimes when she went out of a room and left it empty, she knew as she clicked the door to that THEY were filling it. And there were times in the evenings when she was upstairs, perhaps, and everybody else was down, when she could hardly escape from them. Then she could not hurry, she could not hum a tune; if

51

she tried to say ever so carelessly — "Bother that old thimble" — THEY were not deceived. THEY knew how frightened she was; THEY saw how she turned her head away as she passed the mirror. What Linda always felt was that THEY wanted something of her, and she knew that if she gave herself up and was quiet, more than quiet, silent, motionless, something would really happen.

"It's very quiet now," she thought. She opened her eyes wide, and she heard the silence spinning its soft endless web. How lightly she breathed; she scarcely had to breathe at all.

Yes, everyting had come alive down to the minutest, tiniest particle, and she did not feel her bed, she floated, held up in the air. Only she seemed to be listening with her wide open watchful eyes, waiting for someone to come who just did not come, watching for something to happen that just did not happen.

VI

In the kitchen at the long deal table under the two windows old Mrs. Fairfield was washing the breakfast dishes. The kitchen window looked out on to a big grass patch that led down to the vegetable garden and the rhubarb beds. On one side the grass patch was bordered by the scullery and wash-house and over this whitewashed lean-to there grew a knotted vine. She had noticed yesterday that a few tiny corkscrew tendrils had come right through some cracks in the scullery ceiling and all the windows of the lean-to had a thick frill of ruffled green.

"I am very fond of a grape vine," declared Mrs. Fairfield, "but I do not think that the grapes will ripen here. It takes Australian sun." And she remembered how Beryl when she was a baby had been picking some white grapes from the vine on the back veranda of their Tasmanian house and she had been stung on the leg by a huge red ant. She saw Beryl in a little plaid dress with red ribbon tie-ups on the shoulders screaming so dreadfully that half the street rushed in. And how the child's leg had swelled! "T-t-t-t!" Mrs. Fairfield caught her breath remembering. "Poor child, now terrifying it was." And she set her lips tight and went over to the stove for some more hot water. The water frothed up in the big soapy bowl with pink and blue bubbles on top of the foam. Old Mrs. Fairfield's arms were bare to the elbow and stained a bright pink. She wore a grey foulard dress patterned with large purple pansies, a white linen apron and a high cap shaped like a jelly mould of white muslin. At her throat there was a silver crescent moon with five little owls seated on it, and round here neck she wore a watch-guard made of black beads.

It was hard to believe that she had not been in that kitchen for years; she was so much a part of it. She put the crocks away with a sure, precise touch, moving leisurely and ample from the stove to the dresser, looking into the pantry and the larder as though there were not an unfamiliar corner. When she had finished, everything in the kitchen had become part of a series of patterns. She stood in the middle of the room wiping her hands on a check cloth; a smile beamed on her lips; she thought it looked very nice, very satisfactory.

"Mother! Mother! Are you there?" called Beryl.

"Yes, dear. Do you want me?"

"No. I'm coming," and Beryl rushed in, very flushed, dragging with her two big pictures.

"Mother, whatever can I do with these awful hideous Chinese paintings that Chung Wah gave Stanley when he went bankrupt? It's absurd to say that they are valuable, because they were hanging in Chung Wah's fruit shop for months before. I can't make out why Stanley wants them kept. I'm sure he thinks them just as hideous as we do, but it's because of the frames," she said spitefully. "I suppose he thinks the frames might fetch something some day or other."

"Why don't you hang them in the passage?" suggested Mrs. Fairfield; "they would not be much seen there."

"I can't. There is no room. I've hung all the photographs of his office there before and after building, and the signed photos of his business friends, and that awful enlargement of Isabel lying on the mat in her singlet." Her angry glance swept the placid kitchen. "I know what I'll do. I'll hang them here. I will tell Stanley they got a little damp in the moving so I have put them in here for the time being."

She dragged a chair forward, jumped on it, took a hammer and a big nail out of her pinafore pocket and banged away.

"There! That is enough! Hand me the picture, mother."

"One moment, child." Her mother was wiping over the carved ebony frame.

"Oh, mother, really you need not dust them. It would take years to dust all those little holes." And she frowned at the top of her mother's head and bit her lip with impatience. Mother's deliberate way of doing things was simply maddening. It was old age, she supposed, loftily.

At last the two pictures were hung side by side. She jumped off the chair, stowing away the little hammer.

"They don't look so bad there, do they?" said she. "And at any rate nobody need gaze at them except Pat and the servant girl — have I got a spider's web on my face, mother? I've been poking into the cupboard under the stairs and now something keeps tickling my nose."

But before Mrs. Fairfield had time to look Beryl had turned away. Someone tapped on the window: Linda was there, nodding and smiling. They heard the latch of the scullery door lift and she came in. She had no hat on; her hair stood upon her head in curling rings and she was wrapped up in an old cashmere shawl.

"I'm so hungry," said Linda: "where can I get something to eat, mother? This is the first time I've been in the kitchen. It says 'mother' all over; everything is in pairs."

"I will make you some tea," said Mrs. Fairfield, spreading a clean napkin over a corner of the table, "and Beryl can have a cup with you."

"Beryl, do you want half my gingerbread?" Linda waved the knife at her. "Beryl, do you like the house now that we are here?"

"Oh yes, I like the house immensely and the garden is beautiful, but it feels very far away from everything to me. I can't imagine people coming out from town to see us in that dreadful jolting bus, and I am sure there is not anyone here to come and call. Of course it does not matter to you because — "

"But there's the buggy," said Linda. "Pat can drive you into town whenever you like."

That was a consolation, certainly, but there was something at the back of Beryl's mind, something she did not even put into words for herself.

"Oh, well, at any rate it won't kill us," she said dryly, putting down her empty cup and standing up and stretching. "I am going to hang curtains." And she ran away singing:

"How many thousand birds I see
That sing aloud from every tree...."

"...birds I see That sing aloud from every tree...." But when she reached the dining-room she stopped singing, her face changed; it became gloomy and sullen.

"One may as well rot here as anywhere else," she muttered savagely, digging the stiff brass safety-pins into the red serge curtains.

The two left in the kitchen were quiet for a little. Linda leaned her cheek on her fingers and watched her mother. She thought her mother looked wonderfully beautiful with her back to the leafy window. There was something comforting in the sight of her that Linda felt she could never do without. She needed the sweet smell of her flesh, and the soft feel of her cheeks and her arms and shoulders still softer. She loved the way her hair curled, silver at her forehead, lighter at her neck, and bright brown still in the big coil under the muslin cap. Exquisite were her mother's hands, and the two rings she wore seemed to melt into her creamy skin. And she was always so fresh, so delicious. The old woman could bear nothing but linen next to her body and she bathed in cold water winter and summer.

"Isn't there anything for me to do?" asked Linda.

"No, darling, I wish you would go into the garden and give an eye to your children; but that I know you will not do."

"Of course I will, but you know Isabel is much more grown up than any of us."

"Yes, but Kezia is not," said Mrs. Fairfield.

"Oh, Kezia has been tossed by a bull hours ago," said Linda, winding herself up in her shawl again.

But no, Kezia had seen a bull through a hole in a knot of wood in the paling that separated the tennis lawn from the paddock. But she had not liked the bull frightfully, so she had walked away back through the orchard, up the grassy slope, along the path by the lace-bark tree and so into the spread tangled garden. She did not believe that she would ever not get lost in this garden. Twice she had found her way back to the big iron gates they had driven through the night before, and then had turned to walk up the drive that led to the house, but there were so many little paths on either side. On one side they all led into a tangle of tall dark trees and strange bushes with flat velvet leaves and feathery cream flowers that buzzed with flies when you shook them — this was the frightening side, and no garden at all. The little paths here were wet and clayey with tree roots spanned across them like the marks of big fowls' feet.

But on the other side of the drive there was a high box border and the paths had box edges and all of them led into a deeper and deeper tangle of flowers. The camellias were in bloom, white and crimson and pink and white striped with flashing leaves. You could

Marcus King
A Country Road

not see a leaf on the syringa bushes for the white clusters. The roses were in flower — gentlemen's button-hole roses, little white ones, but far too full of insects to hold under anyone's nose, pink monthly roses with a ring of fallen petals round the bushes, cabbage roses on thick stalks, moss roses, always in bud, pink smooth beauties opening curl on curl, red ones so dark they seemed to turn black as they fell, and a certain exquisite cream kind with a slender red stem and bright scarlet leaves.

There were clumps of fairy bells, and all kinds of geraniums, and there were little trees of verbena and bluish lavender bushes and a bed of pelargoniums with velvet eyes and leaves like moths' wings. There was a bed of nothing but mignonette and another of nothing but pansies — borders of double and single daisies and all kinds of little tufty plants she had never seen before.

The red-hot pokers were taller than she; the Japanese sunflowers grew in a tiny jungle. She sat down on one of the box borders. By pressing hard at first it made a nice seat. But how dusty it was inside! Kezia bent down to look and sneezed and rubbed her nose.

And then she found herself at the top of the rolling grassy slope that led down to the orchard.... She looked down at the slope a moment; then she lay down on her back, gave a squeak and rolled over and over into the thick flowery orchard grass. As she lay waiting for things to stop spinning, she decided to go up to the house and ask the servant girl for an empty matchbox. She wanted to make a surprise for the grandmother.... First she would put a leaf inside with a big violet lying on it, then she would put a very small white picotee, perhaps, on each side of the violet, and then she would sprinkle some lavender on the top, but not to cover their heads.

She often made these surprises for the grandmother, and they were always most successful.

"Do you want a match, my granny?"

"Why, yes, child, I believe a match is just what I'm looking for."

The grandmother slowly opened the box and came upon the picture inside.

"Good gracious, child! How you astonished me!"

"I can make her one every day here," she thought, scrambling up the grass on her slippery shoes.

But on her way back to the house she came to that island that lay in the middle of the drive, dividing the drive into two arms that met in front of the house. The island was made of grass banked up high. Nothing grew on the top except one huge plant with thick, grey-green, thorny leaves, and out of the middle there sprang up a tall stout stem. Some of the leaves of the plant were so old that they curled up in the air no longer; they turned back, they were split and broken; some of them lay flat and withered on the ground.

Whatever could it be? She had never seen anything like it before. She stood and stared. And then she saw her mother coming down the path.

"Mother, what is it?" asked Kezia.

Linda looked up at the fat swelling plant with its cruel leaves and fleshy stem. High above them, as though becalmed in the air, and yet holding so fast to the earth it grew from, it might have had claws instead of roots. The curving leaves seemed to be hiding something; the blind stem cut into the air as if no wind could ever shake it.

"That is an aloe, Kezia," said her mother.

"Does it ever have any flowers?"

"Yes, Kezia," and Linda smiled down at her, and half shut her eyes. "Once every hundred years."

VII

On his way home from the office Stanley Burnell stopped the buggy at the Bodega, got out and bought a large bottle of oysters. At the Chinaman's shop next door he bought a pineapple in the pink of condition, and noticing a basket of fresh black cherries he told John to put him in a pound of those as well. The oysters and the pine he stowed away in the box under the front seat, but the cherries he kept in his hand.

Pat, the handy-man, leapt off the box and tucked him up again in the brown rug.

"Lift yer feet, Mr. Burnell, while I give yer a fold under," said he.

"Right! Right! First-rate!" said Stanley. "You can make straight for home now."

Pat gave the grey mare a touch and the buggy sprang forward.

"I believe this man is a first-rate chap," thought Stanley. He liked the look of him sitting up there in his neat brown coat and brown bowler. He liked the way Pat had tucked him in, and he liked his eyes. There was nothing servile about him — and if there was one thing he hated more than another it was servility. And he looked as if he was pleased with his job — happy and contented already.

The grey mare went very well; Burnell was impatient to be out of the town. He wanted to be home. Ah, it was splendid to live in the country — to get right out of the hole of a town once the office was closed; and this drive in the fresh warm air, knowing all the while that his own house was at the other end, with its garden and paddocks, its three tip-top cows and enough fowls and ducks to keep them in poultry, was splendid too.

As they left the town finally and bowled away up the deserted road his heart beat hard for joy. He rooted in the bag and began to eat the cherries, three or four at a time, chucking the stones over the side of the buggy. They were delicious, so plump and cold, without a spot or a bruise on them.

Look at those two, now — black one side and white the other — perfect! A perfect little pair of Siamese twins. And he stuck them in his button-hole. . . . By Jove, he wouldn't mind giving that chap up there a handful — but no, better not. Better wait until he had been with him a bit longer.

He began to plan what he would do with his Saturday afternoons and his Sundays. He wouldn't go to the club for lunch on Saturday. No, cut away from the office as soon as possible and get them to give him a couple of slices of cold meat and half a lettuce when he got home. And then he'd get a few chaps out from town to play tennis in the afternoon. Not too many — three at most. Beryl was a good player, too. . . . He stretched out his right arm and slowly bent it, feeling the muscle. . . . A bath, a good rub-down, a cigar on the veranda after dinner. . . .

On Sunday morning they would go to church — children and all. Which reminded

Kathleen Walne
Still Life with Cat

him that he must hire a pew, in the sun if possible and well forward so as to be out of the draught from the door. In fancy he heard himself intoning extremely well: "When thou did overcome the *Sharp*ness of Death Thou didst open the *King*dom of Heaven to *all* Believers." And he saw the neat brass-edged card on the corner of the pew — Mr. Stanley Burnell and family. . . . The rest of the day he'd loaf about with Linda. . . . Now they were walking about the garden; she was on his arm, and he was explaining to her at length what he intended doing at the office the week following. He heard her saying: "My dear, I think that is most wise. . . ." Talking things over with Linda was a wonderful help even though they were apt to drift away from the point.

Hang it all! They weren't getting along very fast. Pat had put the brake on again. Ugh! What a brute of a thing it was. He could feel it in the pit of his stomach.

A sort of panic overtook Burnell whenever he approached near home. Before he was well inside the gate he would shout to anyone within sight: "Is everything all right?" And then he did not believe it was until he heard Linda say: "Hullo! Are you home again?" That was the worst of living in the country — it took the deuce of a long time to get back. . . . But now they weren't far off. They were on the top of the last hill; it was a gentle slope all the way now and not more than half a mile.

Pat trailed the whip over the mare's back and he coaxed her: "Goop now. Goop now."

It wanted a few minutes to sunset. Everything stood motionless bathed in bright, metallic light and from the paddocks on either side there streamed the milky scent of ripe grass. The iron gates were open. They dashed through and up the drive and round the island, stopping at the exact middle of the veranda.

"Did she satisfy yer, sir?" said Pat, getting off the box and grinning at his master.

"Very well indeed, Pat," said Stanley.

Linda came out of the glass door; her voice rang in the shadowy quiet. "Hullo! Are you home again!"

At the sound of her his heart beat so hard that he could hardly stop himself dashing up the steps and catching her in his arms.

"Yes, I'm home again. Is everything all right?"

Pat began to lead the buggy round to the side gate that opened into the courtyard.

"Here, half a moment," said Burnell. "Hand me those two parcels." And he said to Linda, "I've brought you back a bottle of oysters and a pineapple," as though he had brought her back all the harvest of the earth.

They went into the hall; Linda carried the oysters in one hand and the pineapple in the other. Burnell shut the glass door, threw his hat down, put his arms round her and strained her to him, kissing the top of her head, her ears, her lips, her eyes.

"Oh, dear! Oh, dear!" said she. "Wait a moment. Let me put down these silly things," and she put the bottle of oysters and the pine on a little carved chair. "What have you got in your button-hole — cherries?" She took them out and hung them over his ear.

"Don't do that, darling. They are for you."

So she took them off his ear again. "You don't mind if I save them. They'd spoil my appetite for dinner. Come and see your children. They are having tea."

The lamp was lighted on the nursery table. Mrs. Fairfield was cutting and spreading bread and butter. The three little girls sat up to table wearing large bibs embroidered with their names. They wiped their mouths as their father came in ready to be kissed. The windows were open; a jar of wild flowers stood on the mantelpiece, and the lamp made a big soft bubble of light on the ceiling.

"You seem pretty snug, mother," said Burnell, blinking at the light. Isabel and Lottie sat one on either side of the table, Kezia at the bottom — the place at the top was empty.

"That's where my boy ought to sit," thought Stanley. He tightened his arm round Linda's shoulder. By God, he was a perfect fool to feel as happy as this!

"We are, Stanley. We are very snug," said Mrs. Fairfield, cutting Kezia's bread into fingers.

"Like it better than town — eh, children?" asked Burnell.

"Oh, yes," said the three little girls, and Isabel added as an after-thought: "Thank you very much indeed, father dear."

"Come upstairs," said Linda. "I'll bring your slippers."

But the stairs were too narrow for them to go up arm in arm. It was quite dark in the room. He heard her ring tapping on the marble mantelpiece as she felt for the matches.

"I've got some, darling. I'll light the candles."

But instead he came up behind her and again he put his arms round her and pressed her head into his shoulder.

"I'm so confoundedly happy," he said.

"Are you?" She turned and put her hands on his breast and looked up at him.

"I don't know what has come over me," he protested.

It was quite dark outside now and heavy dew was falling. When Linda shut the window the cold dew touched her finger tips. Far away a dog barked. "I believe there is going to be a moon," she said.

At the words, and with the cold wet dew on her fingers, she felt as though the moon had risen — that she was being strangely discovered in a flood of cold light. She shivered; she came away from the window and sat down upon the box ottoman beside Stanley.

.   .   .   .   .

In the dining-room, by the flicker of a wood fire, Beryl sat on a hassock playing the guitar. She had bathed and changed all her clothes. Now she wore a white muslin dress with black spots on it and in her hair she had pinned a black silk rose.

> Nature has gone to her rest, love,
>   See, we are alone.
> Give me your hand to press, love,
>   Lightly within my own.

She played and sang half to herself, for she was watching herself playing and singing. The firelight gleamed on her shoes, on the ruddy belly of the guitar, and on her white fingers. . . .

"If I were outside the window and looked in and saw myself I really would be rather struck," thought she. Still more softly she played the accompaniment — not singing now but listening.

"...The first time that I ever saw you, little girl — oh, you had no idea that you were not alone — you were sitting with your little feet upon a hassock, playing the guitar. God, I can never forget...." Beryl flung up her head and began to sing again:

"Even the moon is aweary..."

But there came a loud bang at the door. The servant girl's crimson face popped through. "Please, Miss Beryl, I've got to come and lay."

"Certainly, Alice," said Beryl, in a voice of ice. She put the guitar in a corner. Alice lunged in with a heavy black iron tray.

"Well, I have had a job with that oving," said she. "I can't get nothing to brown."

"Really!" said Beryl.

But no, she could not stand that fool of a girl. She ran into the dark drawing-room and began walking up and down.... Oh, she was restless, restless. There was a mirror over the mantel. She leaned her arms along and looked at her pale shadow in it. How beautiful she looked, but there was nobody to see, nobody.

"Why must you suffer so?" said the face in the mirror. "You were not made for suffering.... Smile!"

Beryl smiled, and really her smile *was* so adorable that she smiled again — but this time because she could not help it.

VIII

"Good morning, Mrs. Jones."

"Oh, good morning, Mrs. Smith. I'm so glad to see you. Have you brought your children?"

"Yes, I've brought both my twins. I have had another baby since I saw you last, but she came so suddenly that I haven't had time to make her any clothes yet. So I left her.... How is your husband?"

"Oh, he is very well, thank you. At least he had an awful cold but Queen Victoria — she's my godmother, you know — sent him a case of pineapples and that cured it im — mediately. Is that your new servant?"

"Yes, her name's Gwen. I've only had her two days. Oh, Gwen, this is my friend, Mrs. Smith."

"Good morning, Mrs. Smith. Dinner won't be ready for about ten minutes."

"I don't think you ought to introduce me to the servant. I think I ought to just begin talking to her."

"Well, she's more of a lady-help than a servant and you do introduce lady-helps, I know, because Mrs. Samuel Josephs had one."

"Oh, well, it doesn't matter," said the servant carelessly, beating up a chocolate custard with half a broken clothes peg. The dinner was baking beautifully on a concrete step. She began to lay the cloth on a pink garden seat. In front of each person she put two geranium leaf plates, a pine needle fork and a twig knife. There were three daisy heads on a laurel leaf for poached eggs, some slices of fuchsia petal cold beef, some lovely little rissoles made of earth and water and dandelion seeds, and the chocolate custard which she had decided to serve in the pawa shell she had cooked it in.

"You needn't trouble about my children," said Mrs. Smith graciously. "If you'll just take this bottle and fill it at the tap — I mean at the dairy."

"Oh, all right," said Gwen, and she whispered to Mrs. Jones: "Shall I go and ask Alice for a little bit of real milk?"

But someone called from the front of the house and the luncheon party melted away, leaving the charming table, leaving the rissoles and the poached eggs to the ants and to an old snail who pushed his quivering horns over the edge of the garden seat and began to nibble a geranium plate.

"Come round to the front, children, Pip and Rags have come."

The Trout boys were the cousins Kezia had mentioned to the storeman. They lived about a mile away in a house called Monkey Tree Cottage. Pip was tall for his age, with lank black hair and a white face, but Rags was very small and so thin that when he was undressed his shoulder blades stuck out like two little wings. They had a mongrel dog with pale blue eyes and a long tail turned up at the end who followed them everywhere; he was called Snooker. They spent half their time combing and brushing Snooker and dosing him with various awful mixtures concocted by Pip, and kept secretly by him in a broken jug covered with an old kettle lid. Even faithful little Rags was not allowed to know the full secret of these mixtures.... Take some carbolic tooth powder and a pinch of sulphur powdered up fine, and perhaps a bit of starch to stiffen up Snooker's coat.... But that was not all; Rags privately thought that the rest was gun-powder.... And he never was allowed to help with the mixing because of the danger.... "Why, if a spot of this flew in your eye, you would be blinded for life," Pip would say, stirring the mixture with an iron spoon. "And there's always the chance — just the chance, mind you — of it exploding if you whack it hard enough.... Two spoons of this in a kerosene tin will be enough to kill thousands of fleas." But Snooker spent all his spare time biting and snuffling, and he stank abominably.

"It's because he is such a grand fighting dog," Pip would say. "All fighting dogs smell."

The Trout boys had often spent the day with the Burnells in town, but now that they lived in this fine house and boncer garden they were inclined to be very friendly. Besides, both of them liked playing with girls — Pip, because he could fox them so, and because Lottie was so easily frightened, and Rags for a shameful reason. He adored dolls. How he would look at a doll as it lay asleep, speaking in a whisper and smiling timidly, and what a treat it was to him to be allowed to hold one....

"Curve your arms round her. Don't keep them stiff like that. You'll drop her," Isabel would say sternly.

Now they were standing on the veranda and holding back Snooker, who wanted to go into the house but wasn't allowed to because Aunt Linda hated decent dogs.

"We came over in the bus with mum," they said, "and we're going to spend the afternoon with you. We brought over a batch of our gingerbread for Aunt Linda. Our Minnie made it. It's all over nuts."

"I skinned the almonds," said Pip. "I just stuck my hand into a saucepan of boiling water and grabbed them out and gave them a kind of pinch and the nuts flew out of the skins, some of them as high as the ceiling. Didn't they, Rags?"

Rags nodded. "When they make cakes at our place," said Pip, "we always stay in the kitchen, Rags and me, and I get the bowl and he gets the spoon and the egg-beater. Sponge cake's best. It's all frothy stuff, then."

He ran down the veranda steps to the lawn, planted his hands on the grass, bent forward, and just did not stand on his head.

"That lawns's all bumpy," he said. "You have to have a flat place for standing on your head. I can walk round the monkey tree on my head at our place. Can't I, Rags?"

"Nearly," said Rags faintly.

"Stand on your head on the veranda. That's quite flat," said Kezia.

"No, smarty," said Pip. "You have to do it on something soft. Because if you give a jerk and fall over, something in your neck goes click and it breaks off. Dad told me."

"Oh, do let's play something," said Kezia.

"Very well," said Isabel quickly, "we'll play hospitals. I will be the nurse and Pip can be the doctor and you and Lottie and Rags can be the sick people."

Lottie didn't want to play that, because last time Pip had squeezed something down her throat and it hurt awfully.

"Pooh," scoffed Pip. "It was only the juice out of a bit of mandarin peel."

"Well, let's play ladies," said Isabel. "Pip can be the father and you can be all our dear little children."

"I hate playing ladies," said Kezia. "You always make us go to church hand in hand and come home and go to bed."

Suddenly Pip took a filthy handerchief out of his pocket. "Snooker! Here, sir," he called. But Snooker, as usual, tried to sneak away, his tail between his legs. Pip leapt on top of him, and pressed him between his knees.

"Keep his head firm, Rags," he said, and he tied the handkerchief round Snooker's head with a funny knot sticking up at the top.

"Whatever is that for?" asked Lottie.

"It's to train his ears to grow more close to his head — see?" said Pip. "All fighting dogs have ears that lie back. But Snooker's ears are a bit too soft."

"I know," said Kezia. "They are always turning inside out. I hate that."

Snooker lay down, made one feeble effort with his paw to get the handerchief off, but finding he could not, trailed after the children, shivering with misery.

IX

Pat came swinging along; in his hand he held a little tomahawk that winked in the sun.

"Come with me," he said to the children, "and I'll show you how the kings of Ireland chop the head off a duck."

They drew back — they didn't believe him, and besides, the Trout boys had never seen Pat before.

"Come on now," he coaxed, smiling and holding out his hand to Kezia.

"Is it a real duck's head? One from the paddock?"

"It is," said Pat. She put her hand in his hard dry one, and he stuck the tomahawk in his belt and held out the other to Rags. He loved little children.

"I'd better keep hold of Snooker's head if there's going to be any blood about," said Pip, "because the sight of blood makes him awfully wild." He ran ahead dragging Snooker by the handkerchief.

"Do you think we ought to go?" whispered Isabel. "We haven't asked or anything. Have we?"

At the bottom of the orchard a gate was set in the paling fence. On the other side a steep bank led down to a bridge that spanned the creek, and once up the bank on the other side you were on the fringe of the paddocks. A little old stable in the first paddock had been turned into a fowl-house. The fowls had strayed far away across the paddock down to a dumping ground in a hollow, but the ducks kept close to that part of the creek that flowed under the bridge.

Tall bushes overhung the stream with red leaves and yellow flowers and clusters of blackberries. At some places the stream was wide and shallow, but at others it tumbled into deep little pools with foam at the edges and quivering bubbles. It was in these pools that the big white ducks had made themselves at home, swimming and guzzling along the weedy banks.

Up and down they swam, preening their dazzling breasts, and other ducks with the same dazzling breasts and yellow bills swam upside down with them.

"There is the little Irish navy," said Pat, "and look at the old admiral there with the green neck and the grand little flagstaff on his tail."

He pulled a handful of grain from his pocket and began to walk towards the fowl-house, lazy, his straw hat with the broken crown pulled over his eyes.

"Lid. Lid-lid-lid-lid-" he called.

"Qua. Qua-qua-qua-qua-" answered the ducks, making for land, and flapping and scrambling up the bank they streamed after him in a long waddling line. He coaxed them, pretending to throw the grain, shaking it in his hands and calling to them until they swept round him in a white ring.

From far away the fowls heard the clamour and they too came running across the paddock, their heads thrust forward, their wings spread, turning in their feet in the silly way fowls run and scolding as they came.

Then Pat scattered the grain and the greedy ducks began to gobble. Quickly he stooped, seized two, one under each arm, and strode across to the children. Their darting heads and round eyes frightened the children — all except Pip.

"Come on, sillies," he cried, "they can't bite. They haven't any teeth. They've only got those two little holes in their beaks for breathing through."

"Will you hold one while I finish with the other?" asked Pat. Pip let go of Snooker. "Won't I? Won't I? Give us one. I don't mind how much he kicks."

He nearly sobbed with delight when Pat gave the white lump into his arms.

There was an old stump beside the door of the fowl-house. Pat grabbed the duck by the legs, laid it flat across the stump, and almost at the same moment down came the little tomahawk and the duck's head flew off the stump. Up the blood spurted over the white feathers and over his hand.

When the children saw the blood they were frightened no longer. They crowded round him and began to scream. Even Isabel leaped about crying: "The blood! The blood!" Pip forgot all about his duck. He simply threw it away from him and shouted, "I saw it. I saw it," and jumped round the wood block.

Rags, with cheeks as white as paper, ran up to the little head, put out a finger as if he wanted to touch it, shrank back again and then again put out a finger. He was shivering all over.

Even Lottie, frightened little Lottie, began to laugh and pointed at the duck and shrieked: "Look, Kezia, look."

"Watch it!" shouted Pat. He put down the body and it began to waddle — with only a long spurt of blood where the head had been; it began to pad away without a sound towards the steep bank that led to the stream. . . . That was the crowning wonder.

"Do you see that? Do you see that?" yelled Pip. He ran among the little girls tugging at their pinafores.

"It's like a little engine. It's like a funny little railway engine," squealed Isabel.

But Kezia suddenly rushed at Pat and flung her arms round his legs and butted her head as hard as she could against his knees.

"Put head back! Put head back!" she screamed.

When he stooped to move her she would not let go or take her head away. She held on as hard as she could and sobbed: "Head back! Head back!" until it sounded like a loud strange hiccup.

"It's stopped. It's tumbled over. It's dead," said Pip.

Pat dragged Kezia up into his arms. Her sun-bonnet had fallen back, but she would not let him look at her face. No, she pressed her face into a bone in his shoulder and clasped her arms around his neck.

The children stopped screaming as suddenly as they had begun. They stood round the dead duck. Rags was not frightened of the head any more. He knelt down and stroked it now.

"I don't think the head is quite dead yet," he said. "Do you think it would keep alive if I gave it something to drink?"

But Pip got very cross: "Bah! You baby." He whistled to Snooker and went off.

When Isabel went up to Lottie, Lottie snatched away.

"What are you always touching me for, Isabel?"

"There now," said Pat to Kezia. "There's the grand little girl."

She put up her hands and touched his ears. She felt something. Slowly she raised her quivering face and looked. Pat wore little round gold ear-rings. She never knew that men wore ear-rings. She was very much surprised.

"Do they come on and off?" she asked huskily.

X

Up in the house, in the warm tidy kitchen, Alice, the servant girl, was getting the afternoon tea. She was "dressed". She had on a black stuff dress that smelt under the arms, a white apron like a large sheet of paper, and a lace bow pinned on to her hair with two jetty pins. Also her comfortable carpet slippers were changed for a pair of black leather ones that pinched her corn on her little toe something dreadful. . . .

It was warm in the kitchen. A blow-fly buzzed, a fan of whity steam came out of the kettle, and the lid kept up a rattling jig as the water bubbled. The clock ticked in the warm air, slow and deliberate, like the click of an old woman's knitting needle, and sometimes — for no reason at all, for there wasn't any breeze — the blind swung out and back, tapping the window.

Alice was making water-cress sandwiches. She had a lump of butter on the table, a barracouta loaf, and the cresses tumbled in a white cloth.

But propped against the butter dish there was a dirty, greasy little book, half unstitched, with curled edges, and while she mashed the butter she read:

"To dream of black-beetles drawing a hearse is bad. Signifies death of one you hold near or dear, either father, husband, brother, son, or intended. If beetles crawl backwards as you watch them it means death from fire or from great height such as flight of stairs, scaffolding, etc.

"Spiders. To dream of spiders creeping over you is good. Signifies large sum of money in near future. Should party be in family way an easy confinement may be expected. But care should be taken in sixth month to avoid eating of probable present of shellfish. . . ."

"How many thousand birds I see."

Oh, life. There was Miss Beryl. Alice dropped the knife and slipped the *Dream Book* under the butter dish. But she hadn't time to hide it quite, for Beryl ran into the kitchen

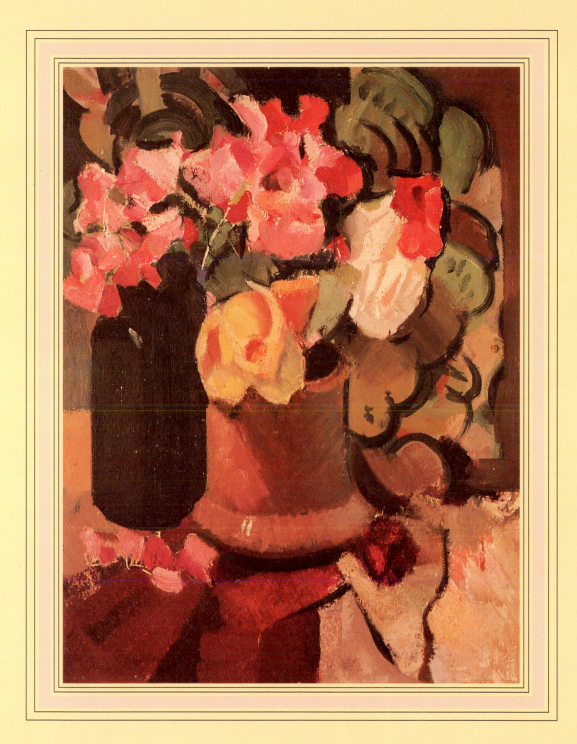

John Weeks
Still Life: Flowers

and up to the table, and the first thing her eye lighted on were those greasy edges. Alice saw Miss Beryl's meaning little smile and the way she raised her eyebrows and screwed up her eyes as though she were not quite sure what that could be. She decided to answer if Miss Beryl should ask her: "Nothing as belongs to you, Miss." But she knew Miss Beryl would not ask her.

Alice was a mild creature in reality, but she had the most marvellous retorts ready for questions that she knew would never be put to her. The composing of them and the turning of them over and over in her mind comforted her just as much as if they'd been expressed. Really, they kept her alive in places where she'd been that chivvied she'd been afraid to go to bed at night with a box of matches on the chair in case she bit the tops off in her sleep, as you might say.

"Oh, Alice," said Miss Beryl. "There's one extra to tea, so heat a plate of yesterday's scones, please. And put on the Victoria sandwich as well as the coffee cake. And don't forget to put little doyleys under the plates — will you? You did yesterday, you know, and the tea looked so ugly and common. And, Alice, don't put that dreadful old pink and green cosy on the afternoon teapot again. That is only for the mornings. Really, I think it ought to be kept for the kitchen — it's so shabby, and quite smelly. Put on the Japanese one. You quite understand, don't you?"

Miss Beryl had finished.

"That sing aloud from every tree . . ."

she sang as she left the kitchen, very pleased with her firm handling of Alice.

Oh, Alice was wild. She wasn't one to mind being told, but there was something in the way Miss Beryl had of speaking to her that she couldn't stand. Oh, that she couldn't. It made her curl up inside, as you might say, and she fair trembled. But what Alice really hated Miss Beryl for was that she made her feel low. She talked to Alice in a special voice as though she wasn't quite all there; and she never lost her temper with her — never. Even when Alice dropped anything or forgot anything important Miss Beryl seemed to have expected it to happen.

"If you please, Mrs. Burnell," said an imaginary Alice, as she buttered the scones, "I'd rather not take my orders from Miss Beryl. I may be only a common servant girl as doesn't know how to play the guitar, but . . ."

This last thrust pleased her so much that she quite recovered her temper.

"The only thing to do," she heard, as she opened the dining-room door, "is to cut the sleeves out entirely and just have a broad band of black velvet over the shoulders instead. . . ."

XI

The white duck did not look as if it had ever had a head when Alice placed it in front of Stanley Burnell that night. It lay, in beautifully basted resignation, on a blue dish —

its legs tied together with a piece of string and a wreath of little balls of stuffing round it.

It was hard to say which of the two, Alice or the duck, looked the better basted; they were both such a rich colour and they both had the same air of gloss and strain. But Alice was fiery red and the duck a Spanish mahogany.

Burnell ran his eye along the edge of the carving knife. He prided himself very much upon his carving, upon making a first-class job of it. He hated seeing a woman carve; they were always too slow and they never seemed to care what the meat looked like afterwards. Now he did; he took a real pride in cutting delicate shaves of cold beef, little wads of mutton, just the right thickness, and in dividing a chicken or duck with nice precision. . . .

"Is this the first of the home products?" he asked, knowing perfectly well that it was.

"Yes, the butcher did not come. We have found out that he only calls twice a week."

But there was no need to apologise. It was a superb bird. It wasn't meat at all, but a kind of very superior jelly. "My father would say," said Burnell, "this must have been one of those birds whose mother played to it in infancy upon the German flute. And the sweet strains of the dulcet instrument acted with such effect upon the infant mind. . . . Have some more, Beryl? You and I are the only ones in this house with a real feeling for food. I'm perfectly willing to state, in a court of law, if necessary, that I love good food."

Tea was served in the drawing-room, and Beryl, who for some reason had been very charming to Stanley ever since he came home, suggested a game of crib. They sat at a little table near one of the open windows. Mrs. Fairfield disappeared, and Linda lay in a rocking-chair, her arms above her head, rocking to and fro.

"You don't want the light — do you, Linda?" said Beryl. She moved the tall lamp so that she sat under its soft light.

How remote they looked, those two, from where Linda sat and rocked. The green table, the polished cards, Stanley's big hands and Beryl's tiny ones, all seemed to be part of one mysterious movement. Stanley himself, big and solid, in his dark suit, took his ease, and Beryl tossed her bright head and pouted. Round her throat she wore an unfamiliar velvet ribbon. It changed her, somehow — altered the shape of her face — but it was charming, Linda decided. The room smelled of lilies; there were two big jars of arums in the fire-place.

"Fifteen two — fifteen four — and a pair is six and a run of three is nine," said Stanley, so deliberately, he might have been counting sheep.

"I've nothing but two pairs," said Beryl, exaggerating her woe because she knew how he loved winning.

The cribbage pegs were like two little people going up the road together, turning round the sharp corner, and coming down the road again. They were pursuing each other. They did not so much want to get ahead as to keep near enough to talk — to keep near, perhaps that was all.

But no, there was always one who was impatient and hopped away as the other came up, and would not listen. Perhaps the white peg was frightened of the red one, or perhaps he was cruel and would not give the red one a chance to speak. . . .

In the front of her dress Beryl wore a bunch of pansies, and once when the little pegs were side by side, she bent over and the pansies dropped out and covered them.

"What a shame," said she, picking up the pansies. "Just as they had a chance to fly into each other's arms."

"Farewell, my girl," laughed Stanley, and away the red peg hopped.

The drawing-room was long and narrow with glass doors that gave on to the veranda. It had a cream paper with a pattern of gilt roses, and the furniture, which had belonged to old Mrs. Fairfield, was dark and plain. A little piano stood against the wall with yellow pleated silk let into the carved front. Above it hung an oil painting by Beryl of a large cluster of surprised-looking clematis. Each flower was the size of a small saucer, with a centre like an astonished eye fringed in black. But the room was not finished yet. Stanley had set his heart on a Chesterfield and two decent chairs. Linda liked it best as it was....

Two big moths flew in through the window and round and round the circle of lamplight.

"Fly away before it is too late. Fly out again."

Round and round they flew; they seemed to bring the silence and the moonlight in with them on their silent wings....

"I've two kings," said Stanley. "Any good?"

"Quite good," said Beryl.

Linda stopped rocking and got up. Stanley looked across. "Anything the matter, darling?"

"No, nothing. I'm going to find mother."

She went out of the room and standing at the foot of the stairs she called, but her mother's voice answered her from the veranda.

The moon that Lottie and Kezia had seen from the storeman's wagon was full, and the house, the garden, the old woman and Linda — all were bathed in dazzling light.

"I have been looking at the aloe," said Mrs. Fairfield. "I believe it is going to flower this year. Look at the top there. Are those buds, or is it only an effect of light?"

As they stood on the steps, the high grassy bank on which the aloe rested rose up like a wave, and the aloe seemed to ride upon it like a ship with the oars lifted. Bright moonlight hung upon the lifted oars like water, and on the green wave glittered the dew.

"Do you feel it, too," said Linda, and she spoke to her mother with the special voice that women use at night to each other as though they spoke in their sleep or from some hollow cave — "Don't you feel that it is coming towards us?"

She dreamed that she was caught up out of the cold water into the ship with the lifted oars and the budding mast. Now the oars fell striking quickly, quickly. They rowed far away over the top of the garden trees, the paddocks and the dark bush beyond. Ah, she heard herself cry: "Faster! Faster!" to those who were rowing.

How much more real this dream was than that they should go back to the house where the sleeping children lay and where Stanley and Beryl played cribbage.

"I believe those are buds," said she. "Let us go down into the garden, mother. I like that aloe. I like it more than anything here. And I am sure I shall remember it long after I've forgotten all the other things."

She put her hand on her mother's arm and they walked down the steps, round the island and on to the main drive that led to the front gates.

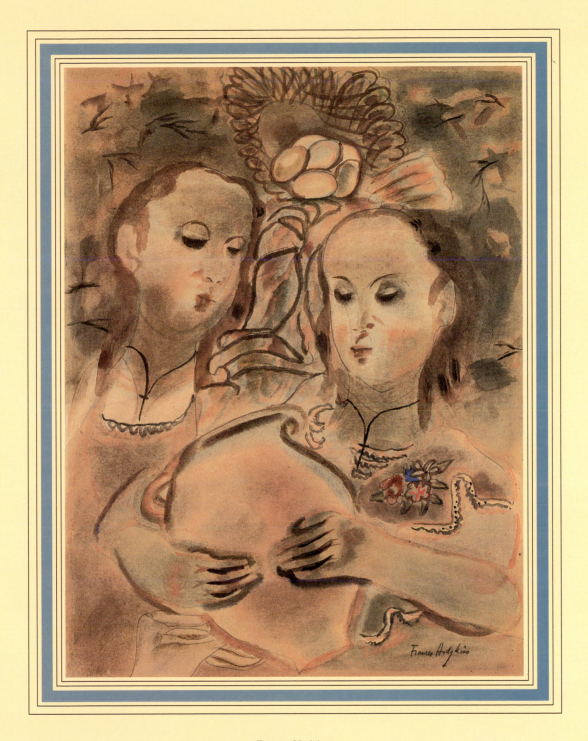

Frances Hodgkins
Two Girls with a Jug

Looking at it from below she could see the long sharp thorns that edged the aloe leaves, and at the sight of them her heart grew hard.... She particularly liked the long sharp thorns.... Nobody would dare to come near the ship or to follow after.

"Not even my Newfoundland dog," thought she, "that I'm so fond of in the daytime."

For she really was fond of him; she loved and admired and respected him tremendously. Oh, better than anyone else in the world. She knew him through and through. He was the soul of truth and decency, and for all his practical experience he was awfully simple, easily pleased and easily hurt....

If only he wouldn't jump at her so, and bark so loudly, and watch her with such eager, loving eyes. He was too strong for her; she had always hated things that rush at her, from a child. There were times when he was frightening — really frightening. When she just had not screamed at the top of her voice: "You are killing me." And at those times she had longed to say the most coarse, hateful things....

"You know I'm very delicate. You know as well as I do that my heart is affected, and the doctor has told you I may die any moment. I have had three great lumps of children already...."

Yes, yes, it was true. Linda snatched her hand from mother's arm. For all her love and respect and admiration she hated him. And how tender he always was after times like those, how submissive, how thoughtful. He would do anything for her; he longed to serve her.... Linda heard herself saying in a weak voice:

"Stanley, would you light a candle?"

And she heard his joyful voice answer: "Of course I will, my darling." And he leapt out of bed as though he were going to leap at the moon for her.

It had never been so plain to her as it was at this moment. There were all her feelings for him, sharp and defined, one as true as the other. And there was this other, this hatred, just as real as the rest. She could have done her feelings up in little packets and given them to Stanley. She longed to hand him that last one, for a surprise. She could see his eyes as he opened that....

She hugged her folded arms and began to laugh silently. How absurd life was — it was laughable, simply laughable. And why this mania of hers to keep alive at all? For it really was a mania, she thought, mocking and laughing.

"What am I guarding myself for so preciously? I shall go on having children and Stanley will go on making money and the children and the gardens will grow bigger and bigger, with whole fleets of aloes in them for me to choose from."

She had been walking with her head bent, looking at nothing. Now she looked up and about her. They were standing by the red and white camellia trees. Beautiful were the rich dark leaves spangled with light and the round flowers that perch among them like red and white birds. Linda pulled a piece of verbena and crumpled it, and held her hands to her mother.

"Delicious," said the old woman. "Are you cold, child? Are you trembling? Yes, your hands are cold. We had better go back to the house."

"What have you been thinking about?" said Linda. "Tell me."

"I haven't really been thinking of anything. I wondered as we passed the orchard what the fruit trees were like and whether we should be able to make much jam this autumn. There are splendid healthy currant bushes in the vegetable garden. I noticed them to-day. I should like to see those pantry shelves thoroughly well stocked with our own jam...."

XII

"My Darling Nan,

Don't think me a piggy wig because I haven't written before. I haven't had a moment, dear, and even now I feel so exhausted that I can hardly hold a pen.

Well, the dreadful deed is done. We have actually left the giddy whirl of town, and I can't see how we shall ever go back again, for my brother-in-law has bought this house 'lock, stock and barrel', to use his own words.

In a way, of course, it is an awful relief, for he has been threatening to take a place in the country ever since I've lived with them— and I must say the house and garden are awfully nice — a million times better than that awful cubby-hole in town.

But buried, my dear. Buried isn't the word.

We have got neighbours, but they are only farmers — big louts of boys who seem to be milking all day, and two dreadful females with rabbit teeth who brought us some scones when we were moving and said they would be pleased to help. But my sister who lives a mile away doesn't know a soul here, so I am sure we never shall. It's pretty certain nobody will ever come out from town to see us, because though there is a bus it's an awful old rattling thing with black leather sides that any decent person would rather die than ride in for six miles.

Such is life. It's a sad ending for poor little B. I'll get to be a most awful frump in a year or two and come and see you in a mackintosh and a sailor hat tied on with a white china silk motor veil. So pretty.

Stanley says that now we are settled — for after the most awful week of my life we really are settled — he is going to bring out a couple of men from the club on Saturday afternoons for tennis. In fact, two are promised as a great treat to-day. But, my dear, if you could see Stanley's men from the club...rather fattish, the type who look frightfully indecent without waistcoats — always with toes that turn in rather — so conspicuous when you are walking about a court in white shoes. And they are pulling up their trousers every minute — don't you know — and whacking at imaginary things with their rackets.

I used to play with them at the club last summer, and I am sure you will know the type when I tell you that after I'd been there about three times they all called me Miss Beryl. It's a weary world. Of course mother simply loves the place, but then I suppose when I am mother's age I shall be content to sit in the sun and shell peas into a basin. But I'm not — not — not.

What Linda thinks about the whole affair, per usual, I haven't the slightest idea. Mysterious as ever....

My dear, you know that white satin dress of mine. I have taken the sleeves out entirely, put bands of black velvet across the shoulders and two big red poppies off my dear sister's *chapeau*. It is a great success, though when I shall wear it I do not know."

Beryl sat writing this letter at a little table in her room. In a way, of course, it was all perfectly true, but in another way it was all the greatest rubbish and she didn't believe a word of it. No, that wasn't true. She felt all those things, but she didn't really feel them like that.

It was her other self who had written that letter. It not only bored, it rather disgusted her real self.

"Flippant and silly," said her real self. Yet she knew that she'd send it and she'd always write that kind of twaddle to Nan Pym. In fact, it was a very mild example of the kind of letter she generally wrote.

Beryl leaned her elbows on the table and read it through again. The voice of the letter seemed to come up to her from the page. It was faint already, like a voice heard over the telephone, high, gushing, with something bitter in the sound. Oh, she detested it to-day.

"You've always got so much animation," said Nan Pym. "That's why men are so keen on you." And she had added, rather mournfully, for men were not at all keen on Nan, who was a solid kind of girl, with fat hips and a high colour — "I can't understand how you can keep it up. But it is your nature, I suppose."

What rot. What nonsense. It wasn't her nature at all. Good heavens, if she had ever been her real self with Nan Pym, Nannie would have jumped out of the window with surprise.... My dear, you know that white satin of mine.... Beryl slammed the letter-case to.

She jumped up and half unconsciously, half consciously she drifted over to the looking-glass.

There stood a slim girl in white — a white serge skirt, a white silk blouse, and a leather belt drawn in very tightly at her tiny waist.

Her face was heart-shaped, wide at the brows and with a pointed chin — but not too pointed. Her eyes, her eyes were perhaps her best feature; they were such a strange uncommon colour — greeny blue with little gold points in them.

She had fine black eyebrows and long lashes — so long, that when they lay on her cheeks you positively caught the light in them, someone or other had told her.

Her mouth was rather large. Too large? No, not really. Her underlip protruded a little; she had a way of sucking it in that somebody else had told her was awfully fascinating.

Her nose was her least satisfactory feature. Not that it was really ugly. But it was not half as fine as Linda's. Linda really had a perfect little nose. Hers spread rather — not badly. And in all probability she exaggerated the spreadiness of it just because it was her nose, and she was so awfully critical of herself. She pinched it with a thumb and first finger and made a little face....

Lovely, lovely hair. And such a mass of it. It had a colour of fresh fallen leaves, brown and red with a glint of yellow. When she did it in a long plait she felt it on her backbone like a long snake. She loved to feel the weight of it dragging her head back, and she loved

Raymond McIntyre
Twilight

to feel it loose, covering her bare arms. "Yes, my dear, there is no doubt about it, you really are a lovely little thing."

At the words her bosom lifted; she took a long breath of delight, half closing her eyes.

But even as she looked the smile faded from her lips and eyes. Oh, God, there she was, back again, playing the same old game. False — false as ever. False as when she'd written to Nan Pym. False even when she was alone with herself, now.

What had that creature in the glass to do with her, and why was she staring? She dropped down to one side of her bed and buried her face in her arms.

"Oh," she cried, "I am so miserable — so frightfully miserable. I know that I'm silly and spiteful and vain; I'm always acting a part. I'm never my real self for a moment." And plainly, plainly, she saw her false self running up and down the stairs, laughing a special trilling laugh if they had visitors, standing under the lamp if a man came to dinner, so that he should see the light on her hair, pouting and pretending to be a little girl when she was asked to play the guitar. Why? She even kept it up for Stanley's benefit. Only last night when he was reading the paper her false self had stood beside him and leaned against his shoulder on purpose. Hadn't she put her hand over his, pointing out something so that he should see how white her hand was beside his brown one.

How despicable! Despicable! Her heart was cold with rage. "It's marvellous how you keep it up," said she to the false self. But then it was only because she was so miserable — so miserable. If she had been happy and leading her own life, her false life would cease to be. She saw the real Beryl — a shadow . . . a shadow. Faint and unsubstantial she shone. What was there of her except the radiance? And for what tiny moments she was really she. Beryl could almost remember every one of them. At those times she had felt: "Life is rich and mysterious and good, and I am rich and mysterious and good, too." Shall I ever be that Beryl for ever? Shall I? How can I? And was there ever a time when I did not have a false self?... But just as she had got that far she heard the sound of little steps running along the passage; the door handle rattled. Kezia came in.

"Aunt Beryl, mother says will you please come down? Father is home with a man and lunch is ready."

Botheration! How she had crumpled her skirt, kneeling in that idiotic way.

"Very well, Kezia." She went over to the dressing-table and powdered her nose.

Kezia crossed too, and unscrewed a little pot of cream and sniffed it. Under her arm she carried a very dirty calico cat.

When Aunt Beryl ran out of the room she sat the cat up on the dressing-table and stuck the top of the cream jar over its ear.

"Now look at yourself," said she sternly.

The calico cat was so overcome by the sight that it toppled over backwards and bumped and bumped on to the floor. And the top of the cream jar flew through the air and rolled like a penny in a round on the linoleum — and did not break.

But for Kezia it had broken the moment it flew through the air, and she picked it up, hot all over, and put it back on the dressing-table.

Then she tiptoed away, far too quickly and airily. . . .

THE DOLL'S HOUSE

WHEN dear old Mrs. Hay went back to town after staying with the Burnells she sent the children a doll's house. It was so big that the carter and Pat carried it into the courtyard, and there it stayed, propped up on two wooden boxes beside the feed-room door. No harm could come to it; it was summer. And perhaps the smell of paint would have gone off by the time it had to be taken in. For, really, the smell of paint coming from that doll's house ("Sweet of old Mrs. Hay, of course; most sweet and generous!") — but the smell of paint was quite enough to make anyone seriously ill, in Aunt Beryl's opinion. Even before the sacking was taken off. And when it was...

There stood the doll's house, a dark, oily, spinach green, picked out with bright yellow. Its two solid little chimneys, glued on to the roof, were painted red and white, and the door, gleaming with yellow varnish, was like a little slab of toffee. Four windows, real windows, were divided into panes by a broad streak of green. There was actually a tiny porch, too, painted yellow, with big lumps of congealed paint hanging along the edge.

But perfect, perfect little house! Who could possibly mind the smell. It was part of the joy, part of the newness.

"Open it quickly, someone!"

The hook at the side was stuck fast. Pat prised it open with his penknife, and the whole house front swung back, and — there you were, gazing at one and the same moment into the drawing-room and dining-room, the kitchen and two bedrooms. That is the way for a house to open! Why don't all houses open like that? How much more exciting than peering through the slit of a door into a mean little hall with a hat-stand and two umbrellas! That is — isn't it? — what you long to know about a house when you put your hand on the knocker. Perhaps it is the way God opens houses at the dead of night when He is taking a quiet turn with an angel....

"Oh-oh!" The Burnell children sounded as though they were in despair. It was too marvellous; it was too much for them. They had never seen anything like it in their lives. All the rooms were papered. There were pictures on the walls, painted on the paper, with gold frames complete. Red carpet covered all the floors except the kitchen; red plush chairs in the drawing-room, green in the dining-room; tables, beds with real bedclothes, a cradle, a stove, a dresser with tiny plates and one big jug. But what Kezia liked more than anything, what she liked frightfully, was the lamp. It stood in the middle of the dining-room table, an exquisite little amber lamp with a white globe. It was even filled all ready for lighting, though, of course, you couldn't light it. But there was something inside that looked like oil and moved when you shook it.

The father and mother dolls, who sprawled very stiff as though they had fainted in the drawing-room, and their two little children asleep upstairs, were really too big for the doll's house. They didn't look as though they belonged. But the lamp was perfect. It seemed to smile at Kezia, to say, "I live here." The lamp was real.

The Burnell children could hardly walk to school fast enough next morning. They burned to tell everybody, to describe, to — well — to boast about their doll's house before the school-bell rang.

"I'm to tell," said Isabel, "because I'm the eldest. And you two can join in after. But I'm to tell first."

There was nothing to answer. Isabel was bossy, but she was always right, and Lottie and Kezia knew too well the powers that went with being eldest. They brushed through the thick buttercups at the road edge and said nothing.

" And I'm to choose who's to come and see it first. Mother said I might."

For it had been arranged that while the doll's house stood in the courtyard they might ask the girls at school, two at a time, to come and look. Not to stay to tea, of course, or to come traipsing through the house. But just to stand quietly in the courtyard while Isabel pointed out the beauties, and Lottie and Kezia looked pleased. . . .

But hurry as they might, by the time they had reached the tarred palings of the boys' playground the bell had begun to jangle. They only just had time to whip off their hats and fall into line before the roll was called. Never mind. Isabel tried to make up for it by looking very important and mysterious and by whispering behind her hand to the girls near her, "Got something to tell you at playtime."

Playtime came and Isabel was surrounded. The girls of her class nearly fought to put their arms round her, to walk away with her, to beam flatteringly, to be her special friend. She held quite a court under the huge pine trees at the side of the play-ground. Nudging, giggling together, the little girls pressed up close. And the only two who stayed outside the ring were the two who were always outside, the little Kelveys. They knew better than to come anywhere near the Burnells.

For the fact was, the school the Burnell children went to was not at all the kind of place their parents would have chosen if there had been any choice. But there was none. It was the only school for miles. And the consequence was all the children of the neighbourhood, the Judge's little girls, the doctor's daughters, the store-keeper's children, the milkman's, were forced to mix together. Not to speak of there being an equal number of rude, rough little boys as well. But the line had to be drawn somewhere. It was drawn at the Kelveys. Many of the children, including the Burnells, were not allowed even to speak to them. They walked past the Kelveys with their heads in the air, and as they set

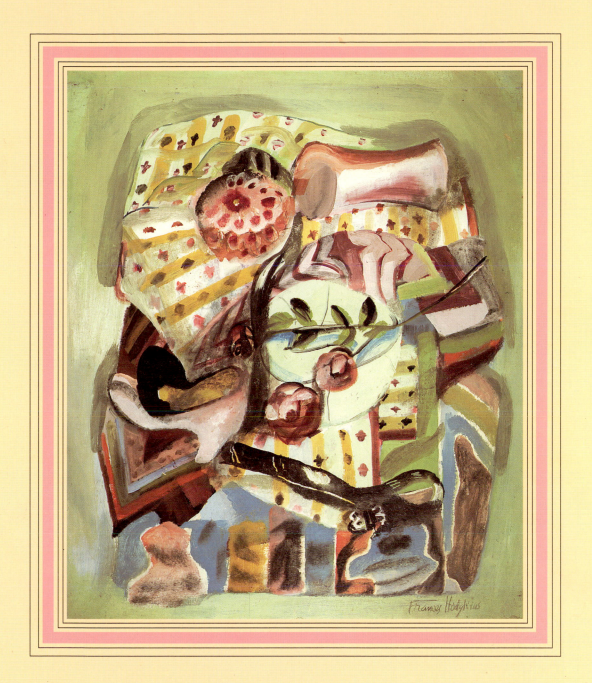

Frances Hodgkins
Self Portrait: Still Life

the fashion in all matters of behaviour, the Kelveys were shunned by everybody. Even the teacher had a special voice for them, and a special smile for the other children when Lil Kelvey came up to her desk with a bunch of dreadfully common-looking flowers.

They were the daughters of a spry, hard-working little washerwoman, who went about from house to house by the day. This was awful enough. But where was Mr. Kelvey? Nobody knew for certain. But everybody said he was in prison. So they were the daughters of a washerwoman and a gaolbird. Very nice company for other people's children! And they looked it. Why Mrs. Kelvey made them so conspicuous was hard to understand. The truth was they were dressed in "bits" given to her by people for whom she worked. Lil, for instance, who was a stout, plain child, with big freckles, came to school in a dress made from a green art-serge tablecloth of the Burnells', with red plush sleeves from the Logans' curtains. Her hat, perched on top of her high forehead, was a grown-up woman's hat, once the property of Miss Lecky, the postmistress. It was turned up at the back and trimmed with a large scarlet quill. What a little guy she looked! It was impossible not to laugh. And her little sister, our Else, wore a long white dress, rather like a nightgown, and a pair of little boy's boots. But whatever our Else wore she would have looked strange. She was a tiny wishbone of a child, with cropped hair and enormous solemn eyes — a little white owl. Nobody had ever seen her smile; she scarcely ever spoke. She went through life holding on to Lil, with a piece of Lil's skirt screwed up in her hand. Where Lil went, our Else followed. In the playground, on the road going to and from school, there was Lil marching in front of our Else holding on behind. Only when she wanted anything, or when she was out of breath, our Else gave Lil a tug, a twitch, and Lil stopped and turned round. The Kelveys never failed to understand each other.

Now they hovered at the edge; you couldn't stop them listening. When the little girls turned round and sneered, Lil, as usual, gave her silly, shamefaced smile, but our Else only looked.

And Isabel's voice, so very proud, went on telling. The carpet made a great sensation, but so did the beds with real bedclothes, and the stove with an oven door.

When she finished Kezia broke in. "You've forgotten the lamp, Isabel."

"Oh, yes," said Isabel, "and there's a teeny little lamp, all made of yellow glass, with a white globe that stands on the dining-room table. You couldn't tell it from a real one."

"The lamp's best of all," cried Kezia. She thought Isabel wasn't making half enough of the little lamp. But nobody paid any attention. Isabel was choosing the two who were to come back with them that afternoon and see it. She chose

Emmie Cole and Lena Logan. But when the others knew they were all to have a chance, they couldn't be nice enough to Isabel. One by one they put their arms round Isabel's waist and walked her off. They had something to whisper to her, a secret. "Isabel's my friend."

Only the little Kelveys moved away forgotten; there was nothing more for them to hear.

Days passed, and as more children saw the doll's house, the fame of it spread. It became the one subject, the rage. The one question was, "Have you seen Burnells' doll's house? Oh, ain't it lovely!" "Haven't you seen it? Oh, I say!"

Even the dinner hour was given up to talking about it. The little girls sat under the pines eating their thick mutton sandwiches and big slabs of johnny cake spread with butter. While always, as near as they could get, sat the Kelveys, our Else holding on to Lil, listening too, while they chewed their jam sandwiches out of a newspaper soaked with large red blobs.

"Mother," said Kezia, "can't I ask the Kelveys just once?"

"Certainly not, Kezia."

"But why not?"

"Run away, Kezia; you know quite well why not."

At last everybody had seen it except them. On that day that day the subject rather flagged. It was the dinner hour. The children stood together under the pine trees, and suddenly, as they looked at the Kelveys eating out of their paper, always by themselves, always listening, they wanted to be horrid to them. Emmie Cole started the whisper.

"Lil Kelvey's going to be a servant when she grows up."

"O-oh, how awful!" said Isabel Burnell, and she made eyes at Emmie.

Emmie swallowed in a very meaning way and nodded to Isabel as she'd seen her mother do on those occasions.

"It's true — it's true — it's true," she snapped. "Shall I ask her?" she whispered.

"Bet you don't," said Jessie May.

"Pooh, I'm not frightened," said Lena. Suddenly she gave a little squeal and danced in front of the other girls. "Watch! Watch me! Watch me now!" said Lena. And sliding, gliding, dragging one foot, giggling behind her hand, Lena went over the the Kelveys.

Lil looked up from her dinner. She wrapped the rest quickly away. Our Else stopped chewing. What was coming now?

"Is it true you're going to be a servant when you grow up, Lil Kelvey?" shrilled Lena.

Dead silence. But instead of answering, Lil only gave her silly, shamefaced smile. She didn't seem to mind the question at all. What a sell for Lena! The girls began to titter.

Lena couldn't stand that. She put her hands on her hips; she shot forward. "Yah, yer father's in prison!" she hissed spitefully.

That was such a marvellous thing to have said that the little girls rushed away in a body, deeply, deeply excited, wild with joy. Someone found a long rope, and they began skipping. And never did they skip so high, run in and out so fast, or do such daring things as on that morning.

In the afternoon Pat called for the Burnell children with the buggy and they drove home. There were visitors. Isabel and Lottie, who liked visitors, went upstairs to change their pinafores. But Kezia thieved out at the back. Nobody was about; she began to swing on the big white gates of the courtyard. Presently, looking along the road, she saw two little dots. They grew bigger, they were coming towards her. Now she could see that one was in front and one close behind. Now she could see that they were the Kelveys. Kezia stopped swinging. She slipped off the gate as if she was going to run away. Then she hesitated. The Kelveys came nearer, and beside them walked their shadows, very long, stretching right across the road with their heads in the buttercups. Kezia clambered back on the gate; she had made up her mind; she swung out.

Hullo," she said to the passing Kelveys.

They were so astounded that they stopped. Lil gave her silly smile. Our Else stared.

"You can come and see our doll's house if you want to," said Kezia, and she dragged one toe on the ground. But at that Lil turned red and shook her head quickly.

"Why not?" asked Kezia.

Lil gasped, then she said, "Your ma told our ma you wasn't to speak to us."

"Oh, well," said Kezia. She didn't know what to reply. "It doesn't matter. You can come and see our doll's house all the same. Come on. Nobody's looking."

But Lil shook her head still harder.

"Don't you want to?" asked Kezia.

Suddenly there was a twitch, a tug at Lil's skirt. She turned round. Our Else was looking at her with big imploring eyes; she was frowning; she wanted to go. For a moment Lil looked at our Else very doubtfully. But then our Else twitched her skirt again. She started forward. Kezia led the way. Like two little stray cats they followed across the courtyard to where the doll's house stood.

"There it is," said Kezia.

There was a pause. Lil breathed loudly, almost snorted; our Else was still as stone.

"I'll open it for you," said Kezia kindly. She undid the hook and they looked inside. "There's the drawing-room and the dining-room, and that's the —"

"Kezia!"

Oh, what a start they gave!

"Kezia!"

It was Aunt Beryl's voice. They turned round. At the back door stood Aunt Beryl, staring as if she couldn't believe what she saw.

"How dare you ask the little Kelveys into the courtyard!" said her cold, furious voice. "You know as well as I do, you're not allowed to talk to them. Run away, children, run away at once. And don't come back again," said Aunt Beryl. And she stepped into the yard and shooed them out as if they were chickens.

"Off you go immediately!" she called, cold and proud.

They did not need telling twice. Burning with shame, shrinking together, Lil huddling along like her mother, our Else dazed, somehow they crossed the big courtyard and squeezed through the white gate.

"Wicked, disobedient little girl!" said Aunty Beryl bitterly to Kezia, and she slammed

Frances Hodgkins
Le Reveil

the doll's house to.

That afternoon had been awful. A letter had come from Willie Brent, a terrifying, threatening letter, saying if she did not meet him that evening in Pulman's Bush, he'd come to the front door and ask the reason why! But now that she had frightened those little rats of Kelveys and given Kezia a good scolding, her heart felt lighter. That ghastly pressure was gone. She went back to the house humming.

When the Kelveys were well out of sight of Burnells', they sat down to rest on a big red drainpipe by the side of the road. Lil's cheeks were still burning; she took off the hat with the quill and held it on her knee. Dreamily they looked over the hay paddocks, past the creek, to the group of wattles where Logan's cows stood waiting to be milked. What were their thoughts?

Presently our Else nudged up close to her sister. But now she had forgotten the cross lady. She put out a finger and stroked her sister's quill; she smiled her rare smile.

"I seen the little lamp," she said softly.

Then both were silent once more.

AT THE BAY

I

VERY early morning. The sun was not yet risen, and the whole of Crescent Bay was hidden under a white sea-mist. The big bush-covered hills at the back were smothered. You could not see where they ended and the paddocks and bungalows began. The sandy road was gone and the paddocks and bungalows the other side of it; there were no white dunes covered with reddish grass beyond them; there was nothing to mark which was beach and where was the sea. A heavy dew had fallen. The grass was blue. Big drops hung on the bushes and just did not fall; the silvery, fluffy toi-toi was limp on its long stalks, and all the marigolds and the pinks in the bungalow gardens were bowed to the earth with wetness. Drenched were the cold fuchsias, round pearls of dew lay on the flat nasturtium leaves. It looked as though the sea had beaten up softly in the darkness, as though one immense wave had come rippling, rippling — how far? Perhaps if you had waked up in the middle of the night you might have seen a big fish flicking in at the window and gone again. . . .

Ah-Aah! sounded the sleepy sea. And from the bush there came the sound of little streams flowing, quickly, lightly, slipping between the smooth stones, gushing into ferny basins and out again; and there was the splashing of big drops on large leaves, and something else — what was it? — a faint stirring and shaking, the snapping of a twig and then such silence that it seemed someone was listening.

Round the corner of Crescent Bay, between the piled-up masses of broken rock, a flock of sheep came pattering. They were huddled together, a small, tossing, woolly mass, and their thin, stick-like legs trotted along quickly as if the cold and the quiet had frightened them. Behind them an old sheep-dog, his soaking paws covered with sand, ran along with his nose to the ground, but carelessly, as if thinking of something else. And then in the rocky gateway the shepherd himself appeared. He was a lean, upright old man, in a frieze coat that was covered with a web of tiny drops, velvet trousers tied under the knee, and a wideawake with a folded blue handkerchief round the brim. One hand was crammed into his belt, the other grasped a beautifully smooth yellow stick. And as he walked, taking his time, he kept up a very soft light whistling, an airy, far-away fluting that sounded mournful and tender. The old dog cut an ancient caper or two and then drew up sharp, ashamed of his levity, and walked a few dignified paces by his master's side. The sheep ran forward in little pattering rushes; they began to bleat, and ghostly flocks and herds answered them from under the sea. "Baa! Baaa!" For a time they seemed to be always on the same piece of ground. There ahead was stretched the sandy road with shallow puddles; the same soaking bushes showed on either side the same shadowy palings. Then something immense came into view; an enormous shock-haired giant with his arms stretched out. It was the big gum tree outside Mrs. Stubb's shop, and as they passed by there was a strong whiff of eucalyptus. And now big spots of light gleamed in the mist. The shepherd stopped whistling; he rubbed his red nose and wet beard on his wet sleeve and, screwing up his eyes, glanced in the direction of the sea. The sun was rising. It was marvellous how quickly the mist thinned, sped away, dissolved from the shallow plain, rolled up from the bush and was gone as if in a hurry to escape; big twists and curls jostled and shouldered each other as the silvery beams broadened. The far-away sky — a bright, pure blue — was reflected in the puddles, and the drops, swimming along the telegraph poles, flashed into points of light. Now the leaping, glittering sea was so bright it made one's eyes ache to look at it. The shepherd drew a pipe, the bowl as small as an acorn, out of his breast-pocket, fumbled for a chunk of speckled tobacco, pared off a few shavings and stuffed the bowl. He was a grave, fine-looking old man. As he lit up and the blue smoke wreathed his head, the dog, watching, looked proud of him.

"Baa! Baaa!" The sheep spread out into a fan. They were just clear of the summer colony before the first sleeper turned over and lifted a drowsy head; their cry sounded in the dreams of little children... who lifted their arms to drag down, to cuddle the darling little woolly lambs of sleep. Then the first inhabitant appeared; it was the Burnells' cat Florrie, sitting on the gatepost, far too early as usual, looking for their milk-girl. When she saw the old sheep-dog she sprang up quickly, arched her back, drew in her tabby head, and seemed to give a little fastidious shiver. "Ugh! What a coarse, revolting creature!" said Florrie. But the old sheep-dog, not looking up, waggled past, flinging out his legs from side to side. Only one of his ears twitched to prove that he saw, and thought her a silly young female.

The breeze of morning lifted in the bush and the smell of leaves and wet black earth mingled with the sharp smell of the sea. Myriads of birds were singing. A goldfinch flew over the shepherd's head and, perching on the tiptop of a spray, it turned to the sun, ruffling its small breast feathers. And now they had passed the fisherman's hut, passed the charred-looking little *whare* where Leila the milk-girl lived with her old Gran. The sheep strayed over a yellow swamp and Wag, the sheep-dog, padded after, rounded them up and headed them for the steeper, narrower rocky pass that led out of Crescent Bay and towards Daylight Cove. "Baa! Baaa!" Faint the cry came as they rocked along the fast-drying road. The shepherd put away his pipe, dropping it into his breast-pocket so that the little bowl hung over. And straightway the soft airy whistling began again. Wag ran out along a ledge of rock after something that smelled, and ran back again disgusted. Then pushing, nudging, hurrying, the sheep rounded the bend and the shepherd followed after out of sight.

II

A few moments later the back door of one of the bungalows opened, and a figure in a broad-striped bathing-suit flung down the paddock, cleared the stile, rushed through the tussock grass into the hollow, staggered up the sandy hillock, and raced for dear life over the big porous stones, over the cold, wet pebbles, on to the hard sand that gleamed like oil. Splish-Splosh! Splish-Splosh! the water bubbled round his legs as Stanley Burnell waded out exulting. First man in as usual! He'd beaten them all again. And he swooped down to souse his head and neck.

"Hail, brother! All hail, Thou Mighty One!" A velvety bass voice came booming over the water.

Great Scott! Damnation take it! Stanley lifted up to see a dark head bobbing far out and an arm lifted. It was Jonathan Trout — there before him! "Glorious morning!" sang the voice.

"Yes, very fine!" said Stanley briefly. Why the dickens didn't the fellow stick to his part of the sea? Why should he come barging over to this exact spot? Stanley gave a kick, a lunge and struck out, swimming overarm. But Jonathan was a match for him. Up he came, his black hair sleek on his forehead, his short beard sleek.

"I had an extraordinary dream last night!" he shouted.

What was the matter with the man? This mania for conversation irritated Stanley beyond words. And it was always the same — always some piffle about a dream he'd had, or some cranky idea he'd got hold if, or some rot he'd been reading. Stanley turned over on his back and kicked with his legs till he was a living water-spout. But even then... "I dreamed I was hanging over a terrifically high cliff, shouting to someone below." You would be! thought Stanley. He could stick no more of it. He stopped splashing. "Look here, Trout," he said, "I'm in rather a hurry this morning."

"You're WHAT?" Jonathan was so surprised — or pretended to be — that he sank under the water, then reappeared again blowing.

"All I mean is," said Stanley, "I'm in a hurry. I've work to do this morning — see?"

Jonathan was gone before Stanley had finished. "Pass, friend!" said the bass voice gently, and he slid away through the water with scarcely a ripple....But curse the fellow! He'd ruined Stanley's bathe. What an unpractical idiot the man was! Stanley struck out to sea again, and then as quickly swam in again, and away he rushed up the beach. He felt cheated.

Jonathan stayed a little longer in the water. He floated, gently moving his hands like fins, and letting the sea rock his long skinny body. It was curious, but in spite of everything he was fond of Stanley Burnell. True, he had a fiendish desire to tease him sometimes, to poke fun at him, but at bottom he was sorry for the fellow. There was something pathetic in his determination to make a job of everything. You couldn't help feeling he'd be caught out one day, and then what an almighty cropper he'd come! At that moment an immense wave lifted Jonathan, rode past him, and broke along the beach with a joyful sound. What a beauty! And now there came another. That was the way to live — carelessly, recklessly, spending oneself. He got on to his feet and began to wade towards the shore, pressing his toes into the firm, wrinkled sand. To take things easy, not to fight against the ebb and flow of life, but to give way to it — that was what was needed. It was this tension that was all wrong. To live — to live! And the perfect morning, so fresh and fair, basking in the light, as though laughing at its own beauty, seemed to whisper, "Why not?"

But now he was out of the water Jonathan turned blue with cold. He ached all over; it was as though someone was wringing the blood out of him. And stalking up the beach, shivering, all his muscles tight, he too felt his bathe was spoilt. He'd stayed in too long.

III

Beryl was alone in the living-room when Stanley appeared, wearing a blue serge suit, a stiff collar and a spotted tie. He looked almost uncannily clean and brushed; he was going to town for the day. Dropping into his chair, he pulled out his watch and put it beside his plate.

"I've just got twenty-five minutes," he said. "You might go and see if the porridge is ready, Beryl?"

"Mother's just gone for it," said Beryl. She sat down at the table and poured out his tea.

"Thanks!" Stanley took a sip. "Hallo!" he said in an astonished voice, "You've forgotten the sugar."

"Oh, sorry!" But even then Beryl didn't help him; she pushed the basin across. What did this mean? As Stanley helped himself his blue eyes widened; they seemed to quiver. He shot a quick glance at his sister-in-law and leaned back.

"Nothing wrong, is there?" he asked carelessly, fingering his collar.

Beryl's head was bent; she turned her plate in her fingers.

"Nothing," said her light voice. Then she too looked up, and smiled at Stanley. "Why should there be?"

"O-oh! No reason at all as far as I know. I thought you seemed rather—"

At that moment the door opened and the three little girls appeared, each carrying a porridge plate. They were dressed alike in blue jerseys and knickers; their brown legs were bare, and each had her hair plaited and pinned up in what was called a horse's tail. Behind them came Mrs. Fairfield with the tray.

"Carefully, children," she warned. But they were taking the very greatest care. They loved being allowed to carry things. "Have you said good-morning to your father?"

"Yes, grandma." They settled themselves on the bench opposite Stanley and Beryl.

Walter Wright
Shelly Beach

"Good morning, Stanley!" Old Mrs. Fairfield gave him his plate.

"Morning, mother! How's the boy?"

"Splendid! He only woke up once last night. What a perfect morning!" The old woman paused, her hand on the loaf of bread, to gaze out of the open door into the garden. The sea sounded. Through the wide-open window streamed the sun on to the yellow varnished walls and bare floor. Everything on the table flashed and glittered. In the middle there was an old salad bowl filled with yellow and red nasturtiums. She smiled, and a look of deep content shone in her eyes.

"You might *cut* me a slice of that bread, mother," said Stanley. "I've only twelve and a half minutes before the coach passes. Has anyone given my shoes to the servant girl?"

"Yes, they're ready for you." Mrs. Fairfield was quite unruffled.

"Oh, Kezia! Why are you such a messy child!" cried Beryl despairingly.

"Me, Aunt Beryl?" Kezia stared at her. What had she done now? She had only dug a river down the middle of her porridge, filled it, and was eating the banks away. But she did that every single morning, and no one had said a word up till now.

"Why can't you eat your food properly like Isabel and Lottie?" How unfair grown-ups are!

"But Lottie always makes a floating island, don't you, Lottie?"

"I don't," said Isabel smartly. "I just sprinkle mine with sugar and put on the milk and finish it. Only babies play with their food."

Stanley pushed back his chair and got up.

"Would you get me those shoes, mother? And, Beryl, if you've finished, I wish you'd cut down to the gate and stop the coach. Run in to your mother, Isabel, and ask her where my bowler hat's been put. Wait a minute — have you children been playing with my stick?"

"No, father!"

"But I put it here," Stanley began to bluster. "I remember distinctly putting it in this corner. Now, who's had it? There's no time to lose. Look sharp! The stick's got to be found."

Even Alice, the servant girl, was drawn into the chase. "You haven't been using it to poke the kitchen fire with by any chance?"

Stanley dashed into the bedroom where Linda was lying. "Most extraordinary thing. I can't keep a single possession to myself. They've made away with my stick, now!"

"Stick, dear? What stick?" Linda's vagueness on these occasions could not be real, Stanley decided. Would nobody sympathise with him?

"Coach! Coach, Stanley!" Beryl's voice cried from the gate.

Stanley waved his arm to Linda. "No time to say good-bye!" he cried. And he meant that as a punishment to her.

He snatched his bowler hat, dashed out of the house, and swung down the garden path. Yes, the coach was there waiting, and Beryl, leaning over the open gate, was laughing up at somebody or other just as if nothing had happened. The heartlessness of women! The way they took it for granted it was your job to slave away for them while they didn't even take the trouble to see that your walking-stick wasn't lost. Kelly trailed his whip across the horses.

"Good-bye, Stanley," called Beryl, sweetly and gaily. It was easy enough to say good-bye! And there she stood, idle, shading her eyes with her hand. The worst of it was Stanley had to shout good-bye too, for the sake of appearances. Then he saw her turn, give a little skip and run back to the house. She was glad to be rid of him!

Yes, she was thankful. Into the living-room she ran and called "He's gone!" Linda cried from her room: "Beryl! Has Stanley gone?" Old Mrs. Fairfield appeared, carrying the boy in his little flannel coatee.

"Gone?"

"Gone!"

Oh, the relief, the difference it made to have the man out of the house. Their very voices were changed as they called to one another; they sounded warm and loving and as if they shared a secret. Beryl went over to the table. "Have another cup of tea, mother. It's still hot." She wanted, somehow, to celebrate the fact that they could do what they liked now. There was no man to disturb them; the whole perfect day was theirs.

"No, thank you, child," said old Mrs. Fairfield, but the way at that moment she tossed the boy up and said "a-goos-a-goos-a-ga!" to him meant that she felt the same. The little girls ran into the paddock like chickens let out of a coop.

Even Alice, the servant girl, washing up the dishes in the kitchen, caught the infection and used the precious tank water in a perfectly reckless fashion.

"Oh, these men!" said she, and she plunged the teapot into the bowl and held it under the water even after it had stopped bubbling, as if it too was a man and drowning was too good for them.

IV

"Wait for me, Isa-bel! Kezia, wait for me!"

There was poor little Lottie, left behind again, because she found it so fearfully hard to get over the stile by herself. When she stood on the first step her knees began to wobble; she grasped the post. Then you had to put one leg over. But which leg? She never could decide. And when she did finally put one leg over with a sort of stamp of despair — then the feeling was awful. She was half in the paddock still and half in the tussock grass. She clutched the post desperately and lifted up her voice. "Wait for me!"

"No, don't you wait for her, Kezia!" said Isabel. "She's such a little silly. She's always making a fuss. Come on!" And she tugged Kezia's jersey. "You can use my bucket if you come with me," she said kindly. "It's bigger than yours." But Kezia couldn't leave Lottie all by herself. She ran back to her. By this time Lottie was very red in the face and breathing heavily.

"Here, put your other foot over," said Kezia.

"Where?"

Lottie looked down at Kezia as if from a mountain height.

"Oh, *there* do you mean?" Lottie gave a deep sigh and put the second foot over.

"Now — sort of turn round and sit down and slide," said Kezia.

"But there's nothing to sit down *on*, Kezia," said Lottie.

She managed it at last, and once it was over she shook herself and began to beam.

"I'm getting better at climbing over stiles, aren't I, Kezia?"

Lottie's was a very hopeful nature.

The pink and the blue sunbonnet followed Isabel's bright red sunbonnet up that sliding, slipping hill. At the top they paused to decide where to go and to have a good stare at who was there already. Seen from behind, standing against the skyline, gesticulating largely with their spades, they looked like minute puzzled explorers.

The whole family of Samuel Josephs was there already with their lady-help, who sat on a camp-stool and kept order with a whistle that she wore tied round her neck, and a small cane with which she directed operations. The Samuel Josephs never played by themselves or managed their own game. If they did, it ended in the boys pouring water down the girls' necks or the girls trying to put little black crabs into the boys' pockets. So Mrs. S. J. and the poor lady-help drew up what she called a "brogramme" every morning to keep them "abused and out of bischief." It was all competitions or races or round games. Everything began with a piercing blast of the lady-help's whistle and ended with another. There were even prizes — large, rather dirty paper parcels which the lady-help with a sour little smile drew out of a bulging string kit. The Samuel Josephs fought fearfully for the prizes and cheated and pinched one another's arms — they were all expert pinchers. The only time the Burnell children ever played with them Kezia had got a prize, and when she undid three bits of paper she found a very small rusty button-hook. She couldn't understand why they made such a fuss. . . .

But they never played with the Samuel Josephs now or even went to their parties. The Samuel Josephs were always giving children's parties at the Bay and there was always the same food. A big washhand basin of very brown fruit salad, buns cut into four and a washhand jug full of something the lady-help called "Limmonadear". And you went away in the evening with half the frill torn off your frock or something spilled all down the front of your openwork pinafore, leaving the Samuel Josephs leaping like savages on their lawn. No! They were too awful.

On the other side of the beach, close down to the water, two little boys, their knickers rolled up, twinkled like spiders. One was digging, the other pattered in and out of the water, filling a small bucket. They were the Trout boys, Pip and Rags. But Pip was so busy digging and Rags was so busy helping that they didn't see their little cousins until they were quite close.

"Look!" said Pip. "Look what I've discovered." And he showed them an old, wet, squashed-looking boot. The three little girls stared.

"Whatever are you going to do with it?" asked Kezia.

"Keep it, of course!" Pip was very scornful. "It's a find — see?"

Yes, Kezia saw that. All the same. . .

"There's lots of things buried in the sand," explained Pip. "They get chucked up from wrecks. Treasure. Why — you might find —"

"But why does Rags have to keep on pouring water in?" asked Lottie.

"Oh, that's to moisten it," said Pip, "to make the work a bit easier. Keep it up, Rags."

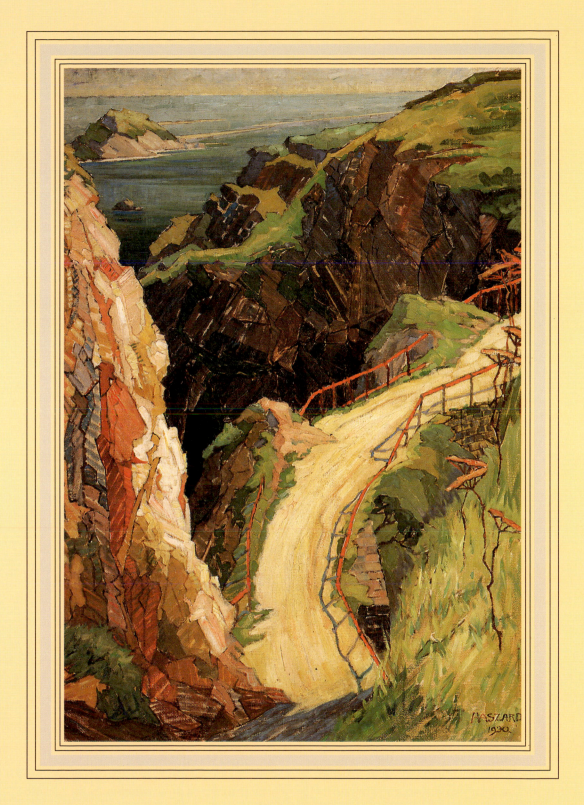

Rhona Haszard
The Road to Little Sark

And good little Rags ran up and down, pouring in the water that turned brown like cocoa.

"Here, shall I show you what I found yesterday?" said Pip mysteriously, and he stuck his spade into the sand. "Promise not to tell."

They promised.

"Say, cross my heart straight dinkum."

The little girls said it.

Pip took something out of his pocket, rubbed it a long time on the front of his jersey, then breathed on it and rubbed it again.

"Now turn round!" he ordered.

They turned round.

"All look the same way! Keep still! Now!"

And his hand opened; he held up to the light something that flashed, that winked, that was a most lovely green.

"It's a nemeral," said Pip solemnly.

"Is it really, Pip?" Even Isabel was impressed.

The lovely green thing seemed to dance in Pip's fingers. Aunt Beryl had a nemeral in a ring, but it was a very small one. This one was as big as a star and far more beautiful.

V

As the morning lengthened whole parties appeared over the sand-hills and came down on the beach to bathe. It was understood that at eleven o'clock the women and children of the summer colony had the sea to themselves. First the women undressed, pulled on their bathing dresses and covered their heads in hideous caps like sponge-bags; then the children were unbuttoned. The beach was strewn with little heaps of clothes and shoes; the big summer hats, with stones on them to keep them from blowing away, looked like immense shells. It was strange that even the sea seemed to sound differently when all those leaping, laughing figures ran into the waves. Old Mrs. Fairfield, in a lilac cotton dress and a black hat tied under the chin, gathered her little brood and got them ready. The little Trout boys whipped their shirts over their heads, and away the five sped, while their grandma sat with one hand in her knitting-bag ready to draw out the ball of wool when she was satisfied they were safely in.

The firm compact little girls were not half so brave as the tender, delicate-looking little boys. Pips and Rags, shivering, crouching down, slapping the water, never hesitated. But Isabel, who could swim twelve strokes, and Kezia, who could nearly swim eight, only followed on the strict understanding they were not to be splashed. As for Lottie, she didn't follow at all. She liked to be left to go in her own way, please. And that way was to sit down at the edge of the water, her legs straight, her knees pressed together, and to make vague motions with her arms as if she expected to be wafted out to sea. But when a bigger wave than usual, an old whiskery one, came lolloping along in her direction, she scrambled to her feet with a face of horror and flew up the beach again.

"Here, mother, keep these for me, will you?"

Two rings and a thin gold chain were dropped into Mrs. Fairfield's lap.

"Yes, dear. But aren't you going to bathe here?"

"No-o," Beryl drawled. She sounded vague. "I'm undressing further along. I'm going to bathe with Mrs. Harry Kember."

"Very well." But Mrs. Fairfield's lips set. She disapproved of Mrs. Harry Kember. Beryl knew it.

Poor old mother, she smiled, as she skimmed over the stones. Poor old mother! Oh, what joy, what bliss it was to be young....

"You looked very pleased," said Mrs. Harry Kember. She sat hunched up on the stones, her arms round her knees, smoking.

"It's such a lovely day," said Beryl, smiling down at her.

"Oh, my *dear*!" Mrs. Harry Kember's voice sounded as though she knew better than that. But then her voice always sounded as though she knew something more about you than you did yourself. She was a long, strange-looking woman with narrow hands and feet. Her face, too, was long and narrow and exhausted-looking; even her fair curled fringe looked burnt out and withered. She was the only woman at the Bay who smoked, and she smoked incessantly, keeping the cigarette between her lips while she talked, and only taking it out when the ash was so long you could not understand why it did not fall. When she was not playing bridge — she played bridge every day of her life — she spent her time lying in the full glare of the sun. She could stand any amount of it; she never had enough. All the same, it did not seem to warm her. Parched, withered, cold, she lay stretched on the stones like a piece of tossed-up driftwood. The women at the Bay thought she was very, very fast. Her lack of vanity, her slang, the way she treated men as though she was one of them, and the fact that she didn't care twopence about her house and called the servant Gladys "Glad-eyes", was disgraceful. Standing on the veranda steps Mrs. Kember would call in her indifferent, tired voice, "I say, Glad-eyes, you might heave me a handkerchief if I've got one, will you?" And Glad-eyes, a red bow in her hair instead of a cap, and white shoes, came running with an impudent smile. It was an absolute scandal! True, she had no children, and her husband...Here the voices were always raised; they became fervent. How can he have married her? How can he, how can he? It must have been money, of course, but even then!

Mrs. Kember's husband was at least ten years younger than she was, and so incredibly handsome that he looked like a mask or a most perfect illustration of an American novel rather than a man. Black hair, dark blue eyes, red lips, a slow sleepy smile, a fine tennis player, a perfect dancer, and with it all a mystery. Harry Kember was like a man walking in his sleep. Men couldn't stand him, they couldn't get a word out of the chap; he ignored his wife just as she ignored him. How did he live? Of course there were stories, but such stories! They simply couldn't be told. The women he'd been seen with, the places he'd been seen in...but nothing was ever certain, nothing definite. Some of the women at the Bay privately thought he'd commit a murder one day. Yes, even while they talked to Mrs. Kember and took in the awful concoction she was wearing, they saw her, stretched as she lay on the beach; but cold, bloody, and still with a cigarette stuck in the corner of her mouth.

Mrs. Kember rose, yawned, unsnapped her belt buckle, and tugged at the tape of her blouse. And Beryl stepped out of her skirt and shed her jersey, and stood up in her short white petticoat, and her camisole with ribbon bows on the shoulders.

"Mercy on us," said Mrs. Harry Kember, "what a little beauty you are!"

"Don't!" said Beryl softly; but, drawing off one stocking and then the other, she felt a little beauty.

"My dear — why not?" said Mrs. Harry Kember, stamping on her own petticoat. Really — her underclothes! A pair of blue cotton knickers and a linen bodice that reminded one somehow of a pillow-case. . . . "And you don't wear stays, do you?" She touched Beryl's waist, and Beryl sprang away with a small affected cry. Then "Never!" she said firmly.

"Lucky little creature," sighed Mrs. Kember, unfastening her own.

Beryl turned her back and began the complicated movements of someone who is trying to take off her clothes and to pull on her bathing-dress all at one and the same time.

"Oh, my dear — don't mind me," said Mrs. Harry Kember. "Why be shy? I shan't eat you. I shan't be shocked like those other ninnies." And she gave her strange neighing laugh and grimaced at the other women.

But Beryl was shy. She never undressed in front of anybody. Was that silly? Mrs. Harry Kember made her feel it was silly, even something to be ashamed of. Why be shy indeed! She glanced quickly at her friend standing so boldly in her torn chemise and lighting a fresh cigarette; and a quick, bold, evil feeling started up in her breast. Laughing recklessly, she drew on the limp, sandy-feeling bathing-dress that was not quite dry and fastened the twisted buttons.

"That's better," said Mrs. Harry Kember. They began to go down the beach together. "Really, it's a sin for you to wear clothes, my dear. Somebody's got to tell you some day."

The water was quite warm. It was that marvellous transparent blue, flecked with silver, but the sand at the bottom looked gold; when you kicked with your toes there rose a little puff of gold-dust. Now the waves just reached her breast. Beryl stood, her arms outstretched, gazing out, and as each wave came she gave the slightest little jump, so that it seemed it was the wave which lifted her so gently.

"I believe in pretty girls having a good time," said Mrs. Harry Kember. "Why not? Don't you make a mistake, my dear. Enjoy yourself." And suddenly she turned turtle, disappeared, and swam away quickly, quickly, like a rat. Then she flicked round and began swimming back. She was going to say something else. Beryl felt that she was being poisoned by this cold woman, but she longed to hear. But oh, how strange, how horrible. As Mrs. Harry

Kember came up close she looked, in her black waterproof bathing-cap, with her sleepy face lifted above the water, just her chin touching, like a horrible caricature of her husband.

VI

In a steamer chair, under a manuka tree that grew in the middle of the front grass patch, Linda Burnell dreamed the morning away. She did nothing. She looked up at the dark, close, dry leaves of the manuka, at the chinks of blue between, and now and again a tiny yellowish flower dropped on her. Pretty — yes, if you held one of those flowers on the palm of your hand and looked at it closely, it was an exquisite small thing. Each pale yellow petal shone as if each was the careful work of a loving hand. The tiny tongue in the centre gave it the shape of a bell. And when you turned it over the outside was a deep bronze colour. But as soon as they flowered, they fell and were scattered. You brushed them off your frock as you talked; the horrid little things got caught in one's hair. Why, then, flower at all? Who takes the trouble — or the joy — to make all these things that are wasted, wasted.... It was uncanny.

On the grass beside her, lying between two pillows, was the boy. Sound asleep he lay, his head turned away from his mother. His fine dark hair looked more like a shadow than like real hair, but his ear was a bright, deep coral. Linda clasped her hands above her head and crossed her feet. It was very pleasant to know that all these bungalows were empty, that everybody was down on the beach, out of sight, out of hearing. She had the garden to herself; she was alone.

Dazzling white the picotees shone; the golden-eyed marigolds glittered; the nasturtiums wreathed the veranda poles in green and gold flame. If only one had time to look at these flowers long enough, time to get over the sense of novelty and strangeness, time to know them! But as soon as one paused to part the petals, to discover the under-side of the leaf, along came Life and one was swept away. And, lying in her cane chair, Linda felt so light; she felt like a leaf. Along came Life like a wind and she was seized and shaken; she had to go. Oh dear, would it always be so? Was there no escape?

...Now she sat on the veranda of their Tasmanian home, leaning against her father's knee. And he promised, "As soon as you and I are old enough, Linny, we'll cut off somewhere, we'll escape. Two boys together. I have a fancy I'd like to sail up a river in China." Linda saw that river, very wide, covered with little rafts and boats. She saw the yellow hats of the boatmen and she heard their high, thin voices as they called...

"Yes, papa."

But just then a very broad young man with bright ginger hair walked slowly past their house, and slowly, solemnly even, uncovered. Linda's father pulled her ear teasingly, in the way he had.

"Linny's beau," he whispered.

"Oh, papa, fancy being married to Stanley Burnell!"

Well, she was married to him. And what was more she loved him. Not the Stanley whom every one saw, not the everyday one; but a timid, sensitive, innocent Stanley who knelt down every night to say his prayers, and who longed to be good. Stanley was simple.

If he believed in people — as he believed in her, for instance — it was with his whole heart. He could not be disloyal; he could not tell a lie. And how terribly he suffered if he thought anyone — she — was not being dead straight, dead sincere with him! "This is too subtle for me!" He flung out the words, but his open, quivering, distraught look was like the look of a trapped beast.

But the trouble was — here Linda felt almost inclined to laugh, though heaven knows it was no laughing matter — she saw *her* Stanley so seldom. There were glimpses, moments, breathing spaces of calm, but all the rest of the time it was like living in a house that couldn't be cured of the habit of catching fire, or a ship that got wrecked every day. And it was always Stanley who was in the thick of the danger. Her whole time was spent in rescuing him, and restoring him, and calming him down, and listening to his story. And what was left of her time was spent in the dread of having children.

Linda frowned; she sat up quickly in her steamer chair and clasped her ankles. Yes, that was her real grudge against life; that was what she could not understand. That was the question she asked and asked, and listened in vain for the answer. It was all very well to say it was the common lot of women to bear children. It wasn't true. She, for one, could prove that wrong. She was broken, made weak, her courage was gone, through child-bearing. And what made it doubly hard to bear was, she did not love her children. It was useless pretending. Even if she had had the strength she never would have nursed and played with the little girls. No, it was as though a cold breath had chilled her through and through on each of those awful journeys; she had no warmth left to give them. As to the boy — well, thank heaven, mother had taken him; he was mother's or Beryl's, or anybody's who wanted him. She had hardly held him in her arms. She was so indifferent about him, that as he lay there...Linda glanced down.

The boy had turned over. He lay facing her, and he was no longer asleep. His dark-blue, baby eyes were open; he looked as though he was peeping at his mother. And suddenly his face dimpled; it broke into a wide, toothless smile, a perfect beam, no less.

"I'm here!" that happy smile seemed to say. "Why don't you like me?"

There was something so quaint, so unexpected about that smile that Linda smiled herself. But she checked herself and said to the boy coldly, "I don't like babies."

"Don't like babies?" The boy couldn't believe her. "Don't like *me*?" He waved his arms foolishly at his mother.

Linda dropped off her chair on to the grass.

"Why do you keep on smiling?" she said severely. "If you knew what I was thinking about, you wouldn't."

But he only squeezed up his eyes, slyly, and rolled his head on the pillow. He didn't believe a word she said.

"We know all about that!" smiled the boy.

Linda was so astonished at the confidence of this little creature.... Ah no, be sincere. That was not what she felt; it was something far different, it was something so new, so... The tears danced in her eyes; she breathed in a small whisper to the boy, "Hallo, my funny!"

But by now the boy had forgotten his mother. He was serious again. Something pink, something soft waved in front of him. He made a grab at it and it immediately disappeared. But when he lay back, another, like the first, appeared. This time he determined to catch it. He made a tremendous effort and rolled right over.

VII

The tide was out; the beach was deserted; lazily flopped the warm sea. The sun beat down, beat down hot and fiery on the fine sand, baking the grey and blue and black and white-veined pebbles. It sucked up the little drop of water that lay in the hollow of the curved shells; it bleached the pink convolvulus that threaded through and through the sand-hills. Nothing seemed to move but the small sand-hoppers. Pit-pit-pit! They were never still.

Over there on the weed-hung rocks that looked at low tide like shaggy beasts come down to the water to drink, the sunlight seemed to spin like a silver coin dropped into each of the small rock pools. They danced, they quivered, and minute ripples laved the porous shores. Looking down, bending over, each pool was like a lake with pink and blue houses clustered on the shores; and oh! the vast mountainous country behind those houses — the ravines, the passes, the dangerous creeks and fearful tracks that led to the water's edge. Underneath waved the sea-forest — pink thread-like trees, velvet anemones, and orange berry-spotted weeds. Now a stone on the bottom moved, rocked, and there was a glimpse of a black feeler; now a thread-like creature wavered by and was lost. Something was happening to the pink, waving trees; they were changing to a cold moonlight blue. And now there sounded the faintest "plop". Who made that sound? What was going on down there? And how strong, how damp the seaweed smelt in the hot sun. . . .

The green blinds were drawn in the bungalows of the summer colony. Over the verandas, prone on the paddock, flung over the fences, there were exhausted-looking bathing-dresses and rough striped towels. Each back window seemed to have a pair of sand-shoes on the sill and some lumps of rock or a bucket or a collection of pawa shells. The bush quivered in a haze of heat; the sandy road was empty except for the Trouts' dog Snooker, who lay stretched in the very middle of it. His blue eye was turned up, his legs stuck out stiffly, and he gave an occasional desperate sounding puff, as much as to say he had decided to make an end of it and was only waiting for some kind cart to come along.

"What are you looking at, my grandma? Why do you keep stopping and sort of staring at the wall?"

Kezia and her grandmother were taking their siesta together. The little girl, wearing only her short drawers and her under-bodice, her arms and legs bare, lay on one of the puffed-up pillows of her grandma's bed, and the old woman, in a white ruffled dressing-gown, sat in a rocker at the window, with a long piece of pink knitting in her lap. This room that they shared, like the other rooms of the bungalow, was of light varnished wood and the floor was bare. The furniture was of the shabbiest, the simplest. The dressing-table, for instance, was a packing-case in a sprigged muslin petticoat, and the mirror above was very strange; it was as though a little piece of forked lightning was imprisoned in it. On the table there stood a jar of sea-pinks, pressed so tightly together they looked more like a velvet pin-cushion, and a special shell which Kezia had given her grandma for a pin-tray, and another even more special which she had thought would make a very nice place for a watch to curl up in.

"Tell me, grandma," said Kezia.

The old woman sighed, whipped the wool twice round her thumb, and drew the bone needle through. She was casting on.

"I was thinking of your Uncle William, darling," she said quietly.

"My Australian Uncle William?" said Kezia. She had another.

"Yes, of course."

"The one I never saw?"

"That was the one."

"Well, what happened to him?" Kezia knew perfectly well, but she wanted to be told again.

"He went to the mines, and he got a sunstroke there and died," said old Mrs. Fairfield.

Kezia blinked and considered the picture again.... A little man fallen over like a tin soldier by the side of a big black hole.

"Does it make you sad to think about him, grandma?" She hated her grandma to be sad.

It was the old woman's turn to consider. Did it make her sad? To look back, back. To stare down the years, as Kezia had seen her doing. To look after *them* as a woman does, long after *they* were out of sight. Did it make her sad? No, life was like that.

"No, Kezia."

"But why?" asked Kezia. She lifted one bare arm and began to draw things in the air. "Why did Uncle William have to die? He wasn't old."

Mrs. Fairfield began counting the stitches in threes. "It just happened," she said in an absorbed voice.

"Does everybody have to die?" asked Kezia.

"Everybody!"

"*Me?*" Kezia sounded fearfully incredulous.

"Some day, my darling."

"But, grandma." Kezia waved her left leg and waggled the toes. They felt sandy. "What if I just won't?"

The old woman sighed again and drew a long thread from the ball.

"We're not asked, Kezia," she said sadly. "It happens to all of us sooner or later."

Kezia lay still thinking this over. She didn't want to die. It meant she would have to leave here, leave everywhere, for ever, leave — leave her grandma. She rolled over quickly.

"Grandma," she said in a startled voice.

"What, my pet!"

"*You're* not to die." Kezia was very decided.

"Ah, Kezia" — her grandma looked up and smiled and shook her head— "don't let's talk about it."

"But you're not to. You couldn't leave me. You couldn't not be there." This was awful. "Promise me you won't ever do it, grandma," pleaded Kezia.

Petrus van der Velden
Stormcloud

101

The old woman went on knitting.

"Promise me! Say never!"

But still her grandma was silent.

Kezia rolled off the bed; she couldn't bear it any longer, and lightly she leapt on to her grandma's knees, clasped her hands round the old woman's throat and began kissing her, under the chin, behind the ear, and blowing down her neck.

"Say never . . . say never . . . say never —" She gasped between the kisses. And then she began, very softly and lightly, to tickle her grandma.

"Kezia!" The old woman dropped her knitting. She swung back in the rocker. She began to tickle Kezia. "Say never, say never, say never," gurgled Kezia, while they lay there laughing in each other's arms. "Come, that's enough, my squirrel! That's enough, my wild pony!" said old Mrs. Fairfield, setting her cap straight. "Pick up my knitting."

Both of them had forgotten what the "Never" was about.

VIII

The sun was still full on the garden when the back door of the Burnells' shut with a bang and a very gay figure walked down the path to the gate. It was Alice, the servant girl, dressed for her afternoon out. She wore a white cotton dress with such large red spots on it, and so many that they made you shudder, white shoes and a leghorn turned up under the brim with poppies. Of course she wore gloves, white ones, stained at the fastenings with iron-mould, and in one hand she carried a very dashed-looking sunshade which she referred to as her *perishall*.

Beryl, sitting in the window, fanning her freshly washed hair, thought she had never seen such a guy. If Alice had only blacked her face with a piece of cork before she started out the picture would have been complete. And where did a girl like that go to in a place like this? The heart-shaped Fijian fan beat scornfully at that lovely bright mane. She supposed Alice had picked up some horrible common larrikin and they'd go off into the bush together. Pity to make herself so conspicuous; they'd have hard work to hide with Alice in that rig-out.

But no, Beryl was unfair. Alice was going to tea with Mrs. Stubbs, who'd sent her an "invite" by the little boy who called for orders. She had taken ever such a liking to Mrs. Stubbs ever since the first time she went to the shop to get something for her mosquitoes.

"Dear heart!" Mrs. Stubbs had clapped her hand to her side. "I never seen anyone so eaten. You might have been attacked by canningbals."

Alice did wish there'd been a bit of life on the road though. Made her feel so queer, having nobody behind her. Made her feel all weak in the spine. She couldn't believe that someone wasn't watching her. And yet it was silly to turn round; it gave you away. She pulled up her gloves, hummed to herself and said to the distant gum tree, "Shan't be long now." But that was hardly company.

Mrs. Stubbs's shop was perched on a little hillock just off the road. It had two big windows for eyes, a broad veranda for a hat, and the sign on the roof, scrawled MRS. STUBBS'S, was like a little card stuck rakishly in the hat crown.

On the veranda there hung a long string of bathing-dresses, clinging together as though they'd just been rescued from the sea rather than waiting to go in, and beside them there hung a cluster of sand-shoes so extraordinarily mixed that to get at one pair you had to tear apart and forcibly separate at least fifty. Even then it was the rarest thing to find the left that belonged to the right. So many people had lost patience and gone off with one shoe that fitted and one that was a little too big. . . . Mrs. Stubbs prided herself on keeping something of everything. The two windows, arranged in the form of precarious pyramids, were crammed so tight, piled so high, that it seemed only a conjuror could prevent them from toppling over. In the left-hand corner of one window, glued to the pane by four gelatine lozenges, there was — and there had been from time immemorial — a notice:

LOST! HANSOME GOLE BROOCH
SOLID GOLD
ON OR NEAR BEACH
REWARD OFFERED

Alice pressed open the door. The bell jangled, the red serge curtains parted, and Mrs. Stubbs appeared. With her broad smile and the long bacon knife in her hand she looked like a friendly brigand. Alice was welcomed so warmly that she found it quite difficult to keep up her "manners". They consisted of persistent little coughs and hems, pulls at her gloves, tweaks at her skirt, and a curious difficulty in seeing what was set before her or understanding what was said.

Tea was laid on the parlour table — ham, sardines, a whole pound of butter, and such a large johnny cake that it looked like an advertisement for somebody's baking powder. But the Primus stove roared so loudly that it was useless to try to talk above it. Alice sat down on the edge of a basket-chair while Mrs. Stubbs pumped the stove still higher. Suddenly Mrs. Stubbs whipped the cushion off a chair and disclosed a large brown paper parcel.

"I've just had some new photers taken, my dear," she shouted cheerfully to Alice. "Tell me what you think of them."

In a very dainty, refined way Alice wet her finger and put the tissue back from the first one. Life! How many there were! There were three dozzing at least. And she held hers up to the light.

Mrs. Stubbs sat in an arm-chair, leaning very much to one side. There was a look of mild astonishment on her large face, and well there might be. For though the arm-chair stood on a carpet, to the left of it, miraculously skirting the carpet border, there was a dashing waterfall. On her right stood a Grecian pillar with a giant fern tree on either side of it, and in the background towered a gaunt mountain, pale with snow.

"It is a nice style, isn't it?" shouted Mrs. Stubbs; and Alice had just screamed "Sweetly" when the roaring of the Primus stove died down, fizzled out, ceased, and she said "Pretty" in a silence that was frightening.

"Draw up your chair, my dear," said Mrs. Stubbs, beginning to pour out. "Yes," she

Laura Knight
The Bathing Pool

said thoughtfully, as she handed the tea, "but I don't care about the size. I'm having an enlargemint. All very well for Christmas cards, but I never was the one for small photers myself. You get no comfort out of them. To say the truth, I find them dis'eartening."

Alice quite saw what she meant.

"Size," said Mrs. Stubbs. "Give me size. That was what my poor dear husband was always saying. He couldn't stand anything small. Gave him the creeps. And, strange as it may seem, my dear" — here Mrs. Stubbs creaked and seemed to expand herself at the memory — "it was dropsy that carried him off at the larst. Many's the time they drawn one and a half pints from 'im at the 'ospital.... It seemed like a judgmint."

Alice burned to know exactly what it was that was drawn from him. She ventured, "I suppose it was water."

But Mrs. Stubbs fixed Alice with her eyes and replied meaningly, "It was *liquid*, my dear."

Liquid! Alice jumped away from the word like a cat and came back to it, nosing and wary.

"That's 'im!" said Mrs. Stubbs, and she pointed dramatically to the life-size head and shoulders of a burly man with a dead white rose in the button-hole of his coat that made you think of a curl of cold mutton fat. Just below, in silver letters on a red cardboard ground, were the words, "Be not afraid, it is I."

"It's ever such a fine face," said Alice faintly.

The pale-blue bow on the top of Mrs. Stubbs's fair frizzy hair quivered. She arched her plump neck. What a neck she had! It was bright pink where it began and then it changed to warm apricot, and that faded to the colour of a brown egg and then to a deep creamy.

"All the same, my dear," she said surprisingly, "freedom's best!" Her soft, fat chuckle sounded like a purr. "Freedom's best," said Mrs. Stubbs again.

Freedom! Alice gave a loud, silly little titter. She felt awkward. Her mind flew back to her own kitching. Ever so queer! She wanted to be back in it again.

IX

A strange company assembled in the Burnells' washhouse after tea. Round the table there sat a bull, a rooster, a donkey that kept forgetting it was a donkey, a sheep and a bee. The washhouse was the perfect place for such a meeting because they could make as much noise as they liked and nobody ever interrupted. It was a small tin shed standing apart from the bungalow. Against the wall there was a deep trough and in the corner a copper with a basket of clothes-pegs on top of it. The little window, spun over with cobwebs, had a piece of candle and a mouse-trap on the dusty sill. There were clothes-lines criss-crossed overhead and, hanging from a peg on the wall, a very big, a huge, rusty horseshoe. The table was in the middle with a form at either side.

"You can't be a bee, Kezia. A bee's not an animal. It's a ninseck."

"Oh, but I do want to be a bee frightfully," wailed Kezia.... A tiny bee, all yellow-furry, with striped legs. She drew her legs up under her and leaned over the table. She felt she was a bee.

"A ninseck must be an animal," she said stoutly. "It makes a noise. It's not like a fish."

"I'm a bull, I'm a bull!" cried Pip. And he gave such a tremendous bellow — how did he make that noise? — that Lottie looked quite alarmed.

"I'll be a sheep," said little Rags. "A whole lot of sheep went past this morning."

"How do you know?"

"Dad heard them. Baa!" He sounded like the little lamb that trots behind and seems to wait to be carried.

"Cock-a-doodle-do!" shrilled Isabel. With her red cheeks and bright eyes she looked like a rooster.

"What'll I be?" Lottie asked everybody, and she sat there smiling, waiting for them to decide for her. It had to be an easy one.

"Be a donkey, Lottie." It was Kezia's suggestion. "Hee-haw! You can't forget that."

"Hee-haw!" said Lottie solemnly. "When do I have to say it?"

"I'll explain, I'll explain," said the bull. It was he who had the cards. He waved them round his head. "All be quiet! All listen!" And he waited for them. "Look here, Lottie." He turned up a card. "It's got two spots on it — see? Now, if you put that card in the middle and somebody else has one with two spots as well, you say 'Hee-haw', and the card's yours."

"Mine?" Lottie was round-eyed. "To keep?"

"No, silly, Just for the game, see? Just while we're playing." The bull was very cross with her.

"Oh, Lottie, you *are* a little silly," said the proud rooster.

Lottie looked at both of them. Then she hung her head; her lip quivered. "I don't not want to play," she whispered. the others glanced at one another like conspirators. All of them knew what that meant. She would go away and be discovered somewhere standing with her pinny thrown over her head, in a corner, or against a wall, or even behind a chair.

"Yes, you *do*, Lottie. It's quite easy," said Kezia.

And Isabel, repentant, said exactly like a grown-up, "Watch *me*, Lottie, and you'll soon learn."

"Cheer up, Lot," said Pip. "There, I know what I'll do. I'll give you the first one. It's mine, really, but I'll give it to you. Here you are." And he slammed the card down in front of Lottie.

Lottie revived at that. But now she was in another difficulty. "I haven't got a hanky," she said; "I want one badly, too."

"Here, Lottie, you can use mine." Rags dipped into his sailor blouse and brought up a very wet-looking one, knotted together. "Be very careful," he warned her. "Only use that corner. Don't undo it. I've got a little star-fish inside I'm going to try and tame."

"Oh, come on, you girls," said the bull. "And mind — you're not to look at your cards. You've got to keep your hands under the table till I say 'Go'."

Smack went the cards round the table. They tried with all their might to see, but Pip was too quick for them. It was very exciting, sitting there in the washhouse; it was all they could do not to burst into a little chorus of animals before Pip had finished dealing.

"Now, Lottie, you begin."

Timidly Lottie stretched out a hand, took the top card off her pack, had a good look at it — it was plain she was counting the spots — and put it down.

"No, Lottie, you can't do that. You mustn't look first. You must turn it the other way over."

"But then everybody will see it the same time as me," said Lottie.

The game proceeded. Mooe-oo-er! The bull was terrible. He charged over the table and seemed to eat the cards up.

Bss-ss! said the bee.

Cock-a-doodle-do! Isabel stood up in her excitement and moved her elbows like wings.

Baa! Little Rags put down the King of Diamonds and Lottie put down the one they called the King of Spain. She had hardly any cards left.

"Why don't you call out, Lottie?"

"I've forgotten what I am," said the donkey woefully.

"Well, change! Be a dog instead! Bow-wow!"

"Oh yes. that's *much* easier." Lottie smiled again. But when she and Kezia both had one Kezia waited on purpose. The others made signs to Lottie and pointed. Lottie turned very red; she looked bewildered, and at last she said, "Hee-haw! Ke-zia."

"Ss! Wait a minute!" They were in the very thick of it when the bull stopped them, holding up his hand. "What's that? What's that noise?"

"What noise? What do you mean?" asked the rooster.

"Ss! Shut up! Listen!" They were mouse-still. "I thought I heard a — a sort of knocking," said the bull.

"What was it like?" asked the sheep faintly.

No answer.

The bee gave a shudder. "Whatever did we shut the door for?" she said softly. Oh, why, why had they shut the door?

While they were playing, the day had faded; the gorgeous sunset had blazed and died. And now the quick dark came racing over the sea, over the sand-hills, up the paddock. You were frightened to look in the corners of the washhouse, and yet you had to look with all your might. And somewhere, far away, grandma was lighting a lamp. The blinds were being pulled down; the kitchen fire leapt in the tins on the mantelpiece.

"It would be awful now," said the bull, "if a spider was to fall from the ceiling on to the table, wouldn't it?"

"Spiders don't fall from ceilings."

"Yes, they do. Our Min told us she'd seen a spider as big as a saucer, with long hairs on it like a gooseberry."

Quickly all the little heads were jerked up; all the little bodies drew together, pressed together.

"Why doesn't somebody come and call us?" cried the rooster.

Oh, those grown-ups, laughing and snug, sitting in the lamp-light, drinking out of cups! They'd forgotten about them. No, not really forgotten. That was what their smile meant. They had decided to leave them there all by themselves.

Suddenly Lottie gave such a piercing scream that all of them jumped off the forms, all of them screamed too. "A face — a face looking!" shrieked Lottie.

It was true, it was real. Pressed against the window was a pale face, black eyes, a black beard.

"Grandma! Mother! Somebody!"

But they had not got to the door, tumbling over one another, before it opened for Uncle Jonathan. He had come to take the little boys home.

X

He had meant to be there before, but in the front garden he had come upon Linda walking up and down the grass, stopping to pick off a dead pink or give a top-heavy carnation something to lean against, or to take a deep breath of something, and then walking on again, with her little air of remoteness. Over her white frock she wore a yellow, pink-fringed shawl from the Chinaman's shop.

"Hallo, Jonathan!" called Linda. And Jonathan whipped off his shabby panama, pressed it against his breast, dropped on one knee, and kissed Linda's hand.

"Greeting, my Fair One! Greeting, my Celestial Peach Blossom!" boomed the bass voice gently. "Where are the other noble dames?"

"Beryl's out playing bridge and mother's giving the boy his bath. . . . Have you come to borrow something?"

The Trouts were for ever running out of things and sending across to the Burnells' at the last moment.

But Jonathan only answered, "A little love, a little kindness"; and he walked by his sister-in-law's side.

Linda dropped into Beryl's hammock under the manuka tree and Jonathan stretched himself on the grass beside her, pulled a long stalk and began chewing it. They knew each other well. The voices of children cried from the other gardens. A fisherman's light cart shook along the sandy road, and from far away they heard a dog barking; it was muffled as though the dog had its head in a sack. If you listened you could just hear the soft swish of the sea at full tide sweeping the pebbles. The sun was sinking.

"And so you go back to the office on Monday, do you, Jonathan?" asked Linda.

"On Monday the cage door opens and clangs to upon the victim for another eleven months and a week," answered Jonathan.

Linda swung a little. "It must be awful," she said slowly.

"Would ye have me laugh, my fair sister? Would ye have me weep?"

Linda was so accustomed to Jonathan's way of talking that she paid no attention to it.

"I suppose," she said vaguely, "one gets used to it. One gets used to anything."

"Does one? Hum!" was so deep it seemed to boom from underneath the ground. "I wonder how it's done," brooded Jonathan; "I've never managed it."

Looking at him as he lay there, Linda thought again how attractive he was. It was strange to think that he was only an ordinary clerk, that Stanley earned twice as much money as he. What was the matter with Jonathan? He had no ambition; she supposed that was it. And yet one felt he was gifted, exceptional. He was passionately fond

Frank Wright
Morning after Rain

of music; every spare penny he had went on books. He was always full of new ideas, schemes, plans. But nothing came of it all. The new fire blazed in Jonathan; you almost heard it rearing softly as he explained, described and dilated on the new thing; but a moment later it had fallen in and there was nothing but ashes, and Jonathan went about with a look like hunger in his black eyes. At these times he exaggerated his absurd manner of speaking, and he sang in church — he was the leader of the choir — with such fearful dramatic intensity that the meanest hymn put on an unholy splendour.

"It seems to me just as imbecile, just as infernal, to have to go to the office on Monday," said Jonathan, "as it always has done and always will do. To spend all the best years of one's life sitting on a stool from nine to five, scratching in somebody's ledger! It's a queer use to make of one's . . . one and only life, isn't it? Or do I fondly dream?" He rolled over on the grass and looked up at Linda. "Tell me, what is the difference between my life and that of an ordinary prisoner. The only difference I can see is that I put myself in jail and nobody's ever going to let me out. That's a more intolerable situation than the other. For if I'd been — pushed in, against my will — kicking, even — once the door was locked, or at any rate in five years or so I might have accepted the fact and begun to take an interest in the flight of flies or counting the warder's steps along the passage with particular attention to variations of tread and so on. But as it is, I'm like an insect that's flown into a room of its own accord. I dash against the walls, dash against the windows, flop against the ceiling, do everything on God's earth, in fact, except fly out again. And all the while I'm thinking, like that moth, or that butterfly, or whatever it is, 'The shortness of life! The shortness of life!' I've only one night or one day, and there's this vast dangerous garden, waiting out there, undiscovered, unexplored."

"But, if you feel like that, why —" began Linda quickly.

"*Ah!*" cried Jonathan. And that "Ah!" was somehow almost exultant. "There you have me. Why? Why indeed? There's the maddening, mysterious question. Why don't I fly out again? There's the window or the door or whatever it was I came in by. It's not hopelessly shut — is it? Why don't I find it and be off? Answer me that, little sister." But he gave her no time to answer.

"I'm exactly like that insect again. For some reason" — Jonathan paused between the words — "it's not allowed, it's forbidden, it's against the insect law, to stop banging and flopping and crawling up the pane even for an instant. Why don't I leave the office? Why don't I seriously consider, this moment, for instance, what it is that prevents me leaving? It's not as though I'm tremendously tied. I've two boys to provide for, but, after all, they're boys. I could cut off to sea, or get a job up-country, or —" Suddenly he smiled at Linda and said in a changed voice, as if he were confiding a secret, "Weak . . . weak. No stamina. No anchor. No guiding principle, let us call it." But then the dark velvety voice rolled out:

> Would ye hear the story
> How it unfolds itself . . .

and they were silent.

The sun had set. In the western sky there were great masses of crushed-up rose-coloured clouds. Broad beams of light shone through the clouds and beyond them as if they would cover the whole sky. Overhead the blue faded; it turned a pale gold, and the bush outlined against it gleamed dark and brilliant like metal. Sometimes when those beams of light show in the sky they are very awful. They remind you that up there sits Jehovah, the jealous God, the Almighty, Whose eye is upon you, ever watchful, never weary. You remember that at His coming the whole earth will shake into one ruined graveyard; the cold, bright angels will drive you this way and that, and there will be no time to explain what could be explained so simply. . . . But to-night it seemed to Linda there was something infinitely joyful and loving in those silver beams. And now no sound came from the sea. It breathed softly as if it would draw that tender, joyful beauty into its own bosom.

"It's all wrong, it's all wrong," came the shadowy voice of Jonathan. "It's not the scene, it's not the setting for . . . three stools, three desks, three inkpots and a wire blind."

Linda knew that he would never change, but she said, "Is it too late, even now?"

"I'm old — I'm old," intoned Jonathan. He bent towards her, he passed his hand over his head. "Look!" His black hair was speckled all over with silver, like the breast plumage of a black fowl.

Linda was surprised. She had no idea that he was grey. And yet, as he stood up beside her and sighed and stretched, she saw him, for the first time, not resolute, not gallant, not careless, but touched already with age. He looked very tall on the darkening grass, and the thought crossed her mind, "He is like a weed."

Jonathan stopped again and kissed her fingers.

"Heaven reward thy sweet patience, lady mine," he murmured. "I must go seek those heirs to my fame and fortune. . . ." He was gone.

XI

Light shone in the windows of the bungalow. Two square patches of gold fell upon the pinks and the peaked marigolds. Florrie, the cat, came out on to the veranda and sat on the top step, her white paws close together, her tail curled round. She looked content, as though she had been waiting for this moment all day.

"Thank goodness, it's getting late," said Florrie. "Thank goodness, the long day is over." Her greengage eyes opened.

Presently there sounded the rumble of the coach, the crack of Kelly's whip. It came near enough for one to hear the voices of the men from town, talking loudly together. It stopped at the Burnells' gate.

Stanley was half-way up the path before he saw Linda. "Is that you, darling?"

"Yes, Stanley."

He leapt across the flower-bed and seized her in his arms. She was enfolded in that familiar, eager, strong embrace.

"Forgive me, darling, forgive me," stammered Stanley, and he put his hand under her chin and lifted her face to him.

"Forgive you?" smiled Linda. "But whatever for?"

"Good God! You can't have forgotten," cried Stanley Burnell. "I've thought of nothing else all day. I've had the hell of a day. I made up my mind to dash out and telegraph, and then I thought the wire mightn't reach you before I did. I've been in tortures, Linda."

"But, Stanley," said Linda, "what must I forgive you for?"

"Linda!" — Stanley was very hurt — "didn't you realise — you must have realised — I went away without saying good-bye to you this morning? I can't imagine how I can have done such a thing. My confounded temper, of course. But — well" — and he sighed and took her in his arms again — "I've suffered for it enough to-day."

"What's that you've got in your hand?" asked Linda. "New gloves? Let me see."

"Oh, just a cheap pair of wash-leather ones," said Stanley humbly. "I noticed Bell was wearing some in the coach this morning, so, as I was passing the shop, I dashed in and got myself a pair. What are you smiling at? You don't think it was wrong of me, do you?"

"On the con-trary, darling," said Linda, "I think it was most sensible."

She pulled one of the large, pale gloves on her own fingers and looked at her hand, turning it this way and that. She was still smiling.

Stanley wanted to say, "I was thinking of you the whole time I bought them." It was true, but for some reason he couldn't say it. "Let's go in," said he.

XII

Why does one feel so different at night? Why is it so exciting to be awake when everybody else is asleep? Late — it is very late! And yet every moment you feel more and more wakeful, as though you were slowly, almost with every breath, waking up into a new, wonderful, far more thrilling and exciting world than the daylight one. And what is this queer sensation that you're a conspirator? Lightly, stealthily you move about your room. You take something off the dressing-table and put it down again without a sound. And everything, even the bedpost, knows you, responds, shares your secret. . . .

You're not very fond of your room by day. You never think about it. You're in and out, the door opens and slams, the cupboard creaks. You sit down on the side of your bed, change your shoes and dash out again. A dive down to the glass, two pins in your hair, powder your nose and off again. But now — it's suddenly dear to you. It's a darling little funny room. It's yours. Oh, what a joy it is to own things! Mine — my own!

"My very own for ever?"

"Yes." Their lips met.

No, of course, that had nothing to do with it. That was all nonsense and rubbish. But, in spite of herself, Beryl saw so plainly two people standing in the middle of her room. Her

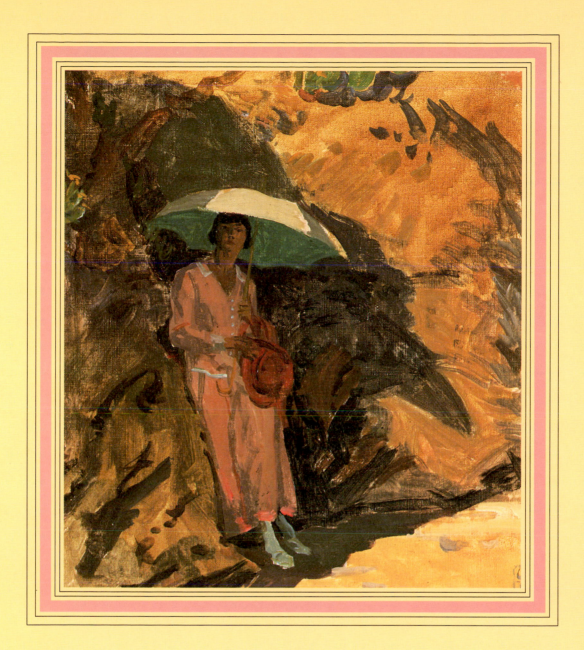

Walter Bayes
Woman with Sunshade

arms were round his neck; he held her. And now he whispered, "My beauty, my little beauty!" She jumped off her bed, ran over to the window and kneeled on the window-seat, with her elbows on the sill. But the beautiful night, the garden, every bush, every leaf, even the white palings, even the stars, were conspirators too. So bright was the moon that the flowers were bright as by day; the shadow of the nasturtiums, exquisite lily-like leaves and wide-open flowers, lay across the silvery veranda. The manuka tree, bent by the southerly winds, was like a bird on one leg stretching out a wing.

But when Beryl looked at the bush, it seemed to her the bush was sad.

"We are dumb trees, reaching up in the night, imploring we know not what," said the sorrowful bush.

It is true when you are by yourself and you think about life, it is always sad. All that excitement and so on has a way of suddenly leaving you, and it's as though, in the silence, somebody called your name, and you heard your name for the first time. "Beryl!"

"Yes, I'm here. I'm Beryl. Who wants me?"

"Beryl!"

"Let me come."

It is lonely living by oneself. Of course, there are relations, friends, heaps of them; but that's not what she means. She wants someone who will find the Beryl they none of them know, who will expect her to be that Beryl always. She wants a lover.

"Take me away from all these other people, my love. Let us go far away. Let us live our life, all new, all ours, from the very beginning. Let us make our fire. Let us sit down to eat together. Let us have long talks at night."

And the thought was almost, "Save me, my love. Save me!"

. . . "Oh, go on! Don't be a prude, my dear. You enjoy yourself while you're young. That's my advice." And a high rush of silly laughter joined Mrs. Harry Kember's loud, indifferent neigh.

You see, it's so frightfully difficult when you've nobody. You're so at the mercy of things. You can't just be rude. And you've always this horror of seeming inexperienced and stuffy like the other ninnies at the Bay. And — and it's fascinating to know you've power over people. Yes, that is fascinating. . . .

Oh why, oh why doesn't "he" come soon?

If I go on living here, thought Beryl, anything may happen to me.

"But how do you know he is coming at all?" mocked a small voice within her.

But Beryl dismissed it. She couldn't be left. Other people, perhaps, but not she. It wasn't possible to think that Beryl Fairfield never married, that lovely, fascinating girl.

"Do you remember Beryl Fairfield?"

"Remember her! As if I could forget her! It was one summer at the Bay that I saw her. She was standing on the beach in a blue" — no pink — "muslin frock,

holding on a big cream" — no, black
— "straw hat. But it's years ago now."

"She's as lovely as ever, more so if
anything."

Beryl smiled, bit her lip, and gazed
over the garden. As she gazed, she saw
somebody, a man, leave the road, step
along the paddock beside their palings as if
he was coming straight towards her. Her
heart beat. Who was it? Who could it
be? It couldn't be a burglar, certainly
not a burglar, for he was smoking

and he strolled lightly. Beryl's heart leapt; it seemed to turn right over and then to stop.
She recognised him.

"Good evening, Miss Beryl," said the voice softly.

"Good evening."

"Won't you come for a little walk?" it drawled.

Come for a walk — at that time of night! "I couldn't. Everybody's in bed. Everybody's
asleep."

"Oh," said the voice lightly, and a whiff of sweet smoke reached her. "What does
everybody matter? Do come! It's such a fine night. There's not a soul about."

Beryl shook her head. But already something stirred in her, something reared its head.

The voice said, "Frightened?" It mocked, "Poor little girl!"

"Not in the least," said she. As she spoke that weak thing within her seemed to uncoil,
to grow suddenly tremendously strong; she longed to go!

And just as if this was quite understood by the other, the voice said, gently and softly,
but finally, "Come along!"

Beryl stepped over her low window, crossed the veranda, ran down the grass to the
gate. He was there before her.

"That's right," breathed the voice, and it teased, "You're not frightened are you? You're
not frightened?"

She was; now she was here she was terrified and it seemed to her everything was different.
The moonlight stared and glittered; the shadows were like bars of iron. Her hand was taken.

"Not in the least," she said lightly. "Why should I be?"

Her hand was pulled gently, tugged. She held back.

"No, I'm not coming any further," said Beryl.

"Oh, rot!" Harry Kember didn't believe her. "Come along! We'll just go as far as that
fuchsia bush. Come along!"

The fuchsia bush was tall. It fell over the fence in a shower. There was a little pit of
darkness beneath.

"No, really, I don't want to," said Beryl.

For a moment Harry Kember didn't answer. Then he came close to her, turned to her, smiled and said quickly, "Don't be silly! Don't be silly!"

His smile was something she'd never seen before. Was he drunk? That bright, blind, terrifying smile froze her with horror. What was she doing? How had she got here? The stern garden asked her as the gate pushed open, and quick as a cat Harry Kember came through and snatched her to him.

"Cold little devil! Cold little devil!" said the hateful voice.

But Beryl was strong. She slipped, ducked, wrenched free. "You are vile, vile," said she.

"Then why in God's name did you come?" stammered Harry Kember.

Nobody answered him.

A cloud, small, serene, floated across the moon. In that moment of darkness the sea sounded deep, troubled. Then the cloud sailed away, and the sound of the sea was a vague murmur, as though it waked out of a dark dream. All was still.

THE VOYAGE

THE Picton boat was due to leave at half-past eleven. It was a beautiful night, mild, starry, only when they got out of the cab and started to walk down the Old Wharf that jutted out into the harbour, a faint wind blowing off the water ruffled under Fenella's hat, and she put up her hand to keep it on. It was dark on the Old Wharf, very dark; the wool sheds, the cattle trucks, the cranes standing up so high, the little squat railway engine, all seemed carved out of solid darkness. Here and there on a rounded wood-pile, that was like the stalk of a huge black mushroom, there hung a lantern, but it seemed afraid to unfurl its timid, quivering light in all that blackness; it burned softly, as if for itself.

Fenella's father pushed on with quick, nervous strides. Beside him her grandma bustled along in her crackling black ulster; they went so fast that she had now and again to give an undignified little skip to keep up with them. As well as her luggage strapped into a neat sausage, Fenella carried clasped to her her grandma's umbrella, and the handle, which was a swan's head, kept giving her shoulder a sharp little peck as if it too wanted her to hurry....
Men, their caps pulled down, their collars turned up, swung by; a few women all muffled scurried along; and one tiny boy, only his little black arms and legs showing out of a white woolly shawl, was jerked along angrily between his father and mother; he looked like a baby fly that had fallen into the cream.

Then suddenly, so suddenly that Fenella and her grandma both leapt, there sounded from behind the largest wool shed, that had a trail of smoke hanging over it, *Mia-oo-oo-O-O!*

"First whistle," said her father briefly, and at that moment they came in sight of the Picton boat. Lying beside the dark wharf, all strung, all beaded with round golden lights, the Picton boat looked as if she was more ready to sail among stars than out into the cold sea. People pressed along the gangway. First went her grandma, then her father, then Fenella. There was a high step down on to the deck, and an old sailor in a jersey standing by gave her his dry, hard hand. They were there; they stepped out of the way of the hurrying people, and standing under a little iron stairway that led to the uppper deck they began to say good-bye.

"There, mother, there's your luggage!" said Fenella's father, giving grandma another strapped-up sausage.

John Holmwood
Wellington Wharf

"Thank you, Frank."

"And you've got your cabin tickets safe?"

"Yes, dear."

"And your other tickets?"

Grandma felt for them inside her glove and showed him the tips.

"That's right."

He sounded stern, but Fenella, eagerly watching him, saw that he looked tired and sad. *Mia-oo-oo-O-O!* The second whistle blared just above their head, and a voice like a cry shouted, "Any more for the gangway?"

"You'll give my love to father," Fenella saw her father's lips say. And her grandma, very agitated, answered, "Of course I will, dear. Go now. You'll be left. Go now, Frank. Go now."

"It's all right, mother. I've got another three minutes." To her surprise Fenella saw her father take off his hat. He clasped grandma in his arms and pressed her to him. "God bless you, mother!" she heard him say.

And grandma put her hand, with the black thread glove that was worn through on her ring finger, against his cheek, and she sobbed," God bless you, my own brave son!"

This was so awful that Fenella quickly turned her back on them, swallowed once, twice, and frowned terribly at a little green star on a mast head. But she had to turn round again; her father was going.

"Good-bye, Fenella. Be a good girl." His cold, wet moustache brushed her cheek. But Fenella caught hold of the lapels of his coat.

"How long am I going to stay?" she whispered anxiously. He wouldn't look at her. He shook her off gently, and gently said, "We'll see about that. Here! Where's your hand?" He pressed something into her palm. "Here's a shilling in case you should need it."

A shilling! She must be going away for ever! "Father!" cried Fenella. But he was gone. He was the last off the ship. The sailors put their shoulders to the gangway. A huge coil of dark rope went flying through the air and fell "thump" on the wharf. A bell rang; a whistle shrilled. Silently the dark wharf began to slip, to slide, to edge away from them. Now there was a rush of water between. Fenella strained to see with all her might. "Was that father turning round?" — or waving? — or standing alone? — or walking off by himself? The strip of water grew broader, darker. Now the Picton boat began to swing round steady, pointing out to sea. It was no good looking any longer. There was nothing to be seen but a few lights, the face of the town clock hanging in the air, and more lights, little patches of them, on the dark hills.

The freshening wind tugged at Fenella's skirts; she went back to her grandma. To her relief grandma seemed no longer sad. She had put the two sausages of luggage one on top of the other, and she was sitting on them, her hands folded, her head a little on one side. There was an intent, bright look on her face. Then Fenella saw that her lips were moving and guessed that she was praying. But the old woman gave her a bright nod as if to say the prayer was nearly over. She unclasped her hands, sighed, clasped them again, bent forward, and at last gave herself a soft shake.

"And now, child," she said, fingering the bow of her bonnet-strings, "I think we ought to see about our cabins. Keep close to me, and mind you don't slip."

"Yes, grandma!"

"And be careful the umbrella isn't caught in the stair rail. I saw a beautiful umbrella broken in half like that on my way over."

"Yes, grandma."

Dark figures of men lounged against the rails. In the glow of their pipes a nose shone out, or the peak of a cap, or a pair of surprised-looking eyebrows. Fenella glanced up. High in the air a little figure, his hands thrust in his short jacket pockets, stood staring out to sea. The ship rocked ever so little and she thought the stars rocked too. And now a pale steward in a linen coat, holding a tray high in the palm of his hand, stepped out of a lighted doorway and skimmed past them. They went through that doorway. Carefully over the high brass-bound step on to the rubber mat and then down such a terribly steep flight of stairs that grandma had to put both feet on each step, and Fenella clutched the clammy brass rail and forgot all about the swan-necked umbrella.

At the bottom grandma stopped; Fenella was rather afraid she was going to pray again. But no, it was only to get out the cabin tickets. They were in the saloon. It was glaring bright and stifling; the air smelled of paint and burnt chop-bones and india-rubber. Fenella wished her grandma would go on, but the old woman was not to be hurried. An immense basket of ham sandwiches caught her eye. She went up to them and touched the top one delicately with her finger.

"How much are the sandwiches?" she asked.

"Tuppence!" bawled a rude steward, slamming down a knife and fork.

Grandma could hardly believe it.

"Twopence *each*?" she asked.

"That's right," said the steward, and he winked at his companion.

Grandma made a small, astonished face. Then she whispered primly to Fenella, "What wickedness!" And they sailed out at the further door and along a passage that had cabins on either side. Such a very nice stewardess came to meet them. She was dressed all in blue and her collar and cuffs were fastened with large brass buttons. She seemed to know grandma well.

"Well, Mrs. Crane," said she, unlocking their washstand. "We've got you back again. It's not often you give yourself a cabin."

"No," said grandma. "But this time my dear son's thoughtfulness —"

"I hope —" began the stewardess. Then she turned round and took a long, mournful look at grandma's blackness and at Fenella's black coat and skirt, black blouse, and hat with a crape rose.

Grandma nodded. "It was God's will," said she. The stewardess shut her lips and, taking a deep breath, she seemed to expand.

"What I always say is," she said,

120

as though it was her own discovery, "sooner or later each of us has to go, and that's a certingty." She paused. "Now, can I bring you anything, Mrs. Crane? A cup of tea? I know it's no good offering you a little something to keep the cold out."

Grandma shook her head. "Nothing, thank you. We've got a few wine biscuits and Fenella has a very nice banana."

"Then I'll give you a look later on," said the stewardess; and she went out, shutting the door.

What a very small cabin it was! It was like being shut up in a box with grandma. The dark round eye above the washstand gleamed at them dully. Fenella felt shy. She stood against the door, still clasping her luggage and the umbrella. Were they going to get undressed in here? Already her grandma had taken off her bonnet, and, rolling up the strings, she fixed each with a pin to the lining before she hung the bonnet up. Her white hair shone like silk; the little bun at the back was covered with a black net. Fenella hardly ever saw her grandma with her head uncovered; she looked strange.

"I shall put on the woollen fascinator your dear mother crocheted for me," said grandma, and, unstrapping the sausage, she took it out and wound it round her head; the fringe of grey bobbles danced at her eyebrows as she smiled tenderly and mournfully at Fenella. Then she undid her bodice, and something under that, and something else underneath that. Then there seemed a short, sharp tussle, and grandma flushed faintly. Snip! Snap! She had undone her stays. She breathed a sigh of relief and, sitting on the plush couch, she slowly and carefully pulled off her elastic-sided boots and stood them side by side.

By the time Fenella had taken off her coat and skirt and put on her flannel dressing-gown grandma was quite ready.

"Must I take off my boots, grandma? They're lace."

Grandma gave them a moment's deep consideration. "You'd feel a great deal more comfortable if you did, child," said she. She kissed Fenella. "Don't forget to say your prayers. Our dear Lord is with us when we are at sea even more than when we are on dry land. And because I am an experienced traveller," said grandma briskly, "I shall take the upper berth."

"But, grandma, how ever will you get up there?"

Three little spider-like steps were all Fenella saw. The old woman gave a small silent laugh before she mounted them nimbly, and she peered over the high bunk at the astonished Fenella.

"You didn't think your grandma could do that, did you?" said she. And as she sank back Fenella heard her light laugh again.

The hard square of brown soap would not lather and the water in the bottle was like a kind of blue jelly. How hard it was, too, to turn down those stiff sheets; you simply had to tear your way in. If everything had been different, Fenella might have got the giggles. . . . At last she was inside, and while she lay there panting, there sounded from above a long, soft whispering, as though someone was gently, gently rustling among tissue paper to find something. It was grandma saying her prayers. . . .

A long time passed. Then the stewardess came in; she trod softly and leaned her hand on grandma's bunk.

"We're just entering the Straits," she said.

"Oh!"

"It's a fine night, but we're rather empty. We may pitch a little."

And indeed at that moment the Picton boat rose and rose and hung in the air just long enough to give a shiver before she swung down again, and there was the sound of heavy water slapping against her sides. Fenella remembered she had left that swan-necked umbrella standing up on the little couch. If it fell over, would it break? But grandma remembered too, at the same time.

"I wonder if you'd mind, stewardess, laying down my umbrella," she whispered.

"Not at all, Mrs. Crane." And the stewardess, coming back to grandma, breathed, "Your little granddaughter's in such a beautiful sleep."

"God be praised for that!" said grandma.

"Poor little motherless mite!" said the stewardess. And grandma was still telling the stewardess all about what happened when Fenella fell asleep.

But she hadn't been asleep long enough to dream before she woke up again to see something waving in the air above her head. What was it? What could it be? It was a small grey foot. Now another joined it. They seemed to be feeling about for something; there came a sigh.

"I'm awake, grandma," said Fenella.

"Oh, dear, am I near the ladder?" asked grandma. "I thought it was this end."

"No, grandma, it's the other. I'll put your foot on it. Are we there?" asked Fenella.

"In the harbour," said grandma. "We must get up, child. You'd better have a biscuit to steady yourself before you move."

But Fenella had hopped out of her bunk. The lamp was still burning, but night was over, and it was cold. Peering through that round eye she could see far off some rocks. Now they were scattered over with foam; now a gull flipped by; and now there came a long piece of real land.

"It's land, grandma," said Fenella, wonderingly, as though they had been at sea for weeks together. She hugged herself; she stood on one leg and rubbed it with the toes of the other foot; she was trembling. Oh, it had all been so sad lately. Was it going to change? But all her grandma said was, "Make haste, child. I should leave your nice banana for the stewardess as you haven't eaten it." And Fenella put on her black clothes again and a button

Dorothy Kate Richmond
Monkey Bay, Picton

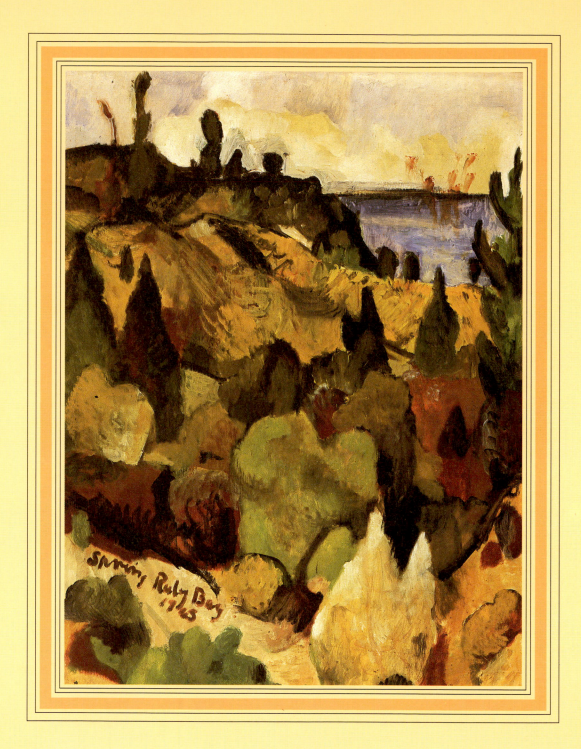

Colin McCahon
Spring, Ruby Bay

sprang off one of her gloves and rolled to where she couldn't reach it. They went up on deck.

But if it had been cold in the cabin, on deck it was like ice. The sun was not up yet, but the stars were dim, and the cold pale sky was the same colour as the cold pale sea. On the land a white mist rose and fell. Now they could see quite plainly dark bush. Even the shapes of the umbrella ferns showed, and those strange silvery withered trees that are like skeletons.... Now they could see the landing-stage and some little houses, pale too, clustered together, like shells on the lid of a box. The other passengers tramped up and down, but more slowly than they had the night before, and they looked gloomy.

And now the landing-stage came out to meet them. Slowly it swam towards the Picton boat and a man holding a coil of rope, and a cart with a small drooping horse and another man sitting on the step, came too.

"It's Mr. Penreddy, Fenella, come for us," said grandma. She sounded pleased. Her white waxen cheeks were blue with cold, her chin trembled, and she had to keep wiping her eyes and her little pink nose.

"You've got my —"

"Yes, grandma." Fenella showed it to her.

The rope came flying through the air and "smack" it fell on to the deck. The gangway was lowered. Again Fenella followed her grandma on to the wharf over to the little cart, and a moment later they were bowling away. The hooves of the little horse drummed over the wooden piles, then sank softly into the sandy road. Not a soul was to be seen; there was not even a feather of smoke. The mist rose and fell and the sea still sounded asleep as slowly it turned on the beach.

"I seen Mr. Crane yestiddy," said Mr. Penreddy. "He looked himself then. Missus knocked him up a batch of scones last week."

And now the little horse pulled up before one of the shell-like houses. They got down. Fenella put her hand on the gate, and the big, trembling dew-drops soaked through her glove-tips. Up a little path of round white pebbles they went, with drenched sleeping flowers on either side. Grandma's delicate white picotees were so heavy with dew that they were fallen, but their sweet smell was part of the cold morning. The blinds were down in the little house; they mounted the steps on to the veranda. A pair of old bluchers was on one side of the door and a large red watering-can on the other.

"Tut! tut! Your grandpa," said grandma. She turned the handle. Not a sound. She called, "Walter!" And immediately a deep voice that sounded half stifled called back, "Is that you, Mary?"

"Wait, dear," said grandma. "Go in there." She pushed Fenella gently into a small dusky sitting-room.

On the table a white cat, that had been folded up like a camel, rose, stretched itself, yawned, and then sprang on to the tips of its toes. Fenella buried one cold little hand in the white, warm fur, and smiled timidly while she stroked and listened to grandma's gentle voice and the rolling tones of grandpa.

A door creaked. "Come in, dear." The old woman beckoned, Fenella followed. There, lying to one side of an immense bed, lay grandpa. Just his head with a white tuft and his rosy face and long silver beard showed over the quilt. He was like a very old, wide-awake bird.

"Well, my girl!" said grandpa. "Give us a kiss!" Fenella kissed him. "Ugh!" said grandpa. "Her little nose is as cold as a button. What's that she's holding? Her grandma's umbrella?"

Fenella smiled again and crooked the swan neck over the bed-rail. Above the bed there was a big text in a deep black frame:

Lost! One Golden Hour
Set with Sixty Diamond Minutes.
No Reward Is Offered
For It Is GONE FOR EVER.

"Yer grandma painted that," said grandpa. And he ruffled his white tuft and looked at Fenella so merrily she almost thought he winked at her.

THE GARDEN-PARTY

AND after all the weather was ideal. They could not have had a more perfect day for a garden-party if they had ordered it. Windless, warm, the sky without a cloud. Only the blue was veiled with a haze of light gold, as it is sometimes in early summer. The gardener had been up since dawn, mowing the lawns and sweeping them, until the grass and the dark flat rosettes where the daisy plants had been seemed to shine. As for the roses, you could not help feeling they understood that roses are the only flowers that impress people at garden-parties; the only flowers that everybody is certain of knowing. Hundreds, yes, literally hundreds, had come out in a single night; the green bushes bowed down as though they had been visited by archangels.

Breakfast was not yet over before the men came to put up the marquee.

"Where do you want the marquee put, mother?"

"My dear child, it's no use asking me. I'm determined to leave everything to you children this year. Forget I am your mother. Treat me as an honoured guest."

But Meg could not possibly go and supervise the men. She had washed her hair before breakfast, and she sat drinking her coffee in a green turban, with a dark wet curl stamped on each cheek. Jose, the butterfly, always came down in a silk petticoat and a kimono jacket.

"You'll have to go, Laura; you're the artistic one."

Away Laura flew, still holding her piece of bread-and-butter. It's so delicious to have an excuse for eating out of doors and, besides, she loved having to arrange things; she always felt she could do it so much better than anybody else.

Four men in their shirt-sleeves stood grouped together on the garden path. They carried staves covered with rolls of canvas and they had big tool-bags slung on their backs. They looked impressive. Laura wished now that she was not holding that piece of bread-and-butter, but there was nowhere to put it and she couldn't possibly throw it away. She blushed and tried to look severe and even a little bit short-sighted as she came up to them.

"Good morning," she said, copying her mother's voice. But that sounded so fearfully affected that she was ashamed, and stammered like a little girl, "Oh — er — have you come — is it about the marquee?"

"That's right, miss," said the tallest of the men, a lanky, freckled fellow, and he shifted his tool-bag, knocked back his straw hat and smiled down at her. "That's about it."

His smile was so easy, so friendly, that Laura recovered. What nice eyes he had, small, but such a dark blue! And now she looked at the others, they were smiling too. "Cheer up, we won't bite," their smile seemed to say. How very nice workmen were! And what a beautiful morning! She mustn't mention the morning; she must be business-like. The marquee.

"Well, what about the lily-lawn? Would that do?"

And she pointed to the lily-lawn with the hand that didn't hold the bread-and-butter. They turned, they stared in the direction. A little fat chap thrust out his underlip and the tall fellow frowned.

"I don't fancy it," said he. "Not conspicuous enough. You see, with a thing like a marquee" — and he turned to Laura in his easy way — "you want to put it somewhere where it'll give you a bang slap in the eye, if you follow me."

Laura's upbringing made her wonder for a moment whether it was quite respectful of a workman to talk to her of bangs slap in the eye. But she did quite follow him.

"A corner of the tennis-court," she suggested. "But the band's going to be in one corner."

"H'm, going to have a band, are you?" said another of the workmen. He was pale. He had a haggard look as his dark eyes scanned the tennis-court. What was he thinking?

"Only a very small band," said Laura gently. Perhaps he wouldn't mind so much if the band was quite small. But the tall fellow interrupted.

"Look here, miss, that's the place. Against those trees. Over there. That'll do fine."

Against the karakas. Then the karaka trees would be hidden. And they were so lovely, with their broad, gleaming leaves, and their clusters of yellow fruit. They were like trees you imagined growing on a desert island, proud, solitary, lifting their leaves and fruits to the sun in a kind of silent splendour. Must they be hidden by a marquee?

They must. Already the men had shouldered their staves and were making for the place. Only the tall fellow was left. He bent down, pinched a sprig of lavender, put his thumb and forefinger to his nose and snuffed up the smell. When Laura saw that gesture she forgot all about the karakas in her wonder at him caring for things like that — caring for the smell of lavender. How many men that she knew would have done such a thing. Oh, how extraordinarily nice workmen were, she thought. Why couldn't she have workmen for friends rather than the silly boys she danced with and who came to Sunday night supper? She would get on much better with men like these.

It's all the fault, she decided, as the tall fellow drew something on the back of an envelope, something that was to be looped up or left to hang, of these absurd class distinctions. Well, for her part, she didn't feel them. Not a bit, not an atom. . . . And now there came the chock-chock of wooden hammers. Someone whistled, someone sang out, "Are you right there, matey?" "Matey!" The friendliness of it, the — the — Just to prove how happy she was, just to show the tall fellow how at home she felt, and how she despised stupid conventions, Laura took a big bite of her bread-and-butter as she stared at the little drawing. She felt just like a work-girl.

"Laura, Laura, where are you? Telephone, Laura!" a voice cried from the house.

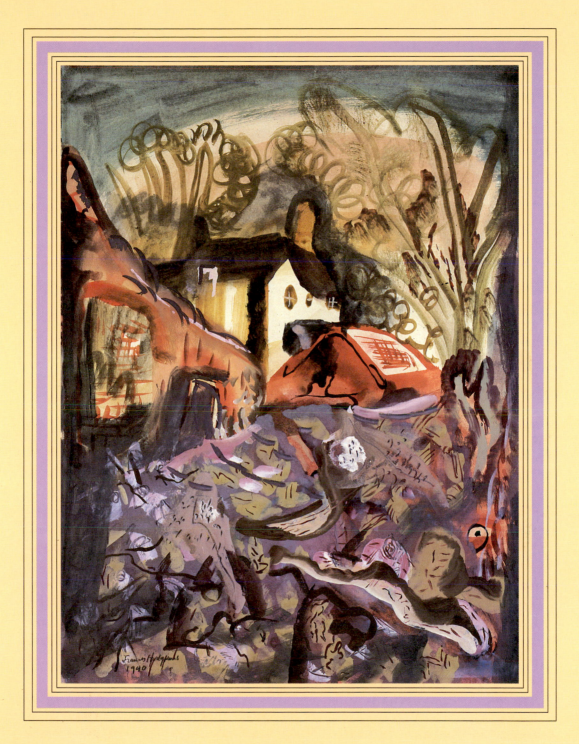

Frances Hodgkins
Bradford-on-Tone, Geoffrey Gorer's Cottage

"Coming!" Away she skimmed, over the lawn, up the path, up the steps, across the veranda and into the porch. In the hall her father and Laurie were brushing their hats ready to go to the office.

"I say, Laura," said Laurie very fast, "you might just give a squiz at my coat before this afternoon. See if it wants pressing."

"I will," said she. Suddenly she couldn't stop herself. She ran at Laurie and gave him a small, quick squeeze. "Oh, I do love parties, don't you?" gasped Laura.

"Ra-ther," said Laurie's warm, boyish voice, and he squeezed his sister too and gave her a gentle push. "Dash off to the telephone, old girl."

The telephone. "Yes, yes; oh yes. Kitty? Good morning, dear. Come to lunch? Do, dear. Delighted, of course. It will only be a very scratch meal — just the sandwich crusts and broken meringue-shells and what's left over. Yes, isn't it a perfect morning? Your white? Oh, I certainly should. One moment — hold the line. Mother's calling." And Laura sat back. "What, mother? Can't hear."

Mrs. Sheridan's voice floated down the stairs. "Tell her to wear that sweet hat she had on last Sunday."

"Mother says you're to wear that *sweet* hat you had on last Sunday. Good. One o'clock. Bye-bye."

Laura put back the receiver, flung her arms over her head, took a deep breath, stretched and let them fall. "Huh," she sighed, and the moment after the sigh she sat up quickly. She was still, listening. All the doors in the house seemed to be open. The house was alive with soft, quick steps and running voices. The green baize door that led to the kitchen regions swung open and shut with a muffled thud. And now there came a long, chuckling absurd sound. It was the heavy piano being moved on its stiff castors. But the air! If you stopped to notice, was the air always like this? Little faint winds were playing chase in at the tops of the windows, out at the doors. And there were two tiny spots of sun, one on the inkpot, one on a silver photograph frame, playing too. Darling little spots. Especially the one on the inkpot lid. It was quite warm. A warm little silver star. She could have kissed it.

The front door bell pealed and there sounded the rustle of Sadie's print skirt on the stairs. A man's voice murmured; Sadie answered, careless, "I'm sure I don't know. Wait. I'll ask Mrs. Sheridan."

"What is it, Sadie?" Laura came into the hall.

"It's the florist, Miss Laura."

It was, indeed. There, just inside the door, stood a wide, shallow tray full of pots of pink lilies. No other kind. Nothing but lilies — canna lilies, big pink flowers, wide open, radiant, almost frighteningly alive on bright crimson stems.

"O-oh, Sadie!" said Laura, and the sound was like a little moan. She crouched down as if to warm herself at that blaze of lilies; she felt they were in her fingers, on her lips, growing in her breast.

"It's some mistake," she said faintly. "Nobody ever ordered so many. Sadie, go and find mother."

But at that moment Mrs. Sheridan joined them.

"It's quite right," she said calmly. "Yes, I ordered them. Aren't they lovely?" She pressed Laura's arm. "I was passing the shop yesterday, and I saw them in the window. And I suddenly thought for once in my life I shall have enough canna lilies. The garden-party will be a good excuse."

"But I thought you said you didn't mean to interfere," said Laura. Sadie had gone. The florist's man was still outside at his van. She put her arm round her mother's neck and gently, very gently, she bit her mother's ear.

"My darling child, you wouldn't like a logical mother, would you? Don't do that. Here's the man."

He carried more lilies still, another whole tray.

"Bank them up, just inside the door, on both sides of the porch, please," said Mrs. Sheridan. "Don't you agree, Laura?"

"Oh I *do*, mother."

In the drawing-room Meg, Jose and good little Hans had at last succeeded in moving the piano.

"Now, if we put this chesterfield against the wall and move everything out of the room except the chairs, don't you think?"

"Quite."

"Hans, move these tables into the smoking-room, and bring a sweeper to take these marks off the carpet and — one moment, Hans —" Jose loved giving orders to the servants and they loved obeying her. She always made them feel they were taking part in some drama. "Tell mother and Miss Laura to come here at once."

"Very good, Miss Jose."

She turned to Meg. "I want to hear what the piano sounds like, just in case I'm asked to sing this afternoon. Let's try over 'This Life is Weary'."

Pom! Ta-ta-ta *Tee*-ta! The piano burst out so passionately that Jose's face changed. She clasped her hands. She looked mournfully and enigmatically at her mother and Laura as they came in.

> This Life is *Wee*-ary,
> A Tear — a Sigh.
> A Love that *Chan*-ges,
>   This Life is *Wee*-ary,
> A Tear — a Sigh.
> A Love that *Chan*-ges,
> And then . . . Good-bye!

But at the word "Good-bye", and although the piano sounded more desperate than ever, her face broke into a brilliant, dreadfully unsympathetic smile.

"Aren't I in good voice, mummy?" she beamed.

This Life is *Wee*-ary,
Hope comes to Die.
A Dream — a *Wa*-kening.

But now Sadie interrupted them. "What is it, Sadie?"

"If you please, m'm, cook says have you got the flags for the sandwiches?"

"The flags for the sandwiches, Sadie?" echoed Mrs. Sheridan dreamily. And the children knew by her face that she hadn't got them. "Let me see." And she said to Sadie firmly, "Tell cook I'll let her have them in ten minutes."

Sadie went.

"Now, Laura," said her mother quickly, "come with me into the smoking-room. I've got the names somewhere on the back of an envelope. You'll have to write them out for me. Meg, go upstairs this minute and take that wet thing off your head. Jose, run and finish dressing this instant. Do you hear me, children, or shall I have to tell your father when he comes home to-night? And — and, Jose, pacify cook if you do go into the kitchen, will you? I'm terrified of her this morning."

The envelope was found at last behind the dining-room clock, though how it had got there Mrs. Sheridan could not imagine.

"One of you children must have stolen it out of my bag, because I remember vividly — cream-cheese and lemon-curd. Have you done that?"

"Yes."

"Egg and —" Mrs. Sheridan held the envelope away from her. "It looks like mice. It can't be mice, can it?"

"Olive, pet," said Laura, looking over her shoulder.

"Yes, of course, olive. What a horrible combination it sounds. Egg and olive."

They were finished at last, and Laura took them off to the kitchen. She found Jose there pacifying the cook, who did not look at all terrifying.

"I have never seen such exquisite sandwiches," said Jose's rapturous voice. "How many kinds did you say there were, cook? Fifteen?"

"Fifteen, Miss Jose."

"Well, cook, I congratulate you."

Cook swept up crusts with the long sandwich knife, and smiled broadly.

"Godber's has come," announced Sadie, issuing out of the pantry. She had seen the man pass the window.

That meant the cream puffs had come. Godber's were famous for their cream puffs. Nobody ever thought of making them at home.

"Bring them in and put them on the table, my girl," ordered cook.

Sadie brought them in and went back to the door. Of course Laura and Jose were far too grown-up to really care about such things. All the same, they couldn't help agreeing that the puffs looked very attractive. Very. Cook began arranging them, shaking off the extra icing sugar.

"Don't they carry one back to all one's parties?" said Laura.

Frances Hodgkins
By the Brook

"I suppose they do," said practical Jose, who never liked to be carried back. "They look beautifully light and feathery, I must say."

"Have one each, my dears," said cook in her comfortable voice. "Yer ma won't know."

Oh, impossible. Fancy cream puffs so soon after breakfast. The very idea made one shudder. All the same, two minutes later Jose and Laura were licking their fingers with that absorbed inward look that only comes from whipped cream.

"Let's go into the garden, out by the back way," suggested Laura. "I want to see how the men are getting on with the marquee. They're such awfully nice men."

But the back door was blocked by cook, Sadie, Godber's man and Hans.

Something had happened.

"Tuk-tuk-tuk," clucked cook like an agitated hen. Sadie had her hand clapped to her cheek as though she had toothache. Han's face was screwed up in the effort to understand. Only Godber's man seemed to be enjoying himself; it was his story.

"What's the matter? What's happened?"

There's been a horrible accident," said cook. "A man killed."

"A man killed! Where? How? When?"

But Godber's man wasn't going to have his story snatched from under his very nose.

"Know those little cottages just below here, miss?" Know them? Of course she knew them. "Well, there's a young chap living there, name of Scott, a carter. His horse shied at a traction-engine, corner of Hawke Street this morning, and he was thrown out on the back of his head. Killed."

"Dead!" Laura stared at Godber's man.

"Dead when they picked him up," said Godber's man with relish. "They were taking the body home as I come up here." And he said to the cook, "He's left a wife and five little ones."

"Jose, come here." Laura caught hold of her sister's sleeve and dragged her through the kitchen to the other side of the green baize door. There she paused and leaned against it. "Jose!" she said, horrified, "However are we going to stop everything?"

"Stop everything, Laura!" cried Jose in astonishment. "What do you mean?"

"Stop the garden-party of course." Why did Jose pretend?

But Jose was still more amazed. "Stop the garden-party? My dear Laura, don't be so absurd. Of course we can't do anything of the kind. Nobody expects us to. Don't be so extravagant."

"But we can't possibly have a garden-party with a man dead just outside the front gate."

That really was extravagant, for the little cottages were in a lane to themselves at the very bottom of a steep rise that led up to the house. A broad road ran between. True, they were far too near. They were the greatest possible eyesore and they had no right to be in that neighbourhood at all. They were little mean dwellings painted a chocolate brown. In the garden patches there was nothing but cabbage stalks, sick hens and tomato cans. The very smoke coming out of their chimneys was poverty-stricken. Little rags and shreds of smoke, so unlike the great silvery plumes that uncurled from the Sheridans' chimneys. Washerwomen lived in the lane and sweeps and a cobbler and a man whose house-front was studded all over with minute bird-cages. Children swarmed. When the Sheridans were little they were forbidden to set foot there because of the revolting language and of what they might catch. But since they were grown up Laura and Laurie on their prowls sometimes walked through. It was disgusting and sordid. They came out with a shudder. But still one must go everywhere; one must see everything. So through they went.

"And just think of what the band would sound like to that poor woman," said Laura.

"Oh, Laura!" Jose began to be seriously annoyed. "If you're going to stop a band playing every time someone has an accident, you'll lead a very strenuous life. I'm every bit as sorry about it as you. I feel just as sympathetic." Her eyes hardened. She looked at her sister just as she used to when they were little and fighting together. "You won't bring a drunken workman back to life by being sentimental," she said softly.

"Drunk! Who said he was drunk?" Laura turned furiously on Jose. She said just as they had used to say on those occasions, "I'm going straight up to tell mother."

"Do, dear," cooed Jose.

"Mother, can I come into your room?" Laura turned the big glass door-knob.

"Of course, child, Why, what's the matter? What's given you such a colour?" And Mrs. Sheridan turned round from her dressing-table. She was trying on a new hat.

"Mother, a man's been killed," began Laura.

"*Not* in the garden?" interrupted her mother.

"No, no!"

"Oh, what a fright you gave me!" Mrs. Sheridan sighed with relief and took off the big hat and held it on her knees.

"But listen, mother," said Laura. Breathless, half choking, she told the dreadful story. "Of course, we can't have our party, can we?" she pleaded. "The band and everybody arriving. They'd hear us, mother; they're nearly neighbours!"

To Laura's astonishment her mother behaved just like Jose; it was harder to bear because she seemed amused. She refused to take Laura seriously.

"But, my dear child, use your common sense. It's only by accident we've heard of it. If someone had died there normally — and I can't understand how they keep alive in those poky little holes — we should still be having our party, shouldn't we?"

Laura had to say "yes" to that, but she felt it was all wrong. She sat down on her mother's sofa and pinched the cushion frill.

"Mother, isn't it really terribly heartless of us?" she asked.

"Darling!" Mrs. Sheridan got up and came over to her, carrying the hat. Before Laura could stop her she had plopped it on. "My child!" said her mother, "the hat is yours. It's made for you. It's much too young for me. I have never seen you look such a picture. Look at yourself!" And she held up her hand-mirror.

"But, mother," Laura began again. She couldn't look at herself; she turned aside.

This time Mrs. Sheridan lost patience just as Jose had done.

"You are being very absurd, Laura," she said coldly. "People like that don't expect sacrifices from us. And it's not very sympathetic to spoil everybody's enjoyment as you're doing now."

135

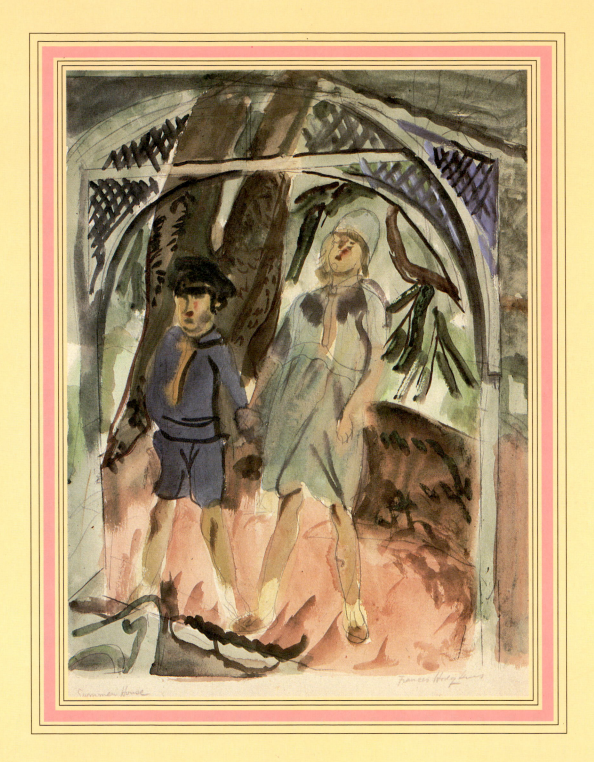

Frances Hodgkins
Summer House

"I don't understand," said Laura, and she walked quickly out of the room into her own bedroom. There, quite by chance, the first thing she saw was this charming girl in the mirror, in her black hat trimmed with gold daisies and a long black velvet ribbon. Never had she imagined she could look like that. Is mother right? she thought. And now she hoped her mother was right. Am I being extravagant? Perhaps it was extravagant. Just for a moment she had another glimpse of that poor woman and those little children and the body being carried into the house. But it all seemed blurred, unreal, like a picture in the newspaper. I'll remember it again after the party's over, she decided. And somehow that seemed quite the best plan. . . .

Lunch was over by half-past one. By half-past two they were all ready for the fray. The green-coated band had arrived and was established in a corner of the tennis-court.

"My dear!" trilled Kitty Maitland, "aren't they too like frogs for words? You ought to have arranged them round the pond with the conductor in the middle on a leaf."

Laurie arrived and hailed them on his way to dress. At the sight of him Laura remembered the accident again. She wanted to tell him. If Laurie agreed with the others, then it was bound to be all right. And she followed him into the hall.

"Laurie!"

"Hallo!" He was half-way upstairs, but when he turned round and saw Laura he suddenly puffed out his cheeks and goggled his eyes at her. "My word, Laura! You do look stunning," said Laurie. "What an absolutely topping hat!"

Laura said faintly "Is it?" and smiled up at Laurie and didn't tell him after all.

Soon after that people began coming in streams. The band struck up; the hired waiters ran from the house to the marquee. Wherever you looked there were couples strolling, bending to the flowers, greeting, moving on over the lawn. They were like bright birds that had alighted in the Sheridans' garden for this one afternoon, on their way to — where? Ah, what happiness it is to be with people who all are happy, to press hands, press cheeks, smile into eyes.

"Darling Laura, how well you look!"

"What a becoming hat, child!"

"Laura, you look quite Spanish. I've never seen you look so striking."

And Laura, glowing, answered softly, "Have you had tea? Won't you have an ice? The passion-fruit ices really are rather special." She ran to her father and begged him: "Daddy darling, can't the band have something to drink?"

And the perfect afternoon slowly ripened, slowly faded, slowly its petals closed.

Party itself meaningless [margin annotation]

"Never a more delightful garden-party. . ." "The greatest success. . ." "Quite the most. . ."

Laura helped her mother with the good-byes. They stood side by side in the porch till it was all over.

"All over, all over, thank heaven," said Mrs. Sheridan. "Round up the others, Laura. Let's go and have some fresh coffee. I'm exhausted. Yes, it's been very successful. But oh, these parties, these parties! Why will you children insist on giving parties!" And they all of them sat down in the deserted marquee.

STOP

"Have a sandwich, daddy dear. I wrote the flag."

"Thanks." Mr. Sheridan took a bite and the sandwich was gone. He took another. "I suppose you didn't hear of a beastly accident that happened to-day?" he said.

"My dear," said Mrs. Sheridan, holding up her hand, "we did. It nearly ruined the party. Laura insisted we should put it off."

"Oh, mother!" Laura didn't want to be teased about it.

"It was a horrible affair all the same," said Mr. Sheridan. "The chap was married too. Lived just below in the lane, and leaves a wife and half a dozen kiddies, so they say."

An awkward little silence fell. Mrs. Sheridan fidgeted with her cup. Really, it was very tactless of father. . . .

Suddenly she looked up. There on the table were all those sandwiches, cakes, puffs, all uneaten, all going to be wasted. She had one of her brilliant ideas.

"I know," she said. "Let's make up a basket. Let's send that poor creature some of this perfectly good food. At any rate, it will be the greatest treat for the children. Don't you agree? And she's sure to have neighbours calling in and so on. What a point to have it all ready prepared. Laura!" She jumped up. "Get me the big basket out of the stairs cupboard."

"But, mother, do you really think it's a good idea?" said Laura.

Again, how curious, she seemed to be different from them all. To take scraps from this party. Would the poor woman really like that?

"Of course! What's the matter with you to-day? An hour or two ago you were insisting on us being sympathetic."

Oh well! Laura ran for the basket. It was filled, it was now heaped by her mother.

"Take it yourself, darling," said she. "Run down just as you are. No, wait, take the arum lilies too. People of that class are so impressed by arum lilies."

"The stems will ruin her lace frock," said practical Jose.

So they would. Just in time. "Only the basket, then. And, Laura!" — her mother followed her out of the marquee — "don't on any account —"

"What, mother?"

No, better not put such ideas into the child's head! "Nothing! Run along."

It was just growing dusky as Laura shut their garden gates. A big dog ran by like a shadow. The road gleamed white, and down below in the hollow the little cottages were in deep shade. How quiet it seemed after the afternoon. Here she was going down the hill to somewhere where a man lay dead, and she couldn't realise it. Why couldn't she? She stopped a minute. And it seemed to her that kisses, voices, tinkling spoons, laughter, the smell of crushed grass were somehow inside her. She had no room for anything else. How strange! She looked up at the pale sky, and all she thought was, "Yes, it was the most successful party."

Now the broad road was crossed. The lane began, smoky and dark. Women in shawls and men's tweed caps hurried by. Men hung over the palings; the children played in the doorways. A low hum came from the mean little cottages. In some of them there was a flicker of light, and a shadow, crab-like, moved across the window. Laura bent her head and hurried on. She wished now she had put on a coat. How her frock shone! And the big hat with the velvet streamer — if only it was another hat! Were the people looking at her? They must be. It was a mistake to have come; she knew all along it was a mistake. Should she go back even now?

No, too late. This was the house. It must be. A dark knot of people stood outside. Beside the gate an old, old woman with a crutch sat in a chair, watching. She had her feet on a newspaper. The voices stopped as Laura drew near. The group parted. It was as though she was expected, as though they had known she was coming here.

Laura was terribly nervous. Tossing the velvet ribbon over her shoulder, she said to a woman standing by, "Is this Mrs. Scott's house?" and the woman, smiling queerly, said, "It is, my lass."

Oh, to be away from this! She actually said, "Help me, God," as she walked up the tiny path and knocked. To be away from those staring eyes, or to be covered up in anything, one of those women's shawls even. I'll just leave the basket and go, she decided. I shan't even wait for it to be emptied.

Then the door opened. A little woman in black showed in the gloom.

Laura said, "Are you Mrs. Scott?" But to her horror the woman answered, "Walk in, please, miss," and she was shut in the passage.

"No," said Laura, "I don't want to come in. I only want to leave this basket. Mother sent —"

The little woman in the gloomy passage seemed not to have heard her. "Step this way, please, miss," she said in an oily voice, and Laura followed her.

She found herself in a wretched little low kitchen, lighted by a smoky lamp. There was a woman sitting before the fire.

"Em," said the little creature who had let her in. "Em! It's a young lady." She turned to Laura. She said meaningly, "I'm 'er sister, miss. You'll excuse 'er, won't you?"

"Oh, but of course!" said Laura. "Please, please don't disturb her. I — I only want to leave —"

But at that moment the woman at the fire turned round. Her face, puffed up, red, with swollen eyes and swollen lips, looked terrible. She seemed as though she couldn't understand why Laura was there. What did it mean? Why was this stranger standing in the kitchen with a basket? What was it all about? And the poor face puckered up again.

"All right, my dear," said the other. "I'll thenk the young lady."

And again she began, "You'll excuse her, miss, I'm sure," and her face, swollen too, tried an oily smile.

139

Laura only wanted to get out, to get away. She was back in the passage. The door opened. She walked straight through into the bedroom, where the dead man was lying.

"You'd like a look at 'im, wouldn't you?" said Em's sister, and she brushed past Laura over to the bed. "Don't be afraid, my lass" — and now her voice sounded fond and sly, and fondly she drew down the sheet — "'e looks a picture. There's nothing to show. Come along, my dear."

Laura came.

There lay a young man, fast asleep — sleeping so soundly, so deeply, that he was far, far away from them both. Oh, so remote, so peaceful. He was dreaming. Never wake him up again. His head was sunk in the pillow, his eyes were closed; they were blind under the closed eyelids. He was given up to his dream. What did garden-parties and baskets and lace frocks matter to him? He was far from all those things. He was wonderful, beautiful. While they were laughing and while the band was playing, this marvel had come to the lane. Happy . . . happy. . . . All is well, said that sleeping face. This is just as it should be. I am content.

But all the same you had to cry, and she couldn't go out of the room without saying something to him. Laura gave a loud childish sob.

"Forgive my hat," she said.

And this time she didn't wait for Em's sister. She found her way out of the door, down the path past all those dark people. At the corner of the lane she met Laurie.

He stepped out of the shadow. "Is that you, Laura?"

"Yes."

"Mother was getting anxious. Was it all right?"

"Yes, quite, Oh, Laurie!" She took his arm, she pressed up against him.

"I say, you're not crying are you?" asked her brother.

Laura shook her head. She was.

Laurie put his arm round her shoulder. "Don't cry," he said in his warm, loving voice. "Was it awful?"

"No," sobbed Laura. "It was simply marvellous. But, Laurie —" She stopped, she looked at her brother. "Isn't life," she stammered, "isn't life —" But what life was she couldn't explain. No matter. He quite understood.

"*Isn't* it, darling?" said Laurie.

THE STRANGER

IT seemed to the little crowd on the wharf that she was never going to move again. There she lay, immense, motionless on the grey crinkled water, a loop of smoke above her, an immense flock of gulls screaming and diving after the galley droppings at the stern. You could just see little couples parading — little flies walking up and down the dish on the grey crinkled tablecloth. Other flies clustered and swarmed at the edge. Now there was a gleam of white on the lower deck — the cook's apron or the stewardess, perhaps. Now a tiny black spider raced up the ladder on to the bridge.

In the front of the crowd a strong-looking, middle-aged man, dressed very well, very snugly in a grey overcoat, grey silk scarf, thick gloves and dark felt hat, marched up and down twirling his folded umbrella. He seemed to be the leader of the little crowd on the wharf and at the same time to keep them together. He was something between the sheep-dog and the shepherd.

But what a fool — what a fool he had been not to bring any glasses! There wasn't a pair of glasses between the whole lot of them.

"Curious thing, Mr. Scott, that none of us thought of glasses. We might have been able to stir 'em up a bit. We might have managed a little signalling. *Don't hesitate to land. Natives harmless.* Or: *A welcome awaits you. All is forgiven.* What? Eh?"

Mr. Hammond's quick, eager glance, so nervous and yet so friendly and confiding, took in everybody on the wharf, roped in even those old chaps lounging against the gangways. They knew, every man-jack of them, that Mrs. Hammond was on that boat, and he was so tremendously excited it never entered his head not to believe that this marvellous fact meant something to them too. It warmed his heart towards them. They were, he decided, as decent a crowd of people — Those old chaps over by the gangways, too — fine, solid old chaps. What chests — by Jove! And he squared his own, plunged his thick-gloved hands into his pockets, rocked from heel to toe.

"Yes, my wife's been in Europe for the last ten months. On a visit to our eldest girl, who was married last year. I brought her up here, as far as Crawford, myself. So I thought I'd better come and fetch her back. Yes, yes, yes." The shrewd grey eyes narrowed again and searched anxiously, quickly, the motionless liner. Again his overcoat was unbuttoned.

Rita Angus
Waikanae

Out came the thin, butter-yellow watch again, and for the twentieth — fiftieth — hundredth time he made the calculation.

"Let me see, now. It was two fifteen when the doctor's launch went off. Two fifteen. It is now exactly twenty-eight minutes past four. That is to say, the doctor's been gone two hours and thirteen minutes. Two hours and thirteen minutes! Whee-ooh!" He gave a queer little half-whistle and snapped his watch to again. "But I think we should have been told if there was anything up- — don't you, Mr. Gaven?"

"Oh yes, Mr. Hammond! I don't think there's anything to — anything to worry about," said Mr. Gaven, knocking out his pipe against the heel of his shoe. "At the same time —"

"Quite so! Quite so!" cried Mr. Hammond. "Dashed annoying!" He paced quickly up and down and came back again to his stand between Mr. and Mrs. Scott and Mr. Gaven. "It's getting quite dark, too," and he waved his folded umbrella as though the dusk at least might have had the decency to keep off for a bit. But the dusk came slowly, spreading like a slow stain over the water. Little Jean Scott dragged at her mother's hand.

"I wan' my tea, mammy!" she wailed.

"I expect you do," said Mr. Hammond. "I expect all these ladies want their tea." And his kind, flushed, almost pitiful glance roped them all in again. He wondered whether Janey was having a final cup of tea in the saloon out there. He hoped so; he thought not. It would be just like her not to leave the deck. In that case perhaps the deck steward would bring her up a cup. If he'd been there he'd have got it for her — somehow. And for a moment he was on deck, standing over her, watching her little hand fold round the cup in the way she had, while she drank the only cup of tea to be got on board.... But now he was back here, and the Lord only knew when that cursed Captain would stop hanging about in the stream. He took another turn, up and down, up and down. He walked as far as the cab-stand to make sure his driver hadn't disappeared; back he swerved again to the little flock, huddled in the shelter of the banana crates. Little Jean Scott was still wanting her tea. Poor little beggar! He wished he had a bit of chocolate on him.

"Here, Jean!" He said. "Like a lift up?" And easily, gently, he swung the little girl on to a higher barrel. The movement of holding her, steadying her, relieved him wonderfully, lightened his heart.

"Hold on," he said, keeping an arm round her.

"Oh, don't worry about *Jean*, Mr. Hammond!" said Mrs. Scott.

"That's all right, Mrs. Scott. No trouble. It's a pleasure. Jean's a little pal of mine, aren't you, Jean?"

"Yes, Mr. Hammond," said Jean, and she ran her finger down the dent of his felt hat.

But suddenly she caught him by the ear and gave a loud scream. "Lo-ok, Mr. Hammond! She's moving! Look, she's coming in!"

By Jove! So she was. At last! She was slowly, slowly turning round. A bell sounded far over the water and a great spout of steam gushed into the air. The gulls rose; they fluttered away like bits of white paper. And whether that deep throbbing was her engines or his heart Mr. Hammond couldn't say. He had to nerve himself to bear it, whatever it was. At that moment old Captain Johnson, the harbour-master, came striding down the wharf, a leather portfolio under his arm.

"Jean'll be all right," said Mr. Scott. "I'll hold her." He was just in time. Mr. Hammond had forgotten about Jean. He sprang away to greet old Captain Johnson.

"Well, Captain," the eager, nervous voice rang out again, "you've taken pity on us at last."

"It's no good blaming me, Mr. Hammond," wheezed old Captain Johnson, staring at the liner. "You got Mrs. Hammond on board, ain't yer?"

"Yes, yes!" said Hammond, and he kept by the harbour-master's side. "Mrs. Hammond's there. Hul-lo! We shan't be long now!"

With her telephone ring-ringing, the thrum of her screw filling the air, the big liner bore down on them, cutting sharp through the dark water so that big white shavings curled to either side. Hammond and the harbour-master kept in front of the rest. Hammond took off his hat; he raked the decks — they were crammed with passengers; he waved his hat and bawled a loud, strange "Hul-lo!" across the water, and then turned round and burst out laughing and said something — nothing — to old Captain Johnson.

"Seen her?" asked the harbour-master.

"No, not yet. Steady — wait a bit!" And suddenly, between two great clumsy idiots — "Get out of the way there!" he signed with his umbrella — he saw a hand raised — a white glove shaking a handkerchief. Another moment, and — thank God, thank God! — there she was. There was Janey. There was Mrs. Hammond, yes, yes, yes — standing by the rail and smiling and nodding and waving her handkerchief.

"Well, that's first class — first class! Well, well, well!" He positively stamped. Like lightning he drew out his cigar-case and offered it to old Captain Johnson. "Have a cigar, Captain! They're pretty good. Have a couple! Here" — and he pressed all the cigars in the case on the harbour-master — "I've a couple of boxes up at the hotel."

"Thanks, Mr. Hammond!" wheezed old Captain Johnson.

Hammond stuffed the cigar-case back. His hands were shaking, but he'd got hold of himself again. He was able to face Janey. There she was, leaning on the rail, talking to some woman and at the same time watching him, ready for him. It struck him, as the gulf of water closed, how small she looked on that huge ship. His heart was wrung with such a spasm that he could have cried out. How little she looked to have come all that long way and back by herself! Just like her, though. Just like Janey. She had the courage of a — And now the crew had come forward and parted the passengers; they had lowered the rails for the gangways.

The voices on shore and the voices on board flew to greet each other.

"All well?"

"All well."

"How's mother?"

"Much better."

"Hullo, Jean!"

"Hillo, Aun' Emily!"

"Had a good voyage?"

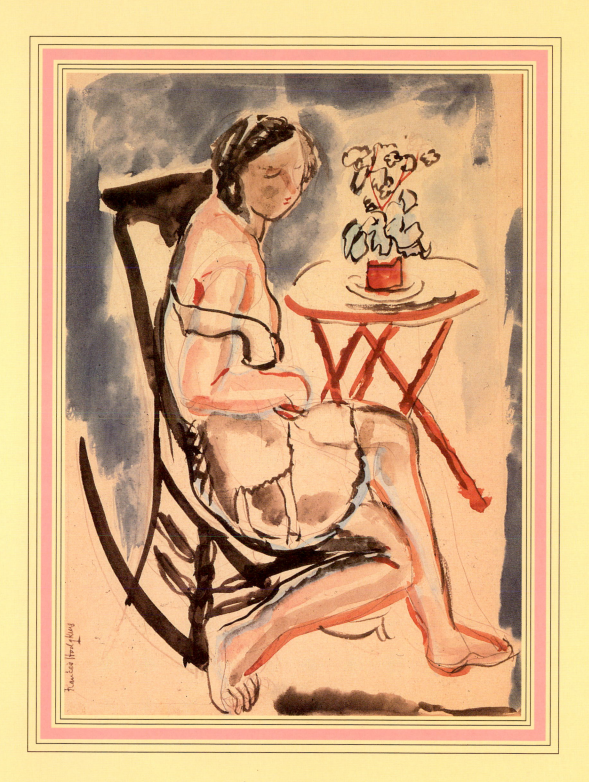

Frances Hodgkins
Study of a Model

"Splendid!"

"Shan't be long now!"

"Not long now."

The engines stopped. Slowly she edged to the wharf-side.

"Make way there — make way — make way!" And the wharf hands brought the heavy gangways along at a sweeping run. Hammond signed to Janey to stay where she was. The old harbour-master stepped forward; he followed. As to "ladies first", or any rot like that, it never entered his head.

"After you, Captain!" he cried genially. And, treading on the old man's heels, he strode up the gangway on to the deck in a bee-line to Janey, and Janey was clasped in his arms.

"Well, well, well! Yes, yes! Here we are at last!" he stammered. It was all he could say. And Janey emerged, and her cool little voice — the only voice in the world for him — said, "Well, darling! Have you been waiting long?"

No; not long. Or, at any rate, it didn't matter. It was over now. But the point was, he had a cab waiting at the end of the wharf. Was she ready to go off? Was her luggage ready? In that case they could cut off sharp with her cabin luggage and let the rest go hang until to-morrow. He bent over her and she looked up with her familiar half-smile. She was just the same. Not a day changed. Just as he'd always known her. She laid her small hand on his sleeve.

"How are the children, John?" she asked.

(Hang the children!) "Perfectly well. Never better in their lives."

"Haven't they sent me letters?"

"Yes, yes — of course! I've left them at the hotel for you to digest later on."

"We can't go quite so fast," said she. "I've got people to say good-bye to — and then there's the Captain." As his face fell she gave his arm a small understanding squeeze. "If the Captain comes off the bridge I want you to thank him for having looked after your wife so beautifully." Well, he'd got her. If she wanted another ten minutes — As he gave way she was surrounded. The whole first-class seemed to want to say good-bye to Janey.

"Good-bye, *dear* Mrs. Hammond! And next time you're in Sydney I'll *expect* you."

"Darling Mrs. Hammond! You won't forget to write to me, will you?"

"Well, Mrs. Hammond, what this boat would have been without you!"

It was as plain as a pikestaff that she was by far the most popular woman on board. And she took it all — just as usual. Absolutely composed. Just her little self — just Janey all over; standing there with her veil thrown back. Hammond never noticed what his wife had on. It was all the same to him whatever she wore. But to-day he did notice that she wore a black "costume" — didn't they call it? — with white frills, trimmings he supposed they were, at the neck and sleeves. All this while Janey handed him round.

"John, dear!" And then: "I want to introduce you to —"

Finally they did escape, and she led the way to her stateroom. To follow Janey down the passage that she knew so well — that was so strange to him; to part the green curtains after her and to step into the cabin that had been hers gave him exquisite happiness. But — confound it! — the stewardess was there on the floor, strapping up the rugs.

"That's the last, Mrs. Hammond," said the stewardess, rising and pulling down her cuffs.

He was introduced again, and then Janey and the stewardess disappeared into the passage. He heard whisperings. She was getting the tipping business over, he supposed. He sat down on the striped sofa and took his hat off. There were the rugs she had taken with her; they looked good as new. All her luggage looked fresh, perfect. The labels were written in her beautiful little clear hand — "Mrs. John Hammond."

"Mrs. John Hammond!" He gave a long sigh of content and leaned back, crossing his arms. The strain was over. He felt he could have sat there for ever sighing his relief — the relief at being rid of that horrible tug, pull, grip on his heart. The danger was over. That was the feeling. They were on dry land again.

But at that moment Janey's head came round the corner.

"Darling — do you mind? I just want to go and say good-bye to the doctor."

Hammond started up. "I'll come with you."

"No, no!" she said. "Don't bother. I'd rather not. I'll not be a minute."

And before he could answer she was gone. He had half a mind to run after her; but instead he sat down again.

Would she really not be long? What was the time now? Out came the watch; he stared at nothing. That was rather queer of Janey, wasn't it? Why couldn't she have told the stewardess to say good-bye for her? Why did she have to go chasing after the ship's doctor? She could have sent a note from the hotel even if the affair had been urgent. Urgent? Did it — could it mean that she had been ill on the voyage — she was keeping something from him? That was it! He seized his hat. He was going off to find that fellow and to wring the truth out of him at all costs. He thought he'd noticed just something. She was just a touch too calm — too steady. From the very first moment —

The curtains rang. Janey was back. He jumped to his feet.

"Janey, have you been ill on this voyage? You have!"

"Ill?" Her airy little voice mocked him. She stepped over the rugs, came up close, touched his breast, and looked up at him.

"Darling," she said, "don't frighten me. Of course I haven't! Whatever makes you think I have? Do I look ill?"

But Hammond didn't see her. He only felt that she was looking at him and that there was no need to worry about anything. She was here to look after things. It was all right. Everything was.

The gentle pressure of her hand was so calming that he put his over hers to hold it there. And she said:

"Stand still. I want to look at you. I haven't seen you yet. You've had your beard beautifully trimmed, and you look — younger, I think, and decidedly thinner! Bachelor life agrees with you."

"Agrees with me!" He groaned for love and caught her close again. And again, as always, he had the feeling he was holding something that never was quite his — his. Something too delicate, too precious, that would fly away once he let go.

"For God's sake let's get off to the hotel so that we can be by ourselves!" And he rang the bell hard for someone to look sharp with the luggage.

Walking down the wharf together she took his arm. He had her on his arm again. And the difference it made to get into the cab after Janey — to throw the red-and-yellow striped blanket round them both — to tell the driver to hurry because neither of them had had any tea. No more going without his tea or pouring out his own. She was back. He turned to her, squeezed her hand, and said gently, teasingly, in the "special" voice he had for her: "Glad to be home again, dearie?" She smiled; she didn't even bother to answer, but gently she drew his hand away as they came to the lighted streets.

"We've got the best room in the hotel," he said. "I wouldn't be put off with another. And I asked the chambermaid to put in a bit of a fire in case you felt chilly. She's a nice, attentive girl. And I thought now we were here we wouldn't bother to go home to-morrow, but spend the day looking round and leave the morning after. Does that suit you? There's no hurry, is there? The children will have you soon enough...I thought a day's sight-seeing might make a nice break in your journey — eh, Janey?"

"Have you taken the tickets for the day after?" she asked.

"I should think I have!" He unbuttoned his overcoat and took out his bulging pocket-book. "Here we are! I reserved a first-class carriage to Salisbury. There it is — 'Mr. *and* Mrs. John Hammond.' I though we might as well do ourselves comfortably, and we don't want other people butting in, do we? But if you'd like to stop here a bit longer —?"

"Oh no!" said Janey quickly. "Not for the world! The day after to-morrow, then. And the children — "

But they had reached the hotel. The manager was standing in the broad, brilliantly lighted porch. He came down to greet them. A porter ran from the hall for their boxes.

"Well, Mr. Arnold, here's Mrs. Hammond at last!"

The manager led them through the hall himself and pressed the elevator-bell. Hammond knew there were business pals of his sitting at the little hall tables having a drink before dinner. But he wasn't going to risk interruption; he looked neither to the right nor the left. They could think what they pleased. If they didn't understand, the more fools they — and he stepped out of the lift, unlocked the door of their room and shepherded Janey in. The door shut. Now, at last, they were alone together. He turned up the light. The curtains were drawn; the fire blazed. He flung his hat on to the huge bed and went towards her.

Frances Hodgkins
The White Urn

But — would you believe it! — again they were interrupted. This time it was the porter with their luggage. He made two journeys of it, leaving the door open in between, taking his time, whistling through his teeth in the corridor. Hammond paced up and down the room, tearing off his gloves, tearing off his scarf. Finally he flung his overcoat on to the bedside.

At last the fool was gone. The door clicked. Now they *were* alone. Said Hammond: "I feel I'll never have you to myself again. These cursed people! Janey" — and he bent his flushed, eager gaze upon her — "let's have dinner up here. If we go down to the restaurant we'll be interrupted, and then there's the confounded music" (the music he'd praised so highly, applauded so loudly last night!). "We shan't be able to hear each other speak. Let's have something up here in front of the fire. It's too late for tea. I'll order a little supper, shall I? How does the idea strike you?"

"Do, darling!" said Janey. "And while you're away — the children's letters — "

"Oh, later on will do!" said Hammond.

"But then we'd get it over," said Janey. "And I'd first have time to — "

"Oh, I needn't go down!" explained Hammond. "I'll just ring and give the order . . . you don't want to send me away, do you?"

Janey shook her head and smiled.

"But you're thinking of something else. You're worrying about something," said Hammond. "What is it? Come and sit here — come and sit on my knee before the fire."

"I'll just unpin my hat," said Janey, and she went over to the dressing-table. "A-ah!" She gave a little cry.

"What is it?"

"Nothing, darling. I've just found the children's letters. That's all right! They will keep. No hurry now!" She turned to him, clasping them. She tucked them into her frilled blouse. She cried quickly, gaily: "Oh, how typical this dressing-table is of you!"

"Why? What's the matter with it?" said Hammond.

"If it were floating in eternity I should say 'John!'" laughed Janey, staring at the big bottle of hair tonic, the wicker bottle of eau-de-Cologne, the two hairbrushes and a dozen new collars tied with pink tape. "Is this all your luggage?"

"Hang my luggage!" said Hammond; but all the same he liked being laughed at by Janey. "Let's talk. Let's get down to things. Tell me" — and as Janey perched on his knees he leaned back and drew her into the deep, ugly chair — "tell me you're really glad to be back, Janey."

"Yes, darling, I am glad," she said.

But just as when he embraced her he felt she would fly away, so Hammond never knew — never knew for dead certain that she was as glad as he was. How could he know? Would he ever know? Would he always have this craving — this pang like hunger, somehow, to make Janey so much part of him that there wasn't any of her to escape? He wanted to blot out everybody, everything. He wished now he'd turned off the light. That might have brought her nearer. And now those letters from the children rustled in her blouse. He could have chucked them into the fire.

"Janey," he whispered.

"Yes, dear?" She lay on his breast, but so lightly, so remotely. Their breathing rose and fell together.

"Janey!"

"What is it?"

"Turn to me," he whispered. A slow, deep flush flowed into his forehead. "Kiss me, Janey! You kiss me!"

It seemed to him there was a tiny pause — but long enough for him to suffer torture — before her lips touched his, firmly, lightly — kissing them as she always kissed him, as though the kiss — how could he describe it? — confirmed what they were saying, signed the contract. But that wasn't what he wanted; that wasn't at all what he thirsted for. He felt suddenly, horribly tired.

"If you knew," he said, opening his eyes, "what it's been like — waiting to-day. I thought the boat never would come in. There we were, hanging about. What kept you so long?"

She made no answer. She was looking away from him at the fire. The flames hurried — hurried over the coals, flickered, fell.

"Not asleep, are you?" said Hammond, and he jumped her up and down.

"No," she said. And then: "Don't do that, dear. No, I was thinking. As a matter of fact," she said, "one of the passengers died last night — a man. That's what held us up. We brought him in — I mean, he wasn't buried at sea. So, of course, the ship's doctor and the shore doctor — "

"What was it?" asked Hammond uneasily. He hated to hear of death. He hated this to have happened. It was, in some queer way, as though he and Janey had met a funeral on their way to the hotel.

"Oh, it wasn't anything in the least infectious!" said Janey. She was speaking scarcely above her breath. "It was *heart*." A pause. "Poor fellow!" she said. "Quite young." And she watched the fire flicker and fall. "He died in my arms," said Janey.

The blow was so sudden that Hammond thought he would faint. He couldn't move; he couldn't breathe. He felt all his strength flowing — flowing into the big dark chair, and the big dark chair held him fast, gripped him, forced him to bear it.

"What?" he said dully. "What's that you say?"

"The end was quite peaceful," said the small voice. "He just" — and Hammond saw her lift her gentle hand — "breathed his life away at the end." And her hand fell.

"Who — else was there?" Hammond managed to ask.

"Nobody. I was alone with him."

Ah, my God, what was she saying! What was she doing to him! This would kill him! And all the while she spoke:

"I saw the change coming and I sent the steward for the doctor, but the doctor was too late. He couldn't have done anything, anyway."

"But — why *you*, why *you?*" moaned Hammond.

At that Janey turned quickly, quickly searched his face.

"You don't *mind*, John, do you?" She asked. "You don't — It's nothing to do with you and me."

Somehow or other he managed to shake some sort of smile at her. Somehow or other he stammered: "No — go — on, go on! I want you to tell me."

"But, John darling — "

"Tell me, Janey!"

"There's nothing to tell," she said, wondering. "He was one of the first-class passengers. I saw he was very ill when he came on board...But he seemed to be so much better until yesterday. He had a severe attack in the afternoon — excitement — nervousness, I think, about arriving. And after that he never recovered."

"But why didn't the stewardess — "

"Oh, my dear — the stewardess!" said Janey. "What would he have felt? And besides...he might have wanted to leave a message...to — "

"Didn't he?" muttered Hammond. "Didn't he say anything?"

"No, darling, not a word!" She shook her head softly. "All the time I was with him he was too weak...he was too weak even to move a finger..."

Janey was silent. But her words, so light, so soft, so chill, seemed to hover in the air, to rain into his breast like snow.

The fire had gone red. Now it fell in with a sharp sound and the room was colder. Cold crept up his arms. The room was huge, immense, glittering. It filled his whole world. There was the great blind bed, with his coat flung across it like some headless man saying his prayers. There was the luggage, ready to be carried away again, anywhere, tossed into trains, carted on to boats.

..."He was too weak. He was too weak to move a finger." And yet he died in Janey's arms. She — who'd never — never once in all these years — never on one single solitary occasion —

No; he mustn't think of it. Madness lay in thinking of it. No, he wouldn't face it. He couldn't stand it. It was too much to bear!

And now Janey touched his tie with her fingers. She pinched the edges of the tie together.

"You're not — sorry I told you, John darling? It hasn't made you sad? It hasn't spoilt our evening — our being alone togehter?"

But at that he had to hide his face. He put his face into her bosom and his arms enfolded her.

Spoilt their evening! Spoilt their being alone together! They would never be alone together again.

HER FIRST BALL

EXACTLY when the ball began Leila would have found it hard to say. Perhaps her first real partner was the cab. It did not matter that she shared the cab with the Sheridan girls and their brother. She sat back in her own little corner of it, and the bolster on which her hand rested felt like the sleeve of an unknown young man's dress suit; and away they bowled, past waltzing lamp-posts and houses and fences and trees.

"Have you really never been to a ball before, Leila? But, my child, how too weird —" cried the Sheridan girls.

"Our nearest neighbour was fifteen miles," said Leila softly, gently opening and shutting her fan.

Oh dear, how hard it was to be indifferent like the others! She tried not to smile too much; she tried not to care. But every single thing was so new and exciting...Meg's tuberoses, Jose's long loop of amber, Laura's little dark head, pushing above her white fur like a flower through snow. She would remember for ever. It even gave her a pang to see her cousin Laurie throw away the wisps of tissue paper he pulled from the fastenings of his new gloves. She would like to have kept those wisps as a keepsake, as a remembrance. Laurie leaned forward and put his hand on Laura's knee.

"Look here, darling," he said. "The third and the ninth as usual. Twig?"

Oh, how marvellous to have a brother! In her excitement Leila felt that if there had been time, if it hadn't been impossible, she couldn't have helped crying because she was an only child and no brother had ever said "Twig?" to her; no sister would ever say, as Meg said to Jose that moment, "I've never known your hair go up more successfully than it has to-night!"

But, of course, there was no time. They were at the drill hall already; there were cabs in front of them and cabs behind. The road was bright on either side with moving fan-like lights, and on the pavement gay couples seemed to float through the air; little satin shoes chased each other like birds.

"Hold on to me, Leila; you'll get lost," said Laura.

"Come on, girls, let's make a dash for it," said Laurie.

Leila put two fingers on Laura's pink velvet cloak, and they were somehow lifted past

153

Raymond McIntyre
Woman in a Broad-Brimmed Hat

the big golden lantern, carried along the passage, and pushed into the little room marked "Ladies". Here the crowd was so great there was hardly space to take off their things; the noise was deafening. Two benches on either side were stacked high with wraps. Two old women in white aprons ran up and down tossing fresh armfuls. And everybody was pressing forward trying to get at the little dressing-table and mirror at the far end.

A great quivering jet of gas lighted the ladies' room. It couldn't wait; it was dancing already. When the door opened again and there came a burst of tuning from the drill hall, it leaped almost to the ceiling.

Dark girls, fair girls were patting their hair, tying ribbons again, tucking handkerchiefs down the fronts of their bodices, smoothing marble-white gloves. And because they were all laughing it seemed to Leila that they were all lovely.

"Aren't there any invisible hairpins?" cried a voice. "How most extraordinary! I can't see a single invisible hairpin."

"Powder my back, there's a darling," cried someone else.

"But I must have a needle and cotton. I've torn simply miles and miles of the frill," wailed a third.

Then, "Pass them along, pass them along!" The straw basket of programmes was tossed from arm to arm. Darling little pink-and-silver programmes, with pink pencils and fluffy tassels. Leila's fingers shook as she took one out of the basket. She wanted to ask someone, "Am I meant to have one too?" but she had just time to read: "Waltz 3. *Two, Two in a Canoe.* Polka 4. *Making the Feathers Fly,*" when Meg cried, "Ready, Leila?" and they pressed their way through the crush in the passage towards the big double doors of the drill hall.

Dancing had not begun yet, but the band had stopped tuning, and the noise was so great it seemed that when it did begin to play it would never be heard. Leila, pressing close to Meg, looking over Meg's shoulder, felt that even the little quivering coloured flags strung across the ceiling were talking. She quite forgot to be shy; she forgot how in the middle of dressing she had sat down on the bed with one shoe off and one shoe on and begged her mother to ring up her cousins and say she couldn't go after all. And the rush of longing she had had to be sitting on the veranda of their forsaken up-country home, listening to the baby owls crying "More pork" in the moonlight, was changed to a rush of joy so sweet that it was hard to bear alone. She clutched her fan, and, gazing at the gleaming, golden floor, the azaleas, the lanterns, the stage at one end with its red carpet and gilt chairs and the band in a corner, she thought breathlessly, "How heavenly; how simply heavenly!"

All the girls stood grouped together at one side of the doors, the men at the other, and the chaperones in dark dresses, smiling rather foolishly, walked with little careful steps over the polished floor towards the stage.

"This is my little country cousin Leila. Be nice to her. Find her partners; she's under my wing," said Meg, going up to one girl after another.

Strange faces smiled at Leila — sweetly, vaguely. Strange voices answered, "Of course, my dear." But Leila felt the girls didn't really see her. They were looking towards the men. Why didn't the men begin? What were they waiting for? There they stood, smoothing their gloves, patting their glossy hair and smiling among themselves. Then, quite suddenly, as if they had only just made up their minds that that was what they had to do, the men came gliding over the parquet. There was a joyful flutter among the girls. A tall, fair man flew up to Meg, seized her programme, scribbled something; Meg passed him on to Leila. "May I have the pleasure?" He ducked and smiled. There came a dark man wearing an eyeglass, then cousin Laurie with a friend, and Laura with a little freckled fellow whose tie was crooked. Then quite an old man — fat, with a big bald patch on his head — took her programme and murmured, "Let me see, let me see!" And he was a long time comparing his programme, which looked black with names, with hers. It seemed to give him so much trouble that Leila was ashamed. "Oh, please don't bother," she said eagerly. But instead of replying the fat man wrote something, glanced at her again. "Do I remember this bright little face?" he said softly. "Is it known to me of yore?" At that moment the band began playing; the fat man disappeared. He was tossed away on a great wave of music that came flying over the gleaming floor, breaking the groups up into couples, scattering them, sending them spinning. . . .

Leila had learned to dance at boarding school. Every Saturday afternoon the boarders were hurried off to a little corrugated iron mission hall where Miss Eccles (of London) held her "select" classes. But the difference between that dusty-smelling hall — with calico texts on the walls, the poor, terrified little woman in a brown velvet toque with rabbit's ears thumping the cold piano, Miss Eccles poking the girls' feet with her long white wand — and this, was so tremendous that Leila was sure if her partner didn't come and she had to listen to that marvellous music and to watch the others sliding, gliding over the golden floor, she would die at least, or faint, or lift her arms and fly out of one of those dark windows that showed the stars.

"Ours, I think — " Someone bowed, smiled, and offered her his arm; she hadn't to die after all. Someone's hand pressed her waist, and she floated away like a flower that is tossed into a pool.

"Quite a good floor, isn't it?" drawled a faint voice close to her ear.

"I think it's most beautifully slippery," said Leila.

"Pardon!" The faint voice sounded surprised. Leila said it again. And there was a tiny pause before the voice echoed, "Oh, quite!" and she was swung round again.

He steered so beautifully. That was the great difference between dancing with girls and men, Leila decided. Girls banged into each other and stamped on each other's feet; the girl who was gentleman always clutched you so.

The azaleas were separate flowers no longer; they were pink and white flags streaming by.

"Were you at the Bells' last week?" the voice came again. It sounded tired. Leila wondered whether she ought to ask him if he would like to stop.

"No, this is my first dance," said she.

Her partner gave a little gasping laugh. "Oh, I say," he protested.

"Yes, it is really the first dance I've ever been to." Leila was most fervent. It was such a relief to be able to tell somebody. "You see, I've lived in the country all my life up till now...."

At that moment the music stopped and they went to sit on two chairs against the wall. Leila tucked her pink satin feet under and fanned herself, while she blissfully watched the other couples passing and disappearing through the swing doors.

"Enjoying yourself, Leila?" asked Jose, nodding her golden head.

Laura passed and gave her the faintest little wink; it made Leila wonder for a moment whether she was quite grown up after all. Certainly her partner did not say very much. He coughed, tucked his handkerchief away, pulled down his waistcoat, took a minute thread off his sleeve. But it didn't matter. Almost immediately the band started and her second partner seemed to spring from the ceiling.

"Floor's not bad," said the new voice. Did one always begin with the floor? And then, "Were you at the Neaves' on Tuesday?" And again Leila explained. Perhaps it was a little strange that her partners were not more interested. For it was thrilling. Her first ball! She was only at the beginning of everything. It seemed to her that she had never known what the night was like before. Up till now it had been dark, silent, beautiful very often — oh yes — but mournful somehow. Solemn. And now it would never be like that again — it had opened dazzling bright.

"Care for an ice?" said her partner. And they went through the swing doors, down the passage, to the supper-room. Her cheeks burned, she was fearfully thirsty. How sweet the ices looked on little glass plates and how cold the frosted spoon was, iced too! And when they came back to the hall there was the fat man waiting for her by the door. It gave her quite a shock again to see how old he was; he ought to have been on the stage with the fathers and mothers. And when Leila compared him with her other partners he looked shabby. His waistcoat was creased, there was a button off his glove, his coat looked as if it was dusty with French chalk.

"Come along, little lady," said the fat man. He scarcely troubled to clasp her, and they moved away so gently, it was more like walking than dancing. But he said not a word about the floor. "Your first dance, isn't it?" he murmured.

"How *did* you know?"

"Ah," said the fat man, "that's what it is to be old!" He wheezed faintly as he steered her past an awkward couple. "You see, I've been doing this kind of thing for the last thirty years."

"Thirty years?" cried Leila. Twelve years before she was born!

"It hardly bears thinking about, does it?" said the fat man gloomily. Leila looked at his bald head, and she felt quite sorry for him.

"I think it's marvellous to be still going on," she said kindly.

"Kind little lady," said the fat man, and he pressed her a little closer and hummed a bar of the waltz. "Of course," he said, "you can't hope to last anything like as long as that. No-o," said the fat man, "long before that you'll be sitting up there on the stage, looking on, in your nice black velvet. And these pretty arms will have turned into little short fat ones, and you'll beat time with such a different kind of fan — a black ebony one." The fat man seemed to shudder. "And you'll smile away like the poor old dears up there, and point to your daughter, and tell the elderly lady next to you how some dreadful man tried to kiss her at the club ball. And your heart will ache, ache" — the fat man squeezed her closer still, as if he really was sorry for that poor heart — "because no one wants to kiss you now. And you'll say how unpleasant these polished floors are to walk on, how dangerous they are. Eh, Mademoiselle Twinkletoes?" said the fat man softly.

Leila gave a light little laugh, but she did not feel like laughing. Was it — could it all be true? It sounded terribly true. Was this first ball only the beginning of her last ball, after all? At that the music seemed to change; it sounded sad, sad; it rose upon a great sigh. Oh, how quickly things changed! Why didn't happiness last for ever? For ever wasn't a bit too long.

"I want to stop," she said in a breathless voice. The fat man led her to the door.

"No," she said, "I won't go outside. I won't sit down. I'll just stand here, thank you." She leaned against the wall, tapping with her foot, pulling up her gloves and trying to smile. But deep inside here a little girl threw her pinafore over her head and sobbed. Why had he spoiled it all?

"I say, you know," said the fat man, "you mustn't take me seriously, little lady."

"As if I should!" said Leila, tossing her small dark head and sucking her underlip. . . .

Again the couples paraded. The swing doors opened and shut. Now new music was given out by the bandmaster. But Leila didn't want to dance any more. She wanted to be home, or sitting on the veranda listening to those baby owls. When she looked through the dark windows at the stars they had long beams like wings. . . .

But presently a soft, melting, ravishing tune began, and a young man with curly hair bowed before her. She would have to dance, out of politeness, until she could find Meg. Very stiffly she walked into the middle; very haughtily she put her hand on his sleeve. But in one minute, in one turn, her feet glided, glided. The lights, the azaleas, the dresses, the pink faces, the velvet chairs, all became one beautiful flying wheel. And when her next partner bumped her into the fat man he said, "Pardon," she smiled at him more radiantly than ever. She didn't even recognise him again.

AN IDEAL FAMILY

THAT evening for the first time in his life, as he pressed through the swing-door and descended the three broad steps to the pavement, old Mr. Neave felt he was too old for the spring. Spring — warm, eager, restless — was there, waiting for him in the golden light, ready in front of everybody to run up, to blow in his white beard, to drag sweetly on his arm. And he couldn't meet her, no; he couldn't square up once more and stride off, jaunty as a young man. He was tired and, although the late sun was still shining, curiously cold, with a numbed feeling all over. Quite suddenly he hadn't the energy, he hadn't the heart to stand this gaiety and bright movement any longer; it confused him. He wanted to stand still, to wave it away with his stick, to say, "Be off with you!" Suddenly it was a terrible effort to greet as usual — tipping his wide-awake with his stick — all the people whom he knew, the friends, acquaintances, shopkeepers, postmen, drivers. But the gay glance that went with the gesture, the kindly twinkle that seemed to say, "I'm a match and more for any of you" — that old Mr. Neave could not manage at all. He stumped along, lifting his knees high as if he were walking through air that had somehow grown heavy and solid like water. And the homeward-going crowd hurried by, the trams clanked, the light cars clattered, the big swinging cabs bowled along with that reckless, defiant indifference that one knows only in dreams. . . .

It had been a day like other days at the office. Nothing special had happened. Harold hadn't come back from lunch until close on four. Where had he been? What had he been up to? He wasn't going to let his father know. Old Mr. Neave had happened to be in the vestibule, saying good-bye to a caller, when Harold sauntered in, perfectly turned out as usual, cool, suave, smiling that peculiar little half-smile that women found so fascinating.

Ah, Harold was too handsome, too handsome by far; that had been the trouble all along. No man had a right to such eyes, such lashes and such lips, it was uncanny. As for his mother, his sisters, and the servants, it was not too much to say they made a young god of him; they worshipped Harold, they forgave him everything; and he had needed some forgiving ever since the time when he was thirteen and he had stolen his mother's purse, taken the money, and hidden the purse in the cook's bedroom. Old Mr. Neave struck sharply with his stick upon the pavement edge. But it wasn't only his family who spoiled

Harold, he reflected, it was everybody; he had only to look and to smile and down they went before him. So perhaps it wasn't to be wondered at that he expected the office to carry on the tradition. H'm, h'm! But it couldn't be done. No business — not even a successful, established, big paying concern — could be played with. A man had either to put his whole heart and soul into it, or it went all to pieces before his eyes....

And then Charlotte and the girls were always at him to make the whole thing over to Harold, to retire, and to spend his time enjoying himself. Enjoying himself! Old Mr. Neave stopped dead under a group of ancient cabbage palms outside the Government buildings! Enjoying himself! The wind of evening shook the dark leaves to a thin airy cackle. Sitting at home, twiddling his thumbs, conscious all the while that his life's work was slipping away, dissolving, disappearing through Harold's fine fingers, while Harold smiled....

"Why will you be so unreasonable, father? There's absolutely no need for you to go to the office. It only makes it very awkward for us when people persist in saying how tired you're looking. Here's this huge house and garden. Surely you could be happy in — in — appreciating it for a change. Or you could take up some hobby."

And Lola the baby had chimed in loftily, "All men ought to have hobbies. It makes life impossible if they haven't."

Well, well! He couldn't help a grim smile as painfully he began to climb the hill that led into Harcourt Avenue. Where would Lola and her sisters and Charlotte be if he'd gone in for hobbies, he'd like to know? Hobbies couldn't pay for the town house and the seaside bungalow, and their horses, and their golf, and the sixty-guinea gramophone in the music-room for them to dance to. Not that he grudged them these things. No, they were smart, good-looking girls, and Charlotte was a remarkable woman; it was natural for them to be in the swim. As a matter of fact, no other house in the town was as popular as theirs; no other family entertained so much. And how many times old Mr. Neave, pushing the cigar-box across the smoking-room table, had listened to praises of his wife, his girls, of himself even.

"You're an ideal family, sir, an ideal family. It's like something one reads about or sees on the stage."

"That's all right, my boy," old Mr. Neave would reply. "Try one of those; I think you'll like them. And if you care to smoke in the garden, you'll find the girls on the lawn, I dare say."

That was why the girls had never married, so people said. They could have married anybody. But they had too good a time at home. They were too happy together, the girls and Charlotte. H'm, h'm! Well, well! Perhaps so....

By this time he had walked the length of fashionable Harcourt Avenue; he had reached the corner house, their house. The carriage gates were pushed back; there were fresh marks of wheels on the drive. And then he faced the big white-painted house, with its wide-open windows, its tulle curtains floating outwards, its blue jars of hyacinths on the broad sills. On either side of the carriage porch their hydrangeas — famous in the town — were coming into flower; the pinkish, bluish masses of flower lay like light among the spreading leaves. And, somehow, it seemed to old Mr. Neave that the house and the flowers, and even the

Frances Hodgkins
Woman with Pearls

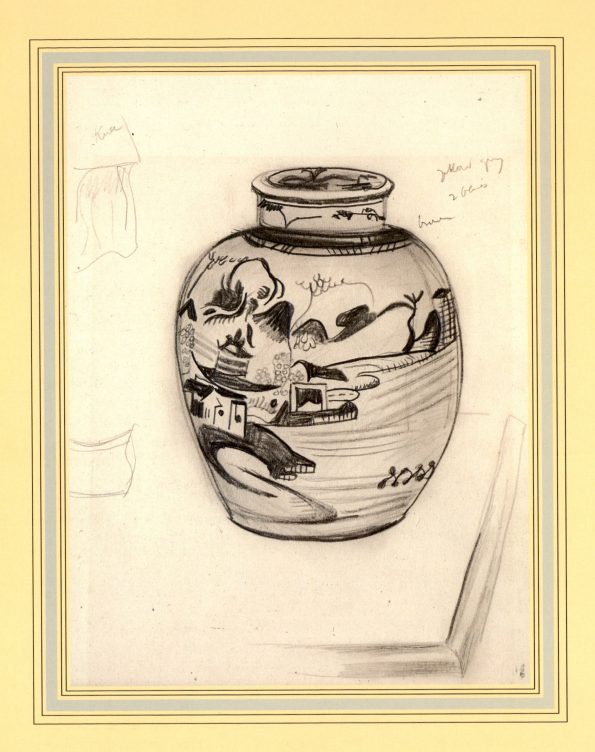

Francès Hodgkins
Chinese Vase

fresh marks on the drive, were saying, "There is young life here. There are girls — "

The hall, as always, was dusky with wraps, parasols, gloves piled on the oak chests. From the music-room sounded the piano, quick, loud and impatient. Through the drawing-room door that was ajar voices floated.

"And were there ices?" came from Charlotte. Then the creak, creak of her rocker.

"Ices!" cried Ethel. "My dear mother, you never saw such ices. Only two kinds. And one a common little strawberry shop ice, in a sopping wet frill."

"The food altogether was too appalling," came from Marion.

"Still, it's rather early for ices," said Charlotte easily.

"But why, if one has them at all..." began Ethel.

"Oh, quite so, darling," crooned Charlotte.

Suddenly the music-room door opened and Lola dashed out. She started, she nearly screamed, at the sight of old Mr. Neave.

"Gracious, father! What a fright you gave me! Have you just come home? Why isn't Charles here to help you off with your coat?"

Her cheeks were crimson from playing, her eyes glittered, the hair fell over her forehead; and she breathed as though she had come running through the dark and was frightened. Old Mr. Neave stared at his youngest daughter; he felt he had never seen her before. So that was Lola, was it? But she seemed to have forgotten her father; it was not for him that she was waiting there. Now she put the tip of her crumpled handkerchief between her teeth and tugged at it angrily. The telephone rang. A-ah! Lola gave a cry like a sob and dashed past him. The door of the telephone-room slammed, and at the same moment Charlotte called, "Is that you, father?"

"You're tired again," said Charlotte reproachfully, and she stopped the rocker and offered him her warm plum-like cheek. Bright-haired Ethel pecked his beard; Marion's lips brushed his ear.

"Did you walk back, father?" asked Charlotte.

"Yes, I walked home," said old Mr. Neave, and he sank into one of the immense drawing-room chairs.

"But why didn't you take a cab?" said Ethel. "There are hundreds of cabs about at that time."

"My dear Ethel," cried Marion, "if father prefers to tire himself out, I really don't see what business of ours it is to interfere."

"Children, children!" coaxed Charlotte.

But Marion wouldn't be stopped. "No, mother, you spoil father, and it's not right. You ought to be stricter with him. He's very naughty." She laughed her hard, bright laugh and patted her hair in a mirror. Strange! When she was a little girl she had such a soft, hesitating voice; she had even stuttered, and now, whatever she said — even if it was only "Jam, please, father" — it rang out as though she were on the stage.

"Did Harold leave the office before you, dear?" asked Charlotte, beginning to rock again.

"I'm not sure," said old Mr. Neave. "I'm not sure. I didn't see him after four o'clock."

"He said — " began Charlotte.

But at that moment Ethel, who was twitching over the leaves of some paper or other, ran to her mother and sank down beside her chair.

"There, you see," she cried. "That's what I mean, mummy. Yellow, with touches of silver. Don't you agree?"

"Give it to me, love," said Charlotte. She fumbled for her tortoise-shell spectacles and put them on, gave the page a little dab with her plump, small fingers, and pursed up her lips. "Very sweet!" she crooned vaguely; she looked at Ethel over her spectacles. "But I shouldn't have the train."

"Not the train!" wailed Ethel tragically. "But the train's the whole point."

"Here, mother, let me decide." Marion snatched the paper playfully from Charlotte. "I agree with mother," she cried trumphantly. "The train overweights it."

Old Mr. Neave, forgotten, sank into the broad lap of his chair, and, dozing, heard them as though he dreamed. There was no doubt about it, he was tired out; he had lost his hold. Even Charlotte and the girls were too much for him to-night. They were too...too...But all his drowsing brain could think of was — too *rich* for him. And somewhere at the back of everything he was watching a little withered ancient man climbing up endless flights of stairs. Who was he?

"I shan't dress to-night," he muttered.

"What do you say, father?"

"Eh, what, what?" Old Mr. Neave woke with a start and stared across at them. "I shan't dress to-night," he repeated.

"But father, we've got Lucile coming, and Henry Davenport, and Mrs. Teddie Walker."

"It will look so *very* out of the picture."

"Don't you feel well, dear?"

"You needn't make any effort. What is Charles *for*?"

"But if you're really not up to it," Charlotte wavered.

"Very well! Very well!" Old Mr. Neave got up and went to join that little old climbing fellow just as far as his dressing-room....

There young Charles was waiting for him. Carefully, as though everything depended on it, he was tucking a towel round the hot-water can. Young Charles had been a favourite of his ever since as a little red-faced boy he had come into the house to look after the fires. Old Mr. Neave lowered himself into the cane lounge by the window, stretched out his legs, and made his little evening joke, "Dress him up, Charles!" And Charles, breathing intensely and frowning, bent forward to take the pin out of his tie.

H'm, h'm! Well, well! It was pleasant by the open window, very pleasant — a fine mild evening. They were cutting the grass on the tennis-court below; he heard the soft churr of the mower. Soon the girls would begin their tennis parties again. And at the thought he seemed to hear Marion's voice ring out, "Good for you, partner....Oh, *played*, partner.... Oh, *very* nice indeed." Then Charlotte calling from the veranda, "Where is Harold?" And Ethel, "He's certainly not here, mother." And Charlotte's vague, "He said — "

Old Mr. Neave sighed, got up, and putting one hand under his beard, he took the

Frances Hodgkins
Jug

comb from young Charles and carefully combed the white beard over. Charles gave him a folded handkerchief, his watch and seals, and spectacle case.

"That will do, my lad." The door shut, he sank back, he was alone. . . .

And now that little ancient fellow was climbing down endless flights that led to a glittering, gay dining-room. What legs he had! They were like a spider's — thin, withered.

"You're an ideal family, sir, an ideal family."

But if that were true, why didn't Charlotte or the girls stop him? Why was he all alone, climbing up and down? Where was Harold? Ah, it was no good expecting anything from Harold. Down, down went the little old spider, and then, to his horror, old Mr. Neave saw him slip past the dining-room and make for the porch, the dark drive, the carriage gates, the office. Stop him, stop him, somebody!

Old Mr. Neave started up. It was dark in his dressing-room; the window shone pale. How long had he been asleep? He listened, and through the big, airy, darkened house there floated far-away voices, far-away sounds. Perhaps, he thought vaguely, he had been asleep for a long time. He'd been forgotten. What had all this to do with him — this house and Charlotte, the girls and Harold — what did he know about them? They were strangers to him. Life had passed him by. Charlotte was not his wife. His wife!

. . . A dark porch, half hidden by a passion-vine, that drooped sorrowful, mournful, as though it understood. Small, warm arms were round his neck. A face, little and pale, lifted to his, and a voice breathed, "Good-bye, my treasure."

My treasure! "Good-bye, my treasure!" Which of them had spoken? Why had they said good-bye? There had been some terrible mistake. *She* was his wife, that little pale girl, and all the rest of his life had been a dream.

Then the door opened, and young Charles, standing in the light, put his hands by his side and shouted like a young soldier, "Dinner is on the table, sir!"

"I'm coming, I'm coming," said old Mr. Neave.

TAKING THE VEIL

IT seemed impossible that anyone should be unhappy on such a beautiful morning. Nobody was, decided Edna, except herself. The windows were flung wide in the houses. From within there came the sound of pianos, little hands chased after each other and ran away from each other, practising scales. The trees fluttered in the sunny gardens, all bright with spring flowers. Street boys whistled, a little dog barked; people passed by, walking so lightly, so swiftly, they looked as though they wanted to break into a run. Now she actually saw in the distance a parasol, peach-coloured, the first parasol of the year.

Perhaps even Edna did not look quite as unhappy as she felt. It is not easy to look tragic at eighteen, when you are extremely pretty, with the cheeks and lips and shining eyes of perfect health. Above all, when you are wearing a French blue frock and your new spring hat trimmed with cornflowers. True, she carried under her arm a book bound in horrid black leather. Perhaps the book provided a gloomy note, but only by accident; it was the ordinary Library binding. For Edna had made going to the Library an excuse for getting out of the house to think, to realise what had happened, to decide somehow what was to be done now.

An awful thing had happened. Quite suddenly, at the theatre last night, when she and Jimmy were seated side by side in the dress-circle, without a moment's warning — in fact, she had just finished a chocolate almond and passed the box to him again — she had fallen in love with an actor. But — fallen — in — love. . . .

The feeling was unlike anything she had ever imagined before. It wasn't in the least pleasant. It was hardly thrilling. Unless you can call the most dreadful sensation of hopeless misery, despair, agony and wretchedness, thrilling. Combined with the certainty that if that actor met her on the pavement after, while Jimmy was fetching their cab, she would follow him to the ends of the earth, at a nod, at a sign, without giving another thought to Jimmy or her father and mother or her happy home and countless friends again. . . .

The play had begun fairly cheerfully. That was at the chocolate almond stage. Then the hero had gone blind. Terrible moment! Edna had cried so much she had to borrow Jimmy's folded, smooth-feeling handkerchief as well. Not that crying mattered. Whole rows were in tears. Even the men blew their noses with a loud trumpeting noise and tried to peer at the programme instead of looking at the stage. Jimmy, most mercifully dry-eyed — for what would she have done without his handkerchief? — squeezed her free hand, and whispered "Cheer up, darling girl!" And it was then she had taken a last chocolate almond to please him and passed the box again. Then there had been that ghastly scene with the hero alone on the stage in a deserted room at twilight, with a band playing outside and the sound of cheering coming from the street. He had tried — ah! how painfully, how pitifully! — to grope his way to the window. He had succeeded at last. There he stood holding the curtain while one beam of light, just one beam, shone full on his raised sightless face, and the band faded away into the distance....

It was — really, it was absolutely — oh, the most — it was simply — in fact, from that moment Edna knew that life could never be the same. She drew her hand away from Jimmy's, leaned back, and shut the chocolate box for ever. This at last was love!

Edna and Jimmy were engaged. She had had her hair up for a year and a half; they had been publicly engaged for a year. But they had known they were going to marry each other ever since they walked in the Botanical Gardens with their nurses, and sat on the grass with a wine biscuit and a piece of barley-sugar each for their tea. It was so much an accepted thing that Edna had worn a wonderfully good imitation of an engagement-ring out of a cracker all the time she was at school. And up till now they had been devoted to each other.

But now it was over. It was so completely over that Edna found it difficult to believe that Jimmy did not realise it too. She smiled wisely, sadly, as she turned into the gardens of the Convent of the Sacred Heart and mounted the path that led through them to Hill Street. How much better to know it now than to wait until after they were married! Now it was possible that Jimmy would get over it. No, it was no use deceiving herself; he would never get over it! His life was wrecked, was ruined; that was inevitable. But he was young.... Time, people always said, Time might make a little, just a little difference. In forty years when he was an old man, he might be able to think of her calmly — perhaps. But she, — what did the future hold for her?

Edna had reached the top of the path. There under a new-leafed tree, hung with little bunches of white flowers, she sat down on a green bench and looked over the Convent flowerbeds. In the one nearest to her there grew tender stocks, with a border of blue, shell-like pansies, with at one corner a clump of creamy freesias, their light spears of green criss-crossed over the flowers. The Convent pigeons were tumbling high in the air, and she could hear the voice of Sister Agnes who was giving a singing lesson. *Ah-me*, sounded the deep tones of the nun, and *Ah-me*, they were echoed....

If she did not marry Jimmy, of course she would marry nobody. The man she was in love with, the famous actor — Edna had far too much common-sense not to realise that would never be. It was very odd. She didn't even want it to be. Her love was too intense for that. It had to be endured, silently; it had to torment her. It was, she supposed, simply that kind of love.

"But, Edna!" cried Jimmy. "Can you never change? Can I never hope again?"

Oh, what sorrow to have to say it, but it must be said. "No, Jimmy, I will never change."

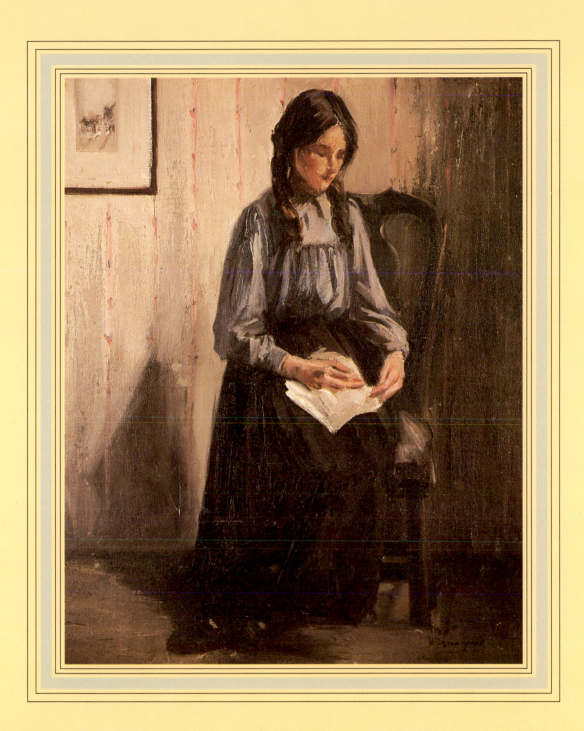

Hermina Arndt
The Blue Blouse

Alexander Roche
One of the Procession

170

Edna bowed her head; and a little flower fell on her lap, and the voice of Sister Agnes cried suddenly *Ah-no*, and the echo came, *Ah-no*. . . .

At that moment the future was revealed. Edna saw it all. She was astonished; it took her breath away at first. But, after all, what could be more natural? She would go into a convent. . . . Her father and mother do everything to dissuade her, in vain. As for Jimmy, his state of mind hardly bears thinking about. Why can't they understand? How can they add to her suffering like this? The world is cruel, terribly cruel! After a last scene when she gives away her jewellery and so on to her best friends — she so calm, they so broken-hearted — into a convent she goes. No, one moment. The very evening of her going is the actor's last evening at Port Willin. He receives by a strange messenger a box. It is full of white flowers. But there is no name, no card. Nothing? Yes, under the roses, wrapped in a white handkerchief, Edna's last photograph with, written underneath,

The world forgetting, by the world forgot.

Edna sat very still under the trees; she clasped the black book in her fingers as though it were her missal. She takes the name of Sister Angela. Snip! Snip! All her lovely hair is cut off. Will she be allowed to send one curl to Jimmy? It is contrived somehow. And in a blue gown with a white headband Sister Angela goes from the convent to the chapel, from the chapel to the convent with something unearthly in her look, in her sorrowful eyes, and in the gentle smile with which they greet the little children who run to her. A saint! She hears it whispered as she paces the chill, wax-smelling corridors. A saint! And visitors to the chapel are told of the nun whose voice is heard above the other voices, of her youth, her beauty, of her tragic, tragic love. "There is a man in this town whose life is ruined. . . ."

A big bee, a golden furry fellow, crept into a freesia, and the delicate flower leaned over, swung, shook; and when the bee flew away it fluttered still as though it were laughing. Happy, careless flower!

Sister Angela looked at it and said, "Now it is winter." One night, lying in her icy cell, she hears a cry. Some stray animal is out there in the garden, a kitten or a lamb or — well, whatever little animal might be there. Up rises the sleepless nun. All in white, shivering but fearless, she goes and brings it in. But next morning, when the bell rings for matins, she is found tossing in high fever. . . in delirium. . . and she never recovers. In three days all is over. The service has been said in the chapel, and she is buried in the corner of the cemetery reserved for the nuns, where there are plain little crosses of wood. Rest in Peace, Sister Angela. . . .

Now it is evening. Two old people leaning on each other come slowly to the grave and kneel down sobbing, "Our daughter! Our only daughter!" Now there comes another. He is all in black; he comes slowly. But when he is there and lifts his black hat, Edna sees to her horror his hair is snow-white. Jimmy! Too late, too late! The tears are running down his face; he is crying *now*. Too late, too late! The wind shakes the leafless trees in the churchyard. He gives one awful bitter cry.

Edna's black book fell with a thud to the garden path. She jumped up, her heart beating. My darling! No, it's not too late. It's all been a mistake, a terrible dream. Oh, that white hair! How could she have done it? She has not done it. Oh, heavens! Oh, what happiness! She is free, young, and nobody knows her secret. Everything is still possible for her and Jimmy. The house they have planned may still be built, the little solemn boy with his hands behind his back watching them plant the standard roses may still be born. His baby sister... But when Edna got as far as his baby sister, she stretched out her arms as though the little love came flying through the air to her, and gazing at the garden, at the white sprays on the tree, at those darling pigeons blue against the blue, and the Convent with its narrow windows, she realised that now at last for the first time in her life — she had never imagined any feeling like it before — she knew what it was to be in love, but — in — love!

THE FLY

"Y'ARE very snug in here," piped old Mr. Woodifield, and he peered out of the great, green-leather armchair by his friend the boss's desk as a baby peers out of its pram. His talk was over; it was time for him to be off. But he did not want to go. Since he had retired, since his . . . stroke, the wife and the girls kept him boxed up in the house every day of the week except Tuesday. On Tuesday he was dressed and brushed and allowed to cut back to the City for the day. Though what he did there the wife and the girls couldn't imagine. Made a nuisance of himself to his friends, they supposed. . . . Well, perhaps so. All the same, we cling to our last pleasures as the tree clings to its last leaves. So there sat old Woodifield, smoking a cigar and staring almost greedily at the boss, who rolled in his office chair, stout, rosy, five years older than he, and still going strong, still at the helm. It did one good to see him.

Wistfully, admiringly, the old voice added, "It's snug in here, upon my word!"

"Yes, it's comfortable enough," agreed the boss, and he flipped the *Financial Times* with a paper-knife. As a matter of fact he was proud of his room; he liked to have it admired, especially by old Woodifield. It gave him a feeling of deep, solid satisfaction to be planted there in the midst of it in full view of that frail old figure in the muffler.

"I've had it done up lately," he explained, as he had explained for the past — how many? — weeks. "New carpet," and he pointed to the bright red carpet with a pattern of large white rings. "New furniture," and he nodded towards the massive bookcase and the table with legs like twisted treacle. "Electric heating!" He waved almost exultantly towards the five transparent, pearly sausages glowing so softly in the tilted copper pan.

But he did not draw old Woodifield's attention to the photograph over the table of a grave-looking boy in uniform standing in one of those spectral photographers' parks with photographers' storm-clouds behind him. It was not new. It had been there for over six years.

"There was something I wanted to tell you," said old Woodifield, and his eyes grew dim remembering. "Now what was it? I had it in my mind when I started out this morning." His hands began to tremble, and patches of red showed above his beard.

Poor old chap, he's on his last pins, thought the boss. And, feeling kindly, he winked at the old man, and said jokingly, "I tell you what. I've got a little drop of something here that'll do you good before you go out into the cold again. It's beautiful stuff. It wouldn't hurt a child." He took a key off his watch-chain, unlocked a cupboard below his desk, and drew forth a dark, squat bottle. "That's the medicine," said he. "And the man from whom I got it told me on the strict Q.T. it came from the cellars at Windsor Castle."

Old Woodifield's mouth fell open at the sight. He couldn't have looked more surprised if the boss had produced a rabbit.

"It's whisky, ain't it?" he piped feebly.

The boss turned the bottle and lovingly showed him the label. Whisky it was.

"D'you know," said he, peering up at the boss wonderingly, "they won't let me touch it at home." And he looked as though he was going to cry.

"Ah, that's where we know a bit more than the ladies," cried the boss, swooping across for two tumblers that stood on the table with the water-bottle, and pouring a generous finger into each. "Drink it down. It'll do you good. And don't put any water with it. It's sacrilege to tamper with stuff like this. Ah!" He tossed off his, pulled out his handkerchief, hastily wiped his moustaches, and cocked an eye at old Woodifield, who was rolling his in his chaps.

The old man swallowed, was silent a moment, and then said faintly, "It's nutty!"

But it warmed him; it crept into his chill old brain — he remembered.

"That was it," he said, heaving himself out of his chair. "I thought you'd like to know. The girls were in Belgium last week having a look at poor Reggie's grave, and they happened to come across your boy's. They're quite near each other, it seems."

Old Woodifield paused, but the boss made no reply. Only a quiver in his eyelids showed that he heard.

"The girls were delighted with the way the place is kept," piped the old voice. "Beautifully looked after. Couldn't be better if they were at home. You've not been across, have yer?"

"No, no!" For various reasons the boss had not been across.

"There's miles of it," quavered old Woodifield, "and it's all as neat as a garden. Flowers growing on all the graves. Nice broad paths." It was plain from his voice how much he liked a nice broad path.

The pause came again. Then the old man brightened wonderfully.

"D'you know what the hotel made the girls pay for a pot of jam?" he piped. "Ten francs! Robbery, I call it. It was a little pot, so Gertrude says, no bigger than a half-crown. And she hadn't taken more than a spoonful when they charged her ten francs. Gertrude brought the pot away with her to teach 'em a lesson. Quite right, too; it's trading on our feelings. They think because we're over there having a look round we're ready to pay anything. That's what it is." And he turned towards the door.

"Quite right, quite right!" cried the boss, though what was quite right he hadn't the least idea. He came round by his desk, followed the shuffling footsteps to the door, and saw the old fellow out. Woodifield was gone.

For a long moment the boss stayed, staring at nothing, while the grey-haired office messenger, watching him, dodged in and out of his cubby-hole like a dog that expects to be taken for a run. Then: "I'll see nobody for half an hour, Macey," said the boss.

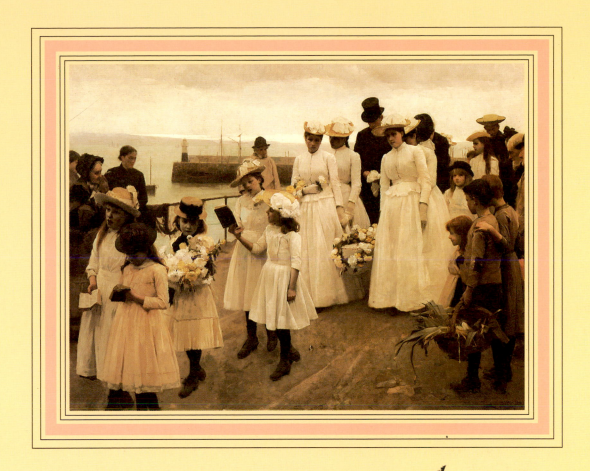

Frank Bramley
For of such is the Kingdom of Heaven

T. Poynter
Wellington Harbour

"Understand? Nobody at all."

"Very good, sir."

The door shut, the firm heavy steps recrossed the bright carpet, the fat body plumped down in the spring chair, and leaning forward, the boss covered his face with his hands. He wanted, he intended, he had arranged to weep....

It had been a terrible shock to him when old Woodifield sprang that remark upon him about the boy's grave. It was exactly as though the earth had opened and he had seen the boy lying there with Woodifield's girls staring down at him. For it was strange. Although over six years had passed away, the boss never thought of the boy except as lying unchanged, unblemished in his uniform, asleep for ever. "My son!" groaned the boss. But no tears came yet. In the past, in the first months and even years after the boy's death, he had only to say those words to be overcome by such grief that nothing short of a violent fit of weeping could relieve him. Time, he had declared then, he had told everybody, could make no difference. Other men perhaps might recover, might live their loss down, but not he. How was it possible? His boy was an only son. Ever since his birth the boss had worked at building up this business for him; it had no other meaning if it was not for the boy. Life itself had come to have no other meaning. How on earth could he have slaved, denied himself, kept going all those years without the promise for ever before him of the boy's stepping into his shoes and carrying on where he left off?

And that promise had been so near being fulfilled. The boy had been in the office learning the ropes for a year before the war. Every morning they had started off together; they had come back by the same train. And what congratulations he had received as the boy's father! No wonder; he had taken to it marvellously. As to his popularity with the staff, every man jack of them down to old Macey couldn't make enough of the boy. And he wasn't in the least spoilt. No, he was just his bright natural self, with the right word for everybody, with that boyish look and his habit of saying, "Simply splendid!"

But all that was over and done with as though it never had been. The day had come when Macey had handed him the telegram that brought the whole place crashing about his head. "Deeply regret to inform you..." And he had left the office a broken man, with his life in ruins.

Six years ago, six years.... How quickly time passed! It might have happened yesterday. The boss took his hands from his face; he was puzzled. Something seemed to be wrong with him. He wasn't feeling as he wanted to feel. He decided to get up and have a look at the boy's photograph. But it wasn't a favourite photograph of his; the expression was unnatural. It was cold, even stern-looking. The boy had never looked like that.

At that moment the boss noticed that a fly had fallen into his broad inkpot, and was trying feebly but desperately to clamber out again. Help! help! said those struggling legs. But the sides of the inkpot were wet and slippery; it fell back again and began to swim. The boss took up a pen, picked the fly out of the ink, and shook it on to a piece of blotting-paper. For a fraction of a second it lay still on the dark patch that oozed round it. Then the front legs waved, took hold, and, pulling its small, sodden body up, it began the immense task of cleaning the ink from its wings. Over and under, over and under, went a leg along a wing as the stone goes over and under the scythe. Then there was a pause, while the fly, seeming to stand on the tips of its toes, tried to expand first one wing and then the other. It succeeded at last, and, sitting down, it began, like a minute cat, to clean its face. Now one could imagine that the little front legs rubbed against each other lightly, joyfully. The horrible danger was over; it had escaped; it was ready for life again.

But just then the boss had an idea. He plunged his pen back into the ink, leaned his thick wrist on the blotting-paper, and as the fly tried its wings down came a great heavy blot. What would it make of that? What indeed! The little beggar seemed absolutely cowed, stunned, and afraid to move because of what would happen next. But then, as if painfully, it dragged itself forward. The front legs waved, caught hold, and more slowly this time, the task began from the beginning.

He's a plucky little devil, thought the boss, and he felt a real admiration for the fly's courage. That was the way to tackle things; that was the right spirit. Never say die; it was only a question of...But the fly had again finished its laborious task, and the boss had just time to refill his pen, to shake fair and square on the new-cleaned body yet another dark drop. What about it this time? A painful moment of suspense followed. But behold, the front legs were again waving; the boss felt a rush of relief. He leaned over the fly and said to it tenderly, "You artful little b..." And he actually had the brilliant notion of breathing on it to help the drying process. All the same, there was something timid and weak about its efforts now, and the boss decided that this time should be the last, as he dipped the pen deep into the inkpot.

It was. The last blot fell on the soaked blotting-paper, and the draggled fly lay in it and did not stir. The back legs were stuck to the body; the front legs were not to be seen.

"Come on," said the boss. "Look sharp!" And he stirred it with his pen — in vain. Nothing happened or was likely to happen. The fly was dead.

The boss lifted the corpse on the end of the paper-knife and flung it into the waste-paper basket. But such a grinding feeling of wretchedness seized him that he felt positively frightened. He started forward and pressed the bell for Macey.

"Bring me some fresh blotting-paper," he said sternly, "and look sharp about it." And while the old dog padded away he fell to wondering what it was he had been thinking about before. What was it? It was...He took out his handkerchief and passed it inside his collar. For the life of him he could not remember.

SIX YEARS AFTER

IT was not the afternoon to be on deck — on the contrary, it was exactly the afternoon when there is no snugger place than a warm cabin, a warm bunk. Tucked up with a rug, a hot-water bottle and a piping hot cup of tea she would not have minded the weather in the least. But he — hated cabins, hated to be inside anywhere more than was absolutely necessary. He had a passion for keeping, as he called it, above board, especially when he was travelling. And it wasn't surprising, considering the enormous amount of time he spent cooped up in the office. So, when he rushed away from her as soon as they got on board and came back five minutes later to say he had secured two deck-chairs on the lee side and the steward was undoing the rugs, her voice through the high sealskin collar murmured "Good"; and because he was looking at her, she smiled with bright eyes and blinked quickly, as if to say, "Yes, perfectly all right — absolutely." And she meant it.

"Then we'd better — " said he, and he tucked her hand inside his arm and began to rush her off to where their chairs stood. But she just had time to breathe, "Not so fast, Daddy, please," when he remembered too and slowed down.

Strange! They had been married twenty-eight years, and it was still an effort to him, each time, to adapt his pace to hers.

"Not cold, are you?" he asked, glancing sideways at her. Her little nose, geranium pink above the dark fur, was answer enough. But she thrust her free hand into the velvet pocket of her jacket and murmured gaily, "I shall be glad of my rug."

He pressed her tighter to his side — a quick, nervous pressure. He knew, of course, that she ought to be down in the cabin; he knew that it was no afternoon for her to be sitting on deck, in this cold and raw mist, lee side or no lee side, rugs or no rugs, and he realised how she must be hating it. But he had come to believe that it really was easier for her to make these sacrifices than it was for him. Take their present case, for instance. If he had gone down to the cabin with her, he would have been miserable the whole time, and he couldn't have helped showing it. At any rate, she would have found him out. Whereas, having made up her mind to fall in with his ideas, he would have betted anybody she would even go so far as to enjoy the experience. Not because she was without personality of her own. Good Lord! She was absolutely brimming with it. But because...but here his thoughts always stopped. Here they always felt the need of a cigar, as it were. And, looking at the cigar-tip, his fine blue eyes narrowed. It was a law of marriage, he supposed....All the same, he always felt guilty when he asked these sacrifices of her. That was what the quick pressure meant. His being said to her being: "You do understand, don't you?" and there was an answering tremor of her fingers, "I *understand*."

Certainly the steward — good little chap — had done all in his power to make them comfortable. He had put up their chairs in whatever warmth there was and out of the smell. She did hope he would be tipped adequately. It was on occasions like these (and her life seemed to be full of such occasions) that she wished it was the woman who controlled the purse.

"Thank you, steward. That will do beautifully."

"Why are stewards so often delicate-looking?" she wondered, as her feet were tucked under. "This poor little chap looks as though he'd got a chest, and yet one would have thought...the sea air..."

The button of the pigskin purse was undone. The tray was tilted. She saw sixpences, shillings, half-crowns.

"I should give him five shillings," she decided, "and tell him to buy himself a good nourishing — "

He was given a shilling, and he touched his cap and seemed genuinely grateful.

Well, it might have been worse. It might have been sixpence. It might, indeed. For at that moment Father turned towards her and said, half apologetically, stuffing the purse back, "I gave him a shilling. I think it was worth it, don't you?"

"Oh, quite! Every bit!" said she.

It is extraordinary how peaceful it feels on a little steamer once the bustle of leaving port is over. In a quarter of an hour one might have been at sea for days. There is something almost touching, childish, in the way people submit themselves to the new conditions. They go to bed in the early afternoon, they shut their eyes and "it's night" like little children who turn the table upside down and cover themselves with the tablecloth. And those who remain on deck — they seem to be always the same, those few hardened men travellers — pause, light their pipes, stamp softly, gaze out to sea, and their voices are subdued as they walk up and down. The long-legged little girl chases after the red-cheeked boy, but soon both are captured; and the old sailor, swinging an unlighted lantern, passes and disappears....

He lay back, the rug up to his chin, and she saw he was breathing deeply. Sea air! If anyone believed in sea air it was he. He had the strongest faith in its tonic qualities. But the great thing was, according to him, to fill the lungs with it the moment you came on board. Otherwise, the sheer strength of it was enough to give you a chill....

She gave a small chuckle, and he turned to her quickly. "What is it?"

"It's your cap," she said. "I never can get used to you in a cap. You look such a thorough burglar."

"Well, what the deuce am I to wear?" He shot up one grey eyebrow and wrinkled his nose. "It's a very good cap, too. Very fine specimen of its kind. It's got a very rich white

Maud Sherwood
Reading

satin lining." He paused. He declaimed, as he had hundreds of times before at this stage, "Rich and rare were the gems she wore."

But she was thinking he really was childishly proud of the white satin lining. He would like to have taken off his cap and made her feel it. "Feel the quality!" How often had she rubbed between finger and thumb his coat, his shirt cuff, tie, sock, linen handkerchief, while he said that.

She slipped down more deeply into her chair.

And the little steamer pressed on, pitching gently, over the grey, unbroken, gently moving water, that was veiled with slanting rain.

Far out, as though idly, listlessly, gulls were flying. Now they settled on the waves, now they beat up into the rainy air and shone against the pale sky like the lights within a pearl. They looked cold and lonely. How lonely it will be when we have passed by, she thought. There will be nothing but the waves and those birds and rain falling.

She gazed through the rust-spotted railing along which big drops trembled, until suddenly she shut her lids. It was as if a warning voice inside her had said, "Don't look!"

"No, I won't," she decided. "It's too depressing, much too depressing."

But, immediately, she opened her eyes and looked again. Lonely birds, water lifting, white pale sky — how were they changed?

And it seemed to her there was a presence far out there, between the sky and the water; someone very desolate and longing watched them pass and cried as if to stop them — but cried to her alone.

"Mother!"

"Don't leave me," sounded the cry. "Don't forget me! You are forgetting me, you know you are!" And it was as though from her own breast there came the sound of childish weeping.

"My son — my precious child — it isn't true!"

Sh! How was it possible that she was sitting there on that quiet steamer beside Father and at the same time she was hushing and holding a little slender boy — so pale — who had just waked out of a dreadful dream?

"I dreamed I was in a wood — somewhere far away from everybody — and I was lying down and a great blackberry vine grew over me. And I called and called to you — and you wouldn't come — you wouldn't come — so I had to lie there for ever."

What a terrible dream! He had always had terrible dreams. How often, years ago, when he was small, she had made some excuse and escaped from their friends in the dining-room or the drawing-room to come to the foot of the stairs and listen. "Mother!" And when he was asleep, his dream had journeyed with her back into the circle of lamplight; it had taken its place there like a ghost. And now —

Far more often — at all times — in all places — like now, for instance — she never settled down, she was never off her guard for a moment but she heard him. He wanted her. "I am coming as fast as I can! As fast as I can!" But the dark stairs have no ending, and the worst dream of all — the one that is always the same — goes for ever and ever uncomforted.

This is anguish! How is it to be borne? Still, it is not the idea of her suffering which

William Sutton
Pastoral

is unbearable — it is his. Can one do nothing for the dead? And for a long time the answer had been — Nothing!

...But softly without a sound the dark curtain has rolled down. There is no more to come. That is the end of the play. But it can't end like that — so suddenly. There must be more. No, it's cold, it's still. There is nothing to be gained by waiting.

But — did he go back again? Or, when the war was over, did he come home for good? Surely, he will marry — later on — not for several years. Surely, one day I shall remember his wedding and my first grandchild — a beautiful dark-haired boy born in the early morning — a lovely morning — spring!

"Oh, Mother, it's not fair to me to put these ideas into my head! Stop, Mother, stop! When I think of all I have missed, I can't bear it."

"I can't bear it!" She sits up breathing the words and tosses the dark rug away. It is colder than ever, and now the dusk is falling, falling like ash upon the pallid water.

And the little steamer, growing determined, throbbed on, pressed on, as if at the end of the journey there waited...

THE CANARY

YOU see that big nail to the right of the front door? I can scarcely look at it . . . even now and yet I could not bear to take it out. I should like to think it was there always even after my time. I sometimes hear the next people saying, "There must have been a cage hanging from there." And it comforts me; I feel he is not quite forgotten.

. . . You cannot imagine how wonderfully he sang. It was not like the singing of other canaries. And that isn't just my fancy. Often, from the window, I used to see people stop at the gate to listen, or they would lean over the fence by the mock-orange for quite a long time — carried away. I suppose it sounds absurd to you — it wouldn't if you had heard him — but it really seemed to me that he sang whole songs with a beginning and an end to them.

For instance, when I'd finished the house in the afternoon, and changed my blouse and brought my sewing on to the veranda here, he used to hop, hop, hop from one perch to another, tap against the bars as if to attract my attention, sip a little water just as a professional singer might, and then break into a song so exquisite that I had to put my needle down to listen to him. I can't describe it; I wish I could. But it was always the same, every afternoon, and I felt that I understood every note of it.

. . . I loved him. How I loved him! Perhaps it does not matter so very much what it is one loves in this world. But love something one must. Of course there was always my little house and the garden, but for some reason they were never enough. Flowers respond wonderfully, but they don't sympathise. Then I loved the evening star. Does that sound foolish? I used to go into the backyard, after sunset, and wait for it until it shone above the dark gum tree. I used to whisper, "There you are, my darling." And just in that first moment it seemed to be shining for me alone. It seemed to understand this . . . something which is like longing, and yet it is not longing. Or regret — it is more like regret. And yet regret for what? I have much to be thankful for.

. . . But after he came into my life I forgot the evening star; I did not need it any more. But it was strange. When the Chinaman who came to the door with birds to sell held him up in his tiny cage, and instead of fluttering, fluttering, like the poor little goldfinches, he gave a faint, small chirp, I found myself saying, just as I had said to the star over the gum tree, "There you are, my darling." From that moment he was mine.

. . . It surprises me even now to remember how he and I shared each other's lives. The moment I came down in the morning and took the cloth off his cage he greeted me with a drowsy little note. I knew it meant "Missus! Missus!" Then I hung him on the nail outside while I got my three young men their breakfasts, and I never brought him in until we had the house to ourselves again. Then, when the washing-up was done, it was quite a little entertainment. I spread a newspaper over a corner of the table, and when I put the cage on it he used to beat with his wings despairingly, as if he didn't know what was coming. "You're a regular little actor," I used to scold him. I scraped the tray, dusted it with fresh sand, filled his seed and water tins, tucked a piece of chickweed and half a chilli between the bars. And I am perfectly certain he understood and appreciated every item of this little performance. You see by nature he was exquisitely neat. There was never a speck on his perch. And you'd only to see him enjoy his bath to realise he had a real small passion for cleanliness. His bath was put in last. And the moment it was in he positively leapt into it. First he fluttered one wing, then the other, then he ducked his head and dabbled his breast feathers. Drops of water were scattered all over the kitchen, but still he would not get out. I used to say to him, "Now that's quite enough. You're only showing off." And at last out he hopped and, standing on one leg, he began to peck himself dry. Finally he gave a shake, a flick, a twitter and he lifted his throat — Oh, I can hardly bear to recall it. I was always cleaning the knives at the time. And it almost seemed to me the knives sang too, as I rubbed them bright on the board.

. . . Company, you see — that was what he was. Perfect company. If you have lived alone you will realise how precious that is. Of course there were my three young men who came in to supper every evening, and sometimes they stayed in the dining-room afterwards reading the paper. But I could not expect them to be interested in the little things that made my day. Why should they be? I was nothing to them. In fact, I overheard them one evening talking about me on the stairs as "the Scarecrow". No matter. It doesn't matter. Not in the least. I quite understand. They are young. Why should I mind? But I remember feeling so especially thankful that I was not quite alone that evening. I told him, after they had gone out. I said, "Do you know what they call Missus?" And he put his head on one side and looked at me with his little bright eye until I could not help laughing. It seemed to amuse him.

. . . Have you kept birds? If you haven't all this must sound, perhaps, exaggerated. People have the idea that birds are heartless, cold little creatures, not like dogs or cats. My washer-woman used to say on Mondays when she wondered why I didn't keep "a nice fox-terrier", "There's no comfort, Miss, in a canary." Untrue. Dreadfully untrue. I remember one night. I had had a very awful dream — dreams can be dreadfully cruel — even after I had woken up I could not get over it. So I put on my dressing-gown and went down to the kitchen for a glass of water. It was a winter night and raining hard. I suppose I was still half asleep, but through the kitchen window, that hadn't a blind, it seemed to me the dark was staring in, spying. And suddenly I felt it was unbearable that I had no one to whom I could say "I've had such a dreadful dream," or — or "Hide me from the dark." I even covered my

Maud Sherwood
Woman in a Boat

face for a minute. And then there came a little "Sweet! Sweet!" His cage was on the table, and the cloth had slipped so that a chink of light shone through. "Sweet, Sweet!" said the darling little fellow again, softly, as much as to say, "I'm here, Missus! I'm here!" That was so beautifully comforting that I nearly cried.

...And now he's gone. I shall never have another bird, another pet of any kind. How could I? When I found him, lying on his back, with his eye dim and his claws wrung, when I realised that never again should I hear my darling sing, something seemed to die in me. My heart felt hollow, as if it was his cage. I shall get over it. Of course. I must. One can get over anything in time. And people always say I have a cheerful disposition. They are quite right. I thank my God I have.

...All the same, without being morbid, and giving way to — to memories and so on, I must confess that there does seem to me something sad in life. It is hard to say what it is. I don't mean the sorrow that we all know, like illness and poverty and death. No, it is something different. It is there, deep down, deep down, part of one, like one's breathing. However hard I work and tire myself I have only to stop to know it is there, waiting. I often wonder if everybody feels the same. One can never know. But isn't it extraordinary that under his sweet, joyful little singing it was just this — sadness? — Ah, what is it? — that I heard.